ALPHA
UNLEASHED

ALSO BY KATHY LYONS

The Bear Who Loved Me
License to Shift
For the Bear's Eyes Only

ALPHA UNLEASHED

Book Four of Grizzlies Gone Wild

Kathy Lyons

FOREVER
YOURS

New York   Boston

Copyright © 2018 by Kathy Lyons
Excerpt from *The Bear Who Loved Me* copyright © 2016 by Kathy Lyons
Cover design by Brian Lemus
Cover copyright © 2018 by Hachette Book Group, Inc.

Forever Yours
Hachette Book Group
1290 Avenue of the Americas
New York, NY 10104
forever-romance.com
twitter.com/foreverromance

First published as an ebook and as a print on demand: March 2018

Forever Yours is an imprint of Grand Central Publishing. The Forever Yours name and logo are trademarks of Hachette Book Group, Inc.

The publisher is not responsible for websites (or their content) that are not owned by the publisher.

The Hachette Speakers Bureau provides a wide range of authors for speaking events. To find out more, go to www.hachettespeakersbureau.com or call (866) 376-6591.

ISBNs: 978-1-5387-6209-7 (ebook), 978-1-5387-6210-3 (print on demand)

ALPHA UNLEASHED

CHAPTER 1

Bear grumbled, the sound low and deep in his belly. The birds squawked and flew straight up, a squirrel took off through the trees, and best of all, a rabbit leapt high and ran, drawing him away from her babies tucked beneath a nearby tree. He didn't follow. It amused him to watch the forest animals scatter at his smallest sound.

He made another sound, this time a chuff of contentment. He rolled onto his back and scratched his rear leg against the tree. He had an itch there. And another slightly higher up between his thighs. There was a female nearby. One who was coming into his territory unaware that he waited for her. He'd been tracking her for a while now and it pleased him that he would soon have his go at her. She was not fertile yet, but his nose told him it might be soon.

He was puzzling, in his dull bear way, about the best way to catch her when a dangerous sound disturbed the morning air. The growl of an engine. It was the call of the worst predator of all: man. He straightened onto all fours, grumbling at the inconvenience. He could not allow such a creature into his territory. Not when a female

was coming. So he shook out his shoulders, hips, and rump, then
went off in search of the danger.

He moved with confidence over this land because it was his. He
knew the rocks, the smells, and the sounds. He knew, too, that when
the engine sound abruptly stopped, the danger increased. It meant
that a human was out of his machine and hunting on foot.

Bear prowled closer, moving toward the structure he called his
own. He sniffed the air and caught the scent of a human woman.
It might have been pleasant if not for the acrid stink of her engine.
She was making a great deal of noise, pounding on the building and
calling out. He didn't put any effort into processing her words. He'd
been a bear too long to want to work that hard. Besides, it didn't
matter what she said. This was his place and he would not allow anyone else inside his dominion.

So when she pounded her fist against the structure again, he
growled, low and threatening.

She spun around and he smelled terror in her scent. She gasped
and moved sideways across his vision. Not at him, but not retreating
either. She made sounds, too, ones that were tight with alarm.

He decided to frighten her away.

He took a deep breath and released a roar. Secretly, he was
pleased with the full, loud sound. It echoed in the trees and startled
birds in the distance. And when he was done, he watched for her to
run away with her engine. He would not give chase. He knew from
experience that he couldn't catch the human prey when it was surrounded in metal. So he would remain where he was with his teeth
bared until she left.

Except she did not run. She stood her ground next to his structure.
Tall and proud as if she were anything but tiny compared to him.

Why would she not leave?

He needed to frighten her again. This time he matched her stance. She needed to see how small she was compared to him. He reared up on his back legs and showed his teeth. He spread his arms and let his claws flash in the sun. He was much larger than her. She should run.

Bam! Bam! Bam!

Something hit him. Powerful somethings. Three times, hard in the chest. He stumbled backward, his bear mind sluggish. Pain hit next, blinding him with fury. He roared again as he struggled to regain his footing.

Bam! Bam!

His leg buckled and he went down on his face. The ground slapped his mouth closed but he was already rolling. Or trying to roll. Something was wrong with his breath. The pain whited out his thoughts, though he tried to scramble to his feet. He had to attack the human predator. He must defend his territory. And yet his breath was wrong. The smell of blood cluttered his senses. His feelings gave no clue beyond pain and fury.

My time, his other self said. *Quickly.*

There were other words, other thoughts, but the mind spoke too quickly and bear was unused to hearing it. He felt pain. He felt anger. And he felt those things being tucked away as the mind began to assert itself.

It came on like a trickle of icy water that quickly became a deluge. It dampened the feelings, then turned everything liquid. His emotions, his body, even his sounds became wet and fluid. Thoughts were still too complicated to follow, but the mind knew enough, had practiced enough, to act without forethought.

He isolated the worst pain—hard points of metal—and shoved them from his body made liquid. It was hard work to push them away. His body was too thin in this in-between place, the energy too insubstantial against something so hard. But he worked at it, holding off the freezing of muscle and bone, until the points—the bullets—were out or at least near the surface.

He didn't have enough time. Three bullets fell away, but two others were trapped in his human body when his cells locked into place. Bone, organs, muscle, skin—all human. All that remained liquid was the blood that flowed inside.

"Holy shit," someone whispered. "It's true."

He opened his eyes. No, they were already open. He focused them now, sorting vision into colors, shapes, and meaning. A woman stood above him, a gun trembling in her hand but aimed unerringly at his heart. Her eyes were wide and her breath stuttered in and out with terror.

Someone wheezed, a sound filled with wet pain. Oh damn. He'd made that sound. His rational mind was coming online now. It was processing information with increasing speed and all the conclusions were bad.

He was lying on the ground after being shot five times.

His body still burned, overwhelmed from the sudden shift. It was all painful, so he could not tell what hurt most. He knew there were two more bullets inside him somewhere, but he couldn't remember where. And an outsider stared at him, terrified and still dangerous.

He had to communicate with her. He had to deliver the message that was uppermost in his brain. They were bear's words, now made intelligible by a human mouth.

"Go. Away."

"Simon?" she whispered, the words half gasp, half squeak of terror.

Had he said the words wrong? Was her brain injured? He tried again, putting more force behind the message though it hurt his chest to do it.

"Go. Away."

"You were a bear! I shot a bear!"

"Human." He tried to push up, but the pain kept him from moving far. Instead, he rolled over onto his back, his breath seizing tight as bolts of agony shot through his ribs.

He focused again on his body, itemizing sensations. His ribs weren't broken but—damn—they ached. The bullets. Trapped in the muscles between ribs. Still sensitive from the shift, he could feel them as hard points inside his body. As his human mind took more control, those sensations would dull. He needed to remove the bullets now while he still had bear's magic strong inside him.

"Get. Knife," he said, his voice stronger now that he had a plan.

"What?"

"Dig. Bullets. Out."

"I... You were a bear!" she said.

"Knife!"

She fumbled to obey, rooting into a purse that he now noticed was slung across her muscular frame. She pulled out a decent-sized Swiss army knife and popped open a blade. "Just remember, I've got a gun."

He didn't respond except to snarl as she extended the blade to him. He had to fully stretch out his arm to get it, and the movement made him hiss with pain. But a part of him admired that she was smart enough to keep back.

He palmed the blade, adjusted it, then reached down to feel where the bullets lodged between ribs. This was going to hurt.

"What are you doing?" she asked. Her tone told him she knew exactly what he was going to do, but couldn't believe it.

Neither could he. But the window was fading on his keen physical awareness. He had to cut the bullets out now. So he did, starting with the one pressed on the inside of his left floater rib. He sliced down precisely, releasing his breath in a slow hiss of pain.

"That's not sterile!" she cried. He hadn't the focus to comment. The good news was that shifters on a whole had really good immune systems.

It sucked to dig around with his fingers to get the bullet. He managed it, though it stole his breath and made him weak with pain. He dropped the bullet and his whole arm to the ground with a grunt of disgust.

One more.

He narrowed his focus, but the bullet was higher on his chest, just on the inside of his right nipple. He'd have no dexterity to use his right hand. The pectoral muscle would move the bullet around while he worked, and he didn't think he could do this one-handed.

He opened his eyes. "You. Now."

"What?"

"Bullet. Here." He pointed, and her eyes widened on horror.

"Hell, no! Jesus, just call a doctor!" Then she grimaced. "Call 911. Why the hell didn't I call 911?"

"You. Shot me."

"You were a bear!"

He looked at her, not even bothering to hide his fury. And he knew his silence challenged her because they both knew no one would believe he'd been a bear. Though there were as many as a million shifters in the United States, their existence was a closely guarded secret. He'd probably get into serious trouble for changing in front of her, but he had to survive first.

"Help. Me," he said, panting the words because of the pain.

She stared at him slack-jawed, her cell phone clutched in her fingers. His rational mind told him that anger wasn't getting him anywhere, so he moderated his tone.

"I'll show you. Bullet. Pretty close." He focused on her face and tried to smile. "I'll heal."

"W-what?"

"Look." He brushed aside the wound where he'd carved out the other bullet. The skin had already knit closed. A light tug would split it open again, but this close to a shift, he healed really fast. "Losing time," he said, pitching his voice to a low threat. "Must do this now."

"W-what?"

"Don't argue. Just do."

Annoyance washed through her features, but was quickly smoothed out. Then she hardened her jaw as she glared down at him.

Oh hell. He knew that look. He knew her face, too, but damned if he could remember how. She was so damned familiar, but he couldn't place her.

"I do this for you, you do something for me."

"You shot me."

"You attacked me."

"I roared."

"You were a freaking bear. Now agree or you dig that shit out yourself."

God, he hated negotiation and time was running out. He was already losing awareness of exactly where the bullet was in his body. "Fine. Dig now." Easy to agree when he had no intention of remembering this promise.

She grimaced and dropped down to her knees beside him. Then she tossed aside her purse and wiped her palms on faded blue jeans before taking the knife from his hand. "This is not smart."

There were a lot stupider things, but he didn't have the breath to say that. He used his left hand to point to where the bullet was. "Cut here. An inch."

She set one palm on his chest, surprisingly cool though there were beads of sweat on her forehead. Or maybe that was because his temperature was still running hot from his shift.

Pain sliced through his consciousness as she cut, but he controlled his breath so that his chest didn't jerk under her.

"Find. Bullet."

"I see it. I think."

Really? Good for her. She was ten times steadier than he expected. As if she had some medical training. Or disaster training. "You. Nurse?"

"No, I'm not a nurse, you sexist pig."

Hope spiked. "Doc?"

"You wish." She dug her fingers in and it took all his attention to not react to the pain. He needed to keep his chest still while she worked, but God, he wanted to scream.

"Got it!" she cried as she pulled it out. "It's done. I'm done. You can heal it now."

He looked at her, his breath still coming in short pants. "Not magic trick. No wand—"

"Whatever. Just do it."

He exhaled and his eyes drifted closed. Let her think he was doing some meditation bullshit. His body would heal as all bodies did. One cell at a time in its own time, which, admittedly, was really fast right now. Of course, it didn't hurt that he could center himself fully inside his human body. He could mentally run through a list of his organs as if tapping each one. Heart, lungs, liver, kidneys. He rolled through the whole litany until he hit his skin. In his mind's eye, it sealed together in a seamless line exactly as it should and the blood vessels beneath worked just as they ought. All perfect human normal.

A few minutes later he heard her move restlessly beside him. "Is it done? Are you all better?"

His eyes opened and shot her a look. Now that the pain was fading, he was better able to think. What he thought about now was her face and body. Caramel skin on a muscular frame. Her dark brown hair was pulled tightly back into a thick bun, and there was a broadness to her nose that should have looked odd, but beneath those large chocolate eyes, she looked absolutely perfect. That is if he ignored the hard jut of her sharp chin.

"I know you," he said.

Her eyes widened for moment, then slowly narrowed the longer he stayed silent. "Don't stop there. Keep thinking."

He was, but there was a lot to process. Sure he was absorbing her physical details, but he was also just realizing that it was cool outside and the air smelled of spring. That the birds were back to twittering and their song was about hatching and feeding young barely out of the shell.

"What day is it?"

"Hell if I—" She cut off her words then thumbed on her phone. "The twenty-second." And when he didn't respond, she added, "Of May."

"Damn." The last time he'd been human it had been mid-July.

"What? Is something else wrong?"

No way to answer that. There were a thousand things wrong. He'd been a bear for ten months. He wasn't sure he remembered how to be human. And yet even as those thoughts rolled through his mind, he managed to push himself upright until he sat facing her. He didn't concentrate on the movement. He'd learned young to just let his body work as it willed. The more he thought about it, the more awkward he got. And besides, his brain was busy parsing other things.

Like who she was and what was she doing up here. His cabin was in the middle of nowhere in Michigan's Upper Peninsula. She sure as hell wasn't a local. To begin with, there weren't that many African Americans up here. But she had found him, sure enough. And that dirty Chevy Malibu in his driveway said she'd driven a long way to get here, even though it did have Michigan plates.

"Your name," he said.

"Can't remember? I'm hurt." She didn't smell hurt. She smelled like cheap floral perfume over something sweet and nutty.

"Do you know who I am?"

"Corporal Simon Gold of the Corps of Engineers. Discharged about a year ago."

That was awful specific for someone he couldn't quite remember. But he knew how to do this. He could look at the individual pieces of her body and connect them with a memory. He could, though it took so much focus. In the end, it was her stubborn chin that triggered his memory, though in his mind's eye it was always paired with a mischievous tilt to the head. Her brother—his closest friend—had always been searching for fun.

"You're Vic's little sister." What was her name? "Alyssa."

Though he and Victor had been nearly inseparable for the last few years, they'd never been stateside together. Not until last year...er, two years ago, when he'd spent a wonderful couple weeks seeing the bars of Detroit while Alyssa had alternately harassed or hung out with them. He remembered her being skinny, sassy, and a ton more fun than his tight-jawed, muscular woman before him. And back then, he was pretty sure she'd never touched a gun much less been able to stand her ground and put five rounds into a roaring grizzly bear. "You've grown up."

"You were a bear, so I'm pretty sure you're the winner in surprising changes."

He looked at her calmly, analyzing her features and stance. Her eyes were steady as they met his gaze, but her hands were twitchy and her nostrils kept flaring as her breath came in and out in a short, tight tempo. Not quite panicked, but certainly not comfortable. Since she'd picked up her gun again, he'd do well to keep her heading toward calm, not terrified.

So he shrugged and was pleased when the motion didn't hurt too badly. "I can explain."

"Really? Have at it soldier. Give me the details."

He frowned. "Um, what details did you want?"

"You an army experiment?"

"No."

"Bit by a radioactive spider or something?"

"That's a comic book."

She arched a brow and he huffed out a breath. "I was born this way."

"As a bear?"

"Human. All human normal. My first shift was at sixteen."

She crinkled her nose. "You make it sound like a shift at a donut shop. You mean you turned into a bear?" It was half statement, half question, so he answered it.

"Yes. Ripped my favorite jeans. Hurt like hell. Wandered until I was in Gladwin."

She frowned. "Where?"

"Middle Michigan. State park. Here." He held up his hand in the shape of Michigan and pointed an inch below the base of his index finger.

"So it's a genetic thing? Your parents can do it, your—"

Her questions were making his head hurt. He was trying to do too much too fast. He couldn't remember how to act. How to answer. And he was starting to think too much. Which meant—oddly enough—that his language ability was about to deteriorate as he tried to function as a man and not a bear. "Not automatic. Can't say more." He pushed to his feet, his coordination awkward.

Don't think about it. Just do it.

He balanced on his feet while she scrambled backward. And though he tried to appear casual, he kept a close eye on where she put that gun. Fortunately, it went back into her purse-satchel after she'd thumbed on the safety. Jesus, she was just now putting on the safety?

He started walking to his front door. His gait was slow and jerky, but eventually it smoothed out. He needed to keep moving to remember how to be a man. He'd never gone bear for so long before, and a sliver of alarm skated down his spine at the realization. Ten months as a bear? Back in July, he'd planned to be bear for a week. Why hadn't he gone insane? Why hadn't someone hunted him down as a feral?

He looked at the woods behind his cabin. Out there was the female he had been tracking. The memory held equal parts temptation and horror. What had he been doing?

And yet as he looked at the woods, his steps faltered. The longing to shift back to grizzly hit him square in the chest, less painful but no less potent than the slugs he'd taken ten minutes before. There was a sweetness out in the woods. A song that he couldn't hear any more and he wanted it like a man wanted that perfect feeling he couldn't quite remember. And as he stood there staring, the woman's voice cut into his thoughts. Her tone was hard and sarcastic, but not enough to cover her fear.

"You're not going furry again, are you? I still have rounds left in my gun."

He turned slowly, his eyes narrowing as he again picked out the details of her face and body. Minute details, the more specific the better because it forced him to process information like a man. Her brows were drawn down in a frown. Her shoulders were tight with fear, but determination glinted in her narrowed eyes and the set of her feet. She was equally prepared for fight or flight, and one of her hands rested inside her purse, no doubt on the butt of her gun.

"You saw a bear turn into a man. Why aren't you freaking out?"

A dull flush crept up her cheeks. "I adapt quickly."

"No one's that flexible." She couldn't know. Shifters were a really big secret and bear-shifters even more so. Sure, someone was always catching sight of the werewolves, but that's because there were so many damned dogs. Then understanding hit. She'd already been told. Because her brother hadn't kept the secret. "Victor has a big mouth."

She shifted awkwardly, but her gaze remained steady. "I didn't believe him. I thought he was hallucinating until…" She swallowed and gestured to where Simon had been lying on the ground in a pool of his own grizzly blood. "I thought a bear was attacking me. I didn't think it was you. I didn't…" No one believed until they saw. And some not even then. He growled, a very animal sound. And when the noise felt too good inside him, he abruptly shifted to words. "Go home. Go back to Victor. Tell him I'm in a shit-ton of trouble because he talked." And because Simon hadn't reported that Victor knew he was a shifter.

"I will," she said. Her voice taking on an edge of panic as he made it to the front porch. "But only if you come with me."

He tried to think of an appropriate human expression. He found it a moment later when he turned to look straight at her and then rolled his eyes. Then in case the message wasn't clear, he added words. "No. Fucking. Way."

"You have to," she said as she rushed to follow him up the steps. "He's turning into one of you." Her voice shook as she said it, but the words rang with conviction.

He ignored it as he unscrewed the case around the porch light and pulled out the key that was taped inside. A moment later he was unlocking the door, but she gripped his elbow. Her fingers were tight hard points, but he'd just survived five rounds. Fingers were nothing.

"I'm serious. He's changing into…into a bear or something. You have to help him."

"It doesn't work that way."

"Really?" she pressed. "Are you sure?"

"Of course—"

"Because this looks like a freaking bear to me."

She pushed her cell phone into his face. It took him a second to focus on the screen, but he managed to pick out the details of his once best friend. Vic was crouched against a wall, his eyes wild and clearly terrified. And was his nose longer? The eyebrows were bushier, and no scissors had ever trimmed that beard. Vic was staring in horror at his left arm. It wasn't human, but it damn sure wasn't fully bear, either. It was thick and furry and came complete with a hairless paw and real claws.

That couldn't be real. It just couldn't. It…

Again, understanding clicked into place. "That's makeup." He shoved open his front door.

"It's true!" she cried as she tried to follow him.

He stopped her, his hand flat and implacable right on her…Um, wow. He'd forgotten what human breasts felt like. His palm was higher up on her chest, but he felt the curve of both her breasts and was startled by how distracting they were. And that pissed him off even more.

"Go home. This wasn't funny."

"This is real and Vic's dying. Your best friend is dying!"

"Bullshit." He shoved her hard, right in the center of her chest. She stumbled backward. Not far enough to land on her ass, but enough that he could slam the door right in her face.

And this kind of nonsense was exactly why he'd been a bear for the last ten months. No one screwed with bears. No one banged on their doors or forced them to think. And because humans—every single one—were assholes.

CHAPTER 2

Alyssa barely caught herself before tumbling onto her ass. Which meant she had no time at all to catch the door before it closed with a resounding *thud*.

"Oh no, no, no! You did not just slam a door in my face!" Except, obviously, he had. But no way in hell had she driven all this way just to end with a shut door. She shoved forward and twisted the knob. To her shock, the thing swung open. How the hell had he forgotten to lock it? Didn't matter. He was standing in the center of the living room staring at a pile of mail that looked like Mount Everest. "Look, Vic is a dick, no question, but he wasn't lying about this," she said as she waved her phone in the air.

Simon wasn't looking. In truth, he just stood there, all bare-assed and frozen. Was that stillness a military thing? Or an animal thing? Didn't matter. She walked around him and got straight in his face.

"Vic is dying. Don't you guys swear to defend each other until death or something? He's your friend and he needs you."

His gaze focused on her. His green eyes shifted then narrowed, and the build in intensity felt like it took eons while her breath caught and held. How could eyes be scary? Like they were picking apart her face piece by piece and memorizing every detail.

"You swore an oath," she tried, her voice weaker than she wanted.

"That's only in the movies." His voice was thick and growly. No other word for it. Like a bear with a sore paw.

"You came to our house."

"Don't care. Shifting is not like that."

"You so sure about that?" she challenged. Then she thumbed on her phone and pulled up a news video. Something about a strange illness killing people all over Detroit. And that some died grossly disfigured. There was only one picture and it was grainy, but it clearly showed a man with a dog face except for human ears.

"Bullshit," he repeated.

"You keep saying that, but the news doesn't lie."

He arched a look at her, and she felt her cheeks flush with embarrassment. Accusations of fake news were everywhere, but this wasn't fake. She'd seen it herself. She'd seen what her brother had become.

"I'm not lying," she stressed. "It really happened, and Vic says you understand it."

"Vic is wrong." He turned away and stomped to the kitchen where he stopped in the middle and frowned. A moment later he went to the refrigerator and opened it. She trailed after him, watching while she scrambled for some argument that would persuade him. And all the while, he just stared into his empty refrigerator. There was nothing inside. Not even beer or stale bread, which were the only things her brother ever bought.

Meanwhile, his naked body was illuminated by the refrigerator light to the point that she could see every cut line of his body, every ropy muscle, every bony ridge, and an abundance of hair that ought to have repulsed her, but honestly, she thought was sexy as hell. She'd never gone for the hairless guys, and God, he was a ruggedly cut he-man if ever there was one.

And damn her libido for noticing something like that when her brother's life was at stake. And double damn him for looking better than he did in her fantasies. The ones that had started nearly two years ago when she'd watched him play basketball shirtless with her brother.

"Just come see him," she said, hating the pleading note in her voice. "You promised to do me a favor. This is it. Just come with me. See for yourself."

"A contract made under duress is not valid." His voice was flat and he still hadn't moved.

"Food is not going to magically appear in there. So turn your hairy ass around and look at me!"

He straightened, his expression clearly startled. Then he did indeed turn around. Sadly, full frontal was no less enticing than his chiseled, not-really-hairy ass. Especially since the man was hung very nicely.

"You are upset," he said.

Well, duh.

"You believe Vic's lie." He gave her a pitying look. "He's tricked you many times before."

Yes, her brother could be a first-class dick, and he loved nothing else than to get her all riled up just so he could laugh his ass off at her. But this wasn't one of those times. "It's real," she repeated. "He's scared shitless and he sent me to find you."

He lifted his hands, palm outward. "I can't help him."

He had a point, especially since looking as he did now—naked and stained with his own blood—it didn't look like he could help himself, much less her brother.

"Vic said you would understand this."

"I don't understand how to turn on the plumbing right now." He rubbed a hand over his face. "I have been too long in the wild." He dropped his hand and his gaze focused past her to stare out the back window.

Oh hell. There was longing on his face. A clear need to go animal again, but she couldn't let that happen. "That's not good for you." She said it as a statement, though it was really more of a guess.

"So they say." It was clear he wasn't sure.

The last thing she needed was another confused man on her hands, but she'd be damned if her brother's only hope—even if it was a Hail Mary pass—didn't help her. But first he needed to get his head on straight.

"You need a shower and clothes. Food, too, unless it's normal for your ribs to stick out like that." Just where the hell did all that mass go to when he shifted back to human? He'd been at least four hundred pounds as a cranky grizzly. Now he looked like a lean two-ten with zero body fat.

"Clothes," he said as he looked down at himself. Holy hell, was he just now realizing he'd been wandering around naked? He looked back at her, a sheepish expression on his face. "You never said a thing."

Like she was going to convince the eye candy to cover up? "I had other things on my mind. Like digging bullets out of you."

He pulled at the skin on his chest. "One bullet. All healed."

"Great. Now get clean and dressed. Got pizza delivery out here?"

She figured the more he did normal human things, the better for him and by extension, for her and Vic. "Never mind. I'll just order ahead and we'll pick it up on the way."

He shook his head. "I am not ready to interact with humans."

No shit, Sherlock. "That's what I'm here for. And, in case you were wondering, I'm human, too, and you're doing just fine."

He tilted his head and arched a brow. It was a strangely awkward gesture. As if he was trying to remember how to give a skeptical look and had to force his features into position. Even so, she found it oddly charming.

"I'll help," she said, gesturing to the stairs. "I'll get the plumbing working. Please tell me I don't need to scrub bear off your back."

His lips curved. "The bear is inside. No amount of scrubbing will get it off." The way he said it made her think he'd once tried to do it, but she didn't have time to delve into that. She had to get back to Vic, and he was all the way down in Detroit.

"Whatever. Just get moving." She fit words to action, putting her hands on him enough to push him toward the stairs. She was a strong woman, but she couldn't have moved him if he hadn't allowed it. And for a moment there, she was pretty sure he wasn't going to cooperate. But something had changed from when he'd slammed the door in her face and now. Something inside this cabin that made him a little malleable.

So when she pushed, he shifted his weight and began to walk. She kept her hands on him, guiding him though he didn't need it. But when else was she going to get her hands on a naked him? Just because he'd lived in her fantasies for years didn't mean that he felt anything toward her. Hell, he hadn't even remembered her at first. And wasn't that a blow to her ego?

The upstairs was simple. Two bedrooms and a large bathroom. She pushed him in the bathroom first. Then while he narrowed his eyes at his reflection, she turned on the bathtub faucet. The water ran—good—but it was pretty cold, so he'd have to wait for it to heat up. Meanwhile, she turned back to him and watched him stroke his hand over his cheeks.

"I never need to shave after a shift. And my hair is always like this." He brushed his fingers through his short, military-style cut. "Even before I enlisted, I always came back like this."

Well that was interesting, but she had no idea what to say about it, so she checked the water again. Toasty warm.

"If you've been gone for months, who's gotten the mail and kept the pipes from freezing?"

"Manny takes care of that." He sniffed the air. "The water's clean and hot."

"Yeah. So get in. I'll look for a towel." There was soap and shampoo in the shower, though a fine coating of dust was on both. Pretty clear no one had used this shower in months.

He obeyed slowly, stepping in as if he were in a daze. But once the water hit him, he gasped and his eyes shuttered as his head tilted back. He was facing directly into the spray and he seemed to stretch his broad chest as if to catch the water.

He didn't have to say a word for her to realize that this was something important to him. Some type of visceral memory that engulfed him. He stood there, water beating at his chest, and he deeply inhaled the mist, which carried the scent of woods and man to her nostrils.

God, what a sight. She felt like she was peeking in on primal man in a moment of joyous oneness with water. It made no sense, but she felt the elemental draw all the way to her womb. Her mouth dried and she stood mesmerized as he slowly tilted his head forward and down. The water hit his face and then the top of his head, running in rivulets down his body. And he breathed. Deep inhales that expanded his shoulders and his barrel chest, while she went wet with lust.

What kind of perv stood there watching a man shower? Especially when he was deep in whatever experience was going on in his head?

Her apparently, because she couldn't force herself to leave.

And then he reached out. The motion was automatic because he didn't look, didn't even open his eyes. His hand connected with the soap and he grabbed it, spinning it slowly as he created a rich lather.

Irish Spring. She remembered that scent from when he'd visited so long ago. It became permanently linked with her fantasies about him, and now she was watching one of her favorites play out right in front of her. If only she dared strip down to join him under the spray. She'd slide against his lathered chest as he pressed her against the tile wall. And when they were both thoroughly slick, he'd lift her knee and impale her. She'd come right then. And she'd keep coming while he pistoned into her. And then he'd erupt just like in her fantasies while pressing kisses into her neck and whispering words of devotion.

Her womb pulsed at the thought, then he inhaled again. God, she'd never tire of watching his chest broaden like that. And then he began to wash. Face first as he leaned back out of the spray. He covered his head in lather, including his hair. With it cut so short, he didn't really need shampoo. She watched the play of his muscles as he moved. Who had biceps that large? Or an abdomen so flat?

Then he tilted forward, and the white foam slid off him like melted ice cream washed away. She wanted to lick it and him, though she told herself sternly that was gross. Didn't seem to matter to her libido. And damn it, with the shower curtain wide open, he was getting water all over the floor—and her pants—but she didn't care. Couldn't move. Not as he started soaping up his arms and chest next.

She watched, her mouth dry, her eyes unblinking. She didn't want to miss a second of this display. When he rubbed the soap over his chest, her nipples tightened unbearably. And that was nothing compared to when he lifted his legs—one by one—to lather every sweet inch.

She even watched when he cleaned his dick. He didn't take any special time with it; was efficient as he rubbed and pulled. But God, what she wouldn't give to do that for him. And extra slow. Especially when he soaped up his ass.

He couldn't reach his back. He tried anyway, rubbing across his shoulders, stretching up behind. And when he turned around to face away from the spray, she got splashed from the movement. Droplets on her face and arms. She might have gasped. She might not. Either way, he abruptly stilled while the water pelted his back.

She froze, her breath trapped in her lungs. Hell, what if he knew she was there? She'd be mortified! But she couldn't turn tail and run now. He'd hear her and know for sure. So she had to remain still and pray, pray, pray that he didn't look her way. It was a losing gambit. Eventually he was going to finish, and she had no idea what she'd do then. But for now, she was frozen in indecision and lust.

Fortunately, he didn't look her way. He stood there while the soapsuds slicked down his body. And together, they breathed deep the misty scent of Irish Spring. Then, three breaths later, she saw his erection. Oh wow.

Right there in profile, his dick thickened until it was high and proud.

Her gaze shot to his face. His eyes were closed, his breathing steady and even. And while she was looking at his face, his hand moved. Oh God. He was touching himself. More than touching, he'd begun a slow, steady stroke.

Seriously? He was jerking off now? She was appalled and intrigued, and a thousand other things. But mostly she was panicked. She couldn't watch. It was depraved.

And yet, she did. She watched as he stroked himself, fisting his impressive penis in a large, soapy hand. His tempo was steady, his breathing barely discernible, but growing faster. She watched as his ass tightened with tiny thrusts. Flex, flex, flex—all as he punched into his fist.

This was exactly how she'd imagined he made love, how she'd fantasized his thrusts inside her would be. Steady and thick. Her belly began to contract in time with him. Her heart beat faster and faster as her breath grew short. And she stared transfixed at the curl of his fist as she imagined herself spread wide as he did that to her.

The head of his penis peaked out above his fist. It grew darker, a reddish purple that fascinated her. But no more so than the rhythmic way that he worked himself. Thrust. Thrust. Thrust. Like a metronome.

His nostrils flared and his breath grew louder. Hers caught as her body flushed hot.

His jaw clenched and his belly seemed to ripple. Hers did, too, a perfect mirror.

Faster. A little faster.

Her toes curled into her shoes and she ached, wanting the finish.

A grunt. Guttural and yet still triumphant.

White shot from his tip. It mixed with the shower spray and the wet on the tiles.

She wanted it, too. She wanted that finish, but it didn't come. Not for her. Not from watching.

He opened his hand and his penis bobbed before him, dark red and still proudly erect.

And he stood there while the water washed the evidence away while she throbbed from nipples to core. She'd never seen anything so raw before. Or so beautiful. A perfect body erupting in the most primal of ways. There'd been power and steady determination in the act. No wild jerks, no exultant crowing like a horny boy.

He was all man and she would remember the sight until the day she died.

And then he turned his head. He turned with his green eyes open and looked straight at her.

She stood, pinned in place. What did she say? What could she do?

He smiled. A slow curve that was arrogant and all male. That look told her he'd known she was there the whole time. He'd been aware of her from the very first moment and that show—that gorgeous erotic display—had been all for her.

That thought rocked her like nothing else. It made her core spasm once hard in the only near-orgasm she would get from this. She was embarrassed, and yet she was also flushed with hunger. She remained poised on her tiptoes, wondering if she could strip down now? Did she dare live out her fantasy? If she asked, would he put her against the wall like she imagined and do that again inside her?

"Closet in the hall," he said. His voice was thick, but the words were clear. The meaning anything but.

"What?"

"The towels," he said. "Closet in the hall."

Oh. Right.

So no enacting the fantasy.

She spun on her heel and fled.

CHAPTER 3

Simon smirked as he cut off the shower and stood to drip dry. Normally he'd have ordered her out of the bathroom the moment he'd stepped into the tub. But the animal inside him was too close to the surface. It had reveled in the lust that had scented the air. It had smelled her attraction the moment she'd stepped into his home. Why else would he stand buck naked in the middle of his kitchen while arguing with her?

So he had let her watch while the water had brought his human body back online. Heat, wet, the feel of the lather on skin without fur. It had taken a while, but he had touched every inch of his body to remember his own dimensions.

And while his mind reacquainted itself with his body, the animal had smelled Alyssa's spicy scent and gloried in showing off his sexual prowess. His loins had thickened and her musk mixed with the steam while he proved his fitness to mate. He'd stroked himself and imagined it was her hand, her lips, her honey that slicked his penis. The orgasm that shot through him had been blindingly intense. His vision had whited out while his body consumed itself with his fantasy of seeding his child in her belly.

When it was done, the man in him had been shocked. The animal had preened. And both had wanted to see Alyssa's reaction.

Flushed cheeks, taut nipples, and eyes that were half dazed, half terrified. That was the sight of a female considering a mate. But then she'd gasped and fled the room. The animal had wanted to leap after her because she was slow and he could overpower her. But the man in him knew human females were different and such a thing was wrong.

So he stood still and let the squabble between animal and man continue in his mind. He knew in this body the man would always win though, damn, it was taking a while.

Suddenly a dark blue towel flew into the room to land drunkenly on the covered toilet.

"Ten minutes," Alyssa snapped in a crisp, authoritarian tone. "We'll get burgers on the way."

Years ago, he'd jumped whenever a sergeant had barked in that tone of voice. Coming from Alyssa, the sound only made him smile.

No point in arguing with her. She couldn't force him to do what she wanted. And he had a system when coming back from weeks as a bear. A process developed as a teen when he'd spent summers in the UP. The return-to-human protocol eased him back safely. And though he'd never been bear for months at a time before, he hoped that the reintegration process would be the same.

He grabbed the towel and began to once again log the sensations of his human body. Fabric rough on skin. The prickle of cold air on wet hair. The flex and strain of remaining upright and balanced on two feet without claws. All these things were being revisited and cataloged in his mind. He was human. He was a man.

The animal slunk back into a corner of his consciousness, sat down with a humph, and sulked. He could even feel the heavy thump of the creature's rear end on the floor of his mind. In time, it would drop its head down onto front paws and snuffle in a pouting doze. It was the way of things with his bear, and he mentally tried to shut the door on the bear's cage.

It didn't close. Not yet. The grizzly was too large to be tucked away so easily. Especially since he had so brazenly demonstrated his prowess to the female just a moment ago. But it would happen in time. Assuming he strictly followed the protocol.

So he hung up his towel to dry and walked upright to his bedroom to get dressed. He went straight to his dresser and opened the first drawer. Tight briefs because humans wore underwear. He pulled them on. Jeans in the next drawer. Loose as he dragged them up over his hips. He had to think how to zip and button, but his fingers found the pattern. Then he stopped to remember what next.

Footwear? Jacket?

His hands opened the third drawer and pulled on an army tee, olive drab. Drawer four had socks. He had to sit down to pull them on, so he bent his knees and dropped onto his bed. A puff of dust blew up from the comforter, and he wrinkled his nose at the odor. He would have to remember to clean the bedding, but that wasn't next on his list. He pulled on his socks. Then when he looked up, he saw his boots set almost exactly in his eye line.

He grabbed them, then jerked them on. Now it was time to tie laces. This, too, he mastered with alacrity, but it was still a reminder that he had to move steadily through his system or find himself hopelessly lost later on.

He was staring at his boots and trying to remember the next step when Alyssa appeared in his bedroom door. "You're dressed. Good. We need to leave now. It's already going to be late when we arrive."

He turned his head, his gaze now able to see details that his animal mind could not. His bear had labeled her beautiful in that she had sturdy bones and smelled healthy. Now he saw that in human terms she had curves that were functional rather than fashionable. Breasts restrained under an athletic bra, jeans that were loose enough to be comfortable and hide what was likely to be strong, shapely legs. Her mocha skin was creamy like a perfect cup of coffee with milk. Her face had nice eyes and full lips, both without makeup. And her ears held tiny gold studs as her only nod to female vanity because her hair was downright severe in the way it was pulled back from her face in a tight bun. This woman didn't even allow a ponytail.

He liked that kind of efficiency, he realized. It spoke of an ordered mind. Except when she spoke, her voice held all the temper of his long-ago sergeant.

"Stand up. Walk to my car. We're leaving."

"You remember me from when I visited with Vic two years ago." A statement, not a question.

Her brows narrowed slightly. "Yes. Why?"

"You tried to order me around then. Did it work?"

Her mouth tightened. "No."

"But you think it will now."

She grimaced. "It did for a moment there. Back in the kitchen."

"When I was vulnerable."

"When you were confused after just being shot. And turning back into…into…"

"A man."

"Yes."

He narrowed his eyes until he saw just her eyes. "It will not work now."

She winced. "Yeah, I'm getting that."

"I control this territory. As a bear or a man, I control it. You cannot win here."

He held her gaze until her eyes dipped in submission. And at that moment, he felt both human and bear ease inside his mind. The man knew it was an illusion. Dominance, control, even leadership could be stripped away in a moment. And then where was the animal's prowess? The man's control? Gone.

A memory flickered in his mind: the reason he had run to the UP and become a bear for ten months. It was because of his need for control. The man knew it to be impossible lie. No one controlled everything. But the bear lived in ignorance. And so he had escaped to the only place where he could believe in his own dominance.

Except now she was here. She forced him back into that uncertain reality where he could not always win. Snowstorms whipped up early. Secrets got out. And commanding officers bounced his ass out of the military.

His gaze dropped to his boots, both hating and loving the familiar feel. Military-issue boots for a man who no longer commanded.

"Okay," Alyssa said, her voice gentle. "What's next on the protocol?"

He didn't have an answer. Not until he looked up from his boots and saw something metal on his dresser. He hadn't noticed it before, but now it seemed to call him.

Computer. And beside it, his phone.

"I need to turn on my computer."

"You can do that in the car."

He ignored her. But just as he reached for his laptop, a folded brochure slipped to the floor. His gaze followed it.

A flyer for pizza.

His stomach rumbled. He was always hungry after a shift. Either from bear to man or the reverse, food was always a need.

"I should order pizza." He had no real desire for the food. In fact, the picture on the flyer was unappetizing. But it was the next step on his list. That's why it had been set there at eye level after he put on his boots.

"Burgers are faster." Alyssa said as she stepped farther into the room. "And burgers have more meat."

He was holding the flyer trying to make sense of the tiny rows of words. Damn it. It would take him a bit to remember how to read. The knowledge made him impatient and his words curt.

"That's not protocol."

He was staring at the words, willing them to make sense. Come on. Come on. Read, damn it!

Then suddenly a brown hand appeared over the text and gently pushed the flyer away. His gaze shot up to hers, anger churning. It was his bear, pouring other resentments into a growl, and her eyes widened at the sound. But she didn't back away. Though fear spiked in her scent, she held her gaze steady.

"You're not in the army anymore. Food isn't protocol. You're getting hangry."

Hell. Now he wasn't hearing right. "Hangry" wasn't a word, was it? And the confusion had his bear rearing up inside him, ready for a fight. He held it back with a mental glare and tried again to slam the cage door. No go. But the beast didn't surge forward, either.

Which meant he had to continue his checklist until he had a better handle on his bear.

"There is a process," he said slowly, every word distinct. "Wash. Dry. Underwear. Jeans." He pointed to his drawers in order. "Shirt, socks, boots." He pulled the flyer from underneath her hand. "Read." Then he growled, "Read!" as if he could order his brain to assimilate the symbols.

He was looking at the paper, so he didn't see the change in her expression. Not until she touched his cheek and forced his gaze up to hers. Her brown eyes were serious as she spoke, the tone without nuances, and for that he was grateful.

"I can help. I can read it for you."

"No." Didn't she understand? He needed to come back to human. She couldn't do that for him. It was a path he had to walk by himself or be trapped as neither one nor the other. Not a bear, and definitely not a whole man.

He glared back down at the paper. Suddenly, one of the symbols made sense. "Two!" He pointed to the printed digit. "That's the number two. Seven. Nine." He was reading. The numbers at least.

"Yes. That's part of the phone number."

He looked up to the smaller metal thing on his dresser. "My phone."

She grabbed it and handed it to him. "Do you want me to dial?"

"No." He understood what he was doing. He could match the numbers on the paper and on his phone now. His fingers fumbled, but he managed it, and soon a thin female voice came through the device, barely heard because the phone remained in his palm in his lap.

"Simon! You're back! Want your usual?"

He swallowed and nodded. Then he remembered to use his voice. "Yes."

"I'll be out there in a half hour," the voice answered.

"No!" Alyssa said loudly. "We'll pick it up."

A pause and then a chuckle. "Got a girl this time? That's new."

It wasn't protocol and he didn't like it. But he didn't have the wherewithal to argue. He never understood why communication was so easy early after a shift back to human but then seemed to abandon him as he brought other functions online. Like reading and manipulating an iPhone. Eventually it would all settle into place. The process usually took anywhere from a day to a week. But right now, he was swimming upstream.

"I want meat," he said.

"Yeah, I know. Fifteen minutes."

He thumbed off the phone. What was next on the list? His gaze rose to the device on his dresser. He pushed Alyssa aside as he stood up to grab it. She moved easily, her expression in the mirror somber.

"Laptop is the next step in this protocol?" she asked.

"Yes. To help with the reading."

"Got it. You can do it in the car."

He turned to look at her and saw that she arched a brow at him. That look was a challenge, clear as day and the bear in him bristled, wanting to fight because that's what his bear did. But he was shifting back to human, so he did the opposite. He nodded and echoed her words, "I can do it in the car."

"Great. Where's your go bag?"

He frowned, taking a moment to process her words. And in that time, she rolled her eyes.

"Don't blank stare me. I know you have one, and I'll bet it's…" She snapped her fingers. "Front door closet."

She turned and tripped lightly down the stairs. He followed, his laptop in one hand, his phone in the other. She was ahead of him, pulling out a black duffel from his closet. She grinned at him, the look triumphant as she slung the pack over one shoulder. Then she pulled open the front door and gestured to her car.

"Come on. Food is waiting."

He took a step, but stopped. "The protocol keeps everyone safe," he said. "I am not at my best now and that is not safe."

She frowned and he was pleased to see that she took his words seriously. Good. It was dangerous to upset a grizzly bear, and he was only 51 percent human right then. Though his higher thought processes were coming on strong, it would take a couple hours at least before he could reliably control his primal instincts. The animal still had a strong grip on his body and it was aiming his feet toward the woods. Go back out to the woods and—

"Oh no, you don't. We're getting in the car."

This was why he got delivery. Because once the scent and sight of the woods hit his body, the grizzly surged forward. It wanted to be back out there. It wanted—

An arm gripped him tight and hauled him around. He was already snarling, showing his teeth at the woman before her.

"Damn it! Get it together!" she snapped.

He was trying. But she had interrupted his protocol. This wasn't going to work—

She yanked on his ears as she jerked his face down until they were nose to nose. "The car. Get in the car."

Her scent filled his nostrils. That nutty tang that surrounded her. He liked it and he liked the lingering echo of musk that clung to her skin. It competed with the rustle of the trees and the scent of summer pine. And since it was a human scent, his mind latched on to it, using it against the bear.

He inhaled deeply, the choice crystallizing in his mind. A human would go with the human. A bear would go back to the woods. And right now, he was human. He stood upright, he wore clothes, and he carried human things in his hands.

"I will be stronger with food," he said.

"So get in the car," she said.

"I need to eat as a man."

She snorted. "You mean grunt and shove handfuls of pizza into your mouth?"

"With a knife and fork."

"On pizza?" She was walking as she spoke and tugging on his arm.

He went because she was human. And she smelled nice. "It is the protocol."

"Of course, it is." Then her tone dropped and grew somber. "I got you, Simon. You'll be okay. And then together, we're going to save Vic."

He sighed. Just because his mind was split into two pieces—human and bear—didn't mean he'd forgotten what she wanted. Her wants had been relegated to a different part of his consciousness while he came back to being fully human. But a part of him did remember, and that was the part who answered.

"There is no saving me. Or Vic."

She clicked the seatbelt around him. He hadn't even realized he'd climbed into the car. "That's bullshit, Simon. Pure drama queen bullshit."

He turned to look her in the eye, his higher consciousness stuttering to a halt in shock. Had she just called him a drama queen? No part of that computed. So he did what he always did when something incomprehensible came at him. He listed the things he did know.

"I was a bear for ten months. You shot me five times. I shifted to human to survive and began my human protocols. You interrupted that. You risk us both by changing what you don't understand." He looked her in the eye. "How does that equate to being a drama queen?"

She met his gaze levelly then shrugged. "It's just pizza and then a quick trip to Detroit."

He knew the human response to that.

"Bullshit."

CHAPTER 4

Alyssa kept her breathing calm. She inhaled and released in slow control and then realized that she wasn't fooling anyone. Her hands gripped the steering wheel like it was her lifeline on the *Titanic*. And though her breath was steady, her pace on the accelerator was anything but. She'd already roared past three trucks only to slow down to grandma speed a moment later. She was losing it and all because of the crazy man sitting much too close in her suddenly tiny car.

She stole a glance to the right. He was watching her with the unceasing stare of a predatory cat. She knew he was a bear, but damn it, he was a predator and she couldn't shake the feeling that he was about to pounce. Or break. Or do something just plain scary while she was driving them to Detroit. But first she had to feed him.

She'd gotten the directions off the flyer and now turned into the large parking lot of a small pizzeria. She breathed a sigh of relief when she saw they had a drive-through and immediately headed for that. A moment later, a stunning redheaded woman with large white teeth grinned at her through the window. The name on the apron read Amanda and she winked at Simon. "You up to talking yet?" she asked.

Simon stared hard at her and said one word, "No."

The woman chuckled and smiled at Alyssa. "He's all grumbly for a few days, but then it'll get better." Then she disappeared.

A moment later, she passed over two thick cheeseburgers and a large pizza loaded down with a half inch of meat. This was Simon's usual order? He ought to weigh five thousand pounds. Though how would she know how many calories it took to shift into a grizzly? Maybe all shifters ate like bears before hibernation.

Alyssa was about to pull away when Amanda held out her hand. "Hold on, sweetie. Let me bring out the case."

Sweetie? Case? There was too much in that sentence to unpack, so she threw the car into park and waited. A moment later, Amanda came out with a case of high-end water bottles. She didn't even know that water could come in glass bottles that looked more like wine than water, but she didn't stop to ask. Just pointed to her backseat.

"Thanks," she said when the water was settled and the car door shut.

"I'll just put it on the tab," Amanda said. Then after another lascivious wink, she waved them on. "Have fun!"

Not likely. Not since she was kidnapping a crazy grizzly man. But what other choice did she have? Vic said he was the only one who could help. But even knowing that, she couldn't stop herself from asking.

"So are you and…um…the redhead dating?"

Simon shook his head. He took his time answering, forming the words slowly as if he had to dredge them up from deep in his memory.

"We dated. Twice. I have gone on two dates with most of the women up here." He looked at her and lifted a shoulder. "We did not suit."

He sounded like he was reading the words—badly—off a cue card. And then she understood.

"It's another system, right? A dating protocol. Two evenings with a woman makes her think you gave her a chance. If you treat her nicely and talk awkwardly, then she doesn't push it when you say you two don't suit. End of story and they stop bothering you." She snorted. "I don't know whether to be impressed or appalled." Then she tilted her head. "You could just tell them you're gay?" She lifted her voice at the end hoping he would answer the implied question.

It worked—sort of. "Lying is too complicated. I don't do it."

Well, that answered that. The man didn't lie. Big point in his favor.

Meanwhile, Simon continued to sit staring at her though the food lay on his lap in neat cardboard boxes. The smell must be driving him crazy. She could hear his stomach rumbling over the road noise. But he just sat there staring at her.

"What?" she finally asked.

"I cannot help Vic. I can barely help myself."

She looked at him. Not just the hard cut to his jaw or the muscles that wrapped his frame. He was a powerful man to be sure, but it was the darkness in his eyes that cut her now. Blue like deep water but shadowed even though he sat in the full sunshine.

Wait. Hadn't his eyes been green? She shoved that thought aside and focused on getting him on board with Vic's plan.

"Vic says you can help him."

"Vic is full of shit."

Often. But she couldn't admit that. If she did, then that meant there was no hope for her only brother. "He was right about you turning into a bear."

Simon's expression didn't change. It was flat. It was emotionless. And it still held shadows of what? Grief? Fear? She didn't know. And worse, she couldn't afford to find out. She only had emotional space in her heart for Vic.

"It's the only Hail Mary pass I've got," she confessed.

His silence told her clearer than anything else that her brother was doomed. She didn't care. She'd been trying for hours to get a hold of Vic and he hadn't answered. Which meant it might already be too late. But she was going to do what she promised. She was going to bring Simon to Detroit. If he couldn't help, if they arrived too late, if any of a thousand terrible things happened, it wasn't her fault. She was doing her part now.

So she put the car into gear and headed for the freeway. "You should eat the food. Your stomach is deafening." And it was. It hadn't stopped growling since the scents of pizza and cheeseburger filled the car.

His gaze turned to the topmost small box and opened it. Thick burger, melted cheese, tomato, mustard. The sight made her mouth water. He lifted it up in both his hands, but he didn't eat.

"Sometimes the food quiets the grizzly. It lets the man take control."

"Good."

"Sometimes the opposite happens."

It took her a moment to process that. So the grizzly would take over? While they were in a car together speeding down a freeway at eighty miles per hour?

She shot him a terrified look. His head was tilted and a single brow arched. It challenged her to turn the car around right then and dump him at the nearest tree. Common sense told her that was the best thing to do. But common sense wasn't trying to save her brother.

"Eat up," she said, her voice ringing with challenge.

He nodded and chomped down.

Swell.

* * *

A short hour later the food was finished, the gas tank was heading toward low, and he remained exactly as he had been before: a predator watching her every breath. Eventually, she had enough. She kept her eyes on the road, but watched him closely out of her peripheral vision.

"So which are you now? Bear or man?"

"Both. I am always both."

Not helpful. "I mean are you about to sprout fur?"

He looked down at his arms. All human normal, as far as she could tell. "Not at the moment. And I must not change again for at least a week. If I do, I will probably stay a bear forever."

"Jesus," she muttered. Like she needed more of an incentive to keep him human? "Can you just tell me if you're about to kill me?"

He straightened as if insulted. "I am not." His tone indicated he thought the question insane.

"Thank you," she snapped, her anxiety coming out in a sharp tone.

He waited a moment, then spoke in that slow monotone of his. "Why are you angry? I am answering your questions."

"Not really," she groused. He was giving her literal answers to direct questions. But none of it told her what she wanted to know because she didn't know what she didn't know. How could she ask the right questions when she hadn't the first clue how to start? Maybe at the beginning. "How did my brother find out you were a bear? Did he shoot you, too?"

"I rescued him. As a bear."

She turned to look at him, annoyance eating at her already frayed nerves. God, she wanted to smack him. Instead she decided to bargain. "What do you need to talk to me like a normal person? To have a conversation where your answers don't create a dozen more questions?"

He tilted his head, the gesture slower than natural. "Communication is hard after a shift. I will get better."

"With practice?" She didn't wait for his answer. "So let's practice now. Tell me the full story of how my brother found out you were a bear."

He looked at her with clear irritation. Not a studied movement at all but a furrowing of his brow and a peeling back of his lips. His teeth flashed white but she pretended she didn't see it. She just kept her hands on the wheel, her gaze steady ahead. Part of her screamed that it wasn't smart to poke at the bear, but she couldn't seem to stop herself.

"Talk. Now," she ordered.

"You cannot command me," he said. "Only my alpha can."

"And now I have another dozen questions." *Okay.* Ordering him around wasn't working. She hadn't really expected it to, so maybe it was time for logic mixed with a little begging. "It's a long way to Detroit. It would help me pass the time and you need the practice. Please?"

His gaze shifted from her face to the road. Then he nodded. "A solid argument." He pursed his lips. "I will tell you the story of your brother's stupidity."

Like that would be a rare story…not.

"We were stationed in Alaska near Mount Denali. He wanted to go climbing, but I said no. The weather would turn. He disagreed."

"Really?" Her brother might be stupid but usually with people. Not with something like the weather.

"The reports said the storm wouldn't come until the next morning." Simon snorted. "The reports were wrong."

She turned to look at him, only now processing what the man was saying. She remembered when Vic had been transferred to Alaska. She'd been thrilled. Sure, it was cold as hell, but he wasn't likely to get shot at. But, of course, her brother would want to explore. Hell, he loved mountain climbing more than anything. And, of course, he would get in trouble. It was just how the boy's luck ran.

"How did you find him?"

He grimaced. "I went with the rescue team. I knew where he meant to go, but the storm came in fast and hard. We were ordered back." He shook his head. "Stupid. Stupid not to listen to me."

"That's Vic all right."

He shot her the most human look she'd seen on his face: a wry almost-smile coupled with a shrug. God, how many times had she done that in response to one of her brother's mad ideas?

"I was very angry. I fell behind the rescuers—told them I was going back—and shifted." He grimaced. "The grizzly was very near to the surface that day. There is something about that mountain that draws it out. I don't know why, but it allowed me to save Vic's life."

She blew out a breath. "You found him…as a bear?"

"Yes." His voice was the same near monotone he'd used before. But she was starting to hear fluctuations in his tones now. And his next sentences seemed to imply curiosity as much as irritation. "My bear was very sharp then. Very smart in that place. Even with the snow and the storm, I could smell Vic."

She felt her hands ease on the steering wheel. Her shoulders relaxed even though the danger had been months ago. Vic had survived and come back to Detroit only to be hit by whatever it was that was changing him now. "So you found him and both made it back to base."

"I was a bear and he was hurt from a fall." Simon looked down at his hands where they seemed to clench his thighs. Like claws digging in? She didn't have the time to ask because the moment she noticed them, he stretched out his fingers until he could set his palms flat on the denim. "It was too cold to shift back to human, and I had already ripped out of my clothing."

Right. They'd been in Alaska in a snowstorm. No way could he just shift back in torn skivvies and travel back to the base. "What did you do?"

"I carried him as a bear." His lips curved and she was startled to see his smile. It softened the harsh angles of his face, but only in a small way. His mouth and cheeks eased, but not his eyes, which stared fixedly ahead. "He was terrified, but I gave him no choice."

She couldn't even imagine how that had gone down. "I'm surprised he didn't shoot you."

"He tried. It took a long time for me to convince him to climb onto my back, but then he did and we made it back to base."

"But you were a bear."

"There is much that can be expressed by pushing with my nose and a well-timed growl."

She snorted. "Wish I had been there to see it."

He flashed her a frown. "You would have frozen to death."

Literal much? "Yeah, I know. I...It's just a figure of speech."

He didn't respond at first, and when she finally glanced at him again, she was startled to see him grinning at her. Like full-blown grinning. It made his face look youthful. She did a double take and then finally figured it out. "You're teasing me. Taking my words really literally just to see if I'll roll with it."

"No, I'm not." His grin widened.

Holy hell, he *was* teasing her. She'd just gotten into the rhythm of the man's hyper-literal speech pattern, and now he was turning the tables on her. Pretending to be more communications-challenged than he really was. Would she ever gain the upper hand with this guy?

"Don't be a dick," she groused, but without much heat. She preferred dealing with someone who had a sense of humor, odd though it might be. "So you're a bear and you convince Vic to climb onto your back. Was he able to hold on as you went back to base?"

"His knee was hurt, not his arms. He held on tight and I was able to move fast." He blew out a breath. "Very fast."

Sounded like it was surprisingly fast, even for Simon. "That's the part about your grizzly being close to the surface, right? Being especially strong?"

"Yes." The word held a wealth of uncertainty. "I have never been that strong or that fast before. Or since."

"Since you saved my brother's life, I can only be grateful."

He blew out a breath, clearly brooding on the experience. She let him do it for a while, hoping that he would talk out his thoughts. He didn't. He was the strong silent type, which made him mysterious and attractive to her twisted libido. Why couldn't she lust after someone who couldn't shut up? Then she'd know exactly what drivel went about in his head.

Eventually she got tired of the silence. "So how did you get him back to base without getting shot?" She couldn't imagine guards allowing a huge grizzly bear to zip up to the front gate.

"There were trees nearby. I shifted to human there, then carried your brother back to base."

Carried? Vic must have been hurt a great deal more than a bad knee. But hell, he was talking about carrying a man through an Alaskan snowstorm while naked.

"It's a miracle you weren't frostbitten."

"I was. But I fixed it on my next shift."

"But there must have been questions. And video, right? Even if the guards didn't see, weren't there cameras?"

He turned and looked directly at her, surprise in the lift of his eyebrows. "I was seen."

He seemed startled that she could think the scenario through. She shot him an arch look. She wasn't just a pretty face.

Meanwhile, he nodded as if he accepted her words though she hadn't said anything. "Enough people saw and then more when I refused to allow them to amputate my feet."

What? Ouch.

"Among many shifters, that is a killing offense."

And now she had another thousand questions, all of them ending in an exclamation point. So she started with the most obvious. "Killing offense because you didn't want your feet amputated?"

He shook his head. "Letting the shifter secret out."

Oh. Right. "So you'd be killed for telling? Or they'd be killed for knowing?" And how soon were angry grizzly-shifters going to come for her because she knew about the fur?

He sighed. "Both. Sometimes. That's why I didn't tell anyone."

Oh shit. "So, um, the military knows about shifters now because you saved my brother's life?"

"Yes."

"And you haven't confessed that particular detail to your alpha." She was guessing at the power structure among his kind, but he seemed to confirm it all with a nod.

"Many human things are forgotten when being a bear. And they don't come always come back." He glanced at her. "It slipped my mind."

Yeah, right. "I thought you said you didn't lie."

"I don't. I came back home and everything about my clan had changed. We had a new alpha and new rules, plus there had been some sort of attack on the children."

"What?" A very real surge of fury went through her. She despised it when kids were targeted.

"I was angry about leaving the army, and I would not submit to Carl. I decided since I had left the army, I didn't have to take orders from anyone anymore." He swallowed loud enough for her to hear. "I was very angry."

She heard the pain in the very emptiness of his tone. Her brother had cost him everything, and here she was demanding he help Vic again. But rather than face his pain, she shifted to her questions. "Who is Carl?"

"The new alpha." His gaze wandered out the window to the passing trees as he clearly longed to be outside as a bear. Which meant she had to keep him talking.

"That's why you went bear for so long? Because you were avoiding a showdown with your alpha?" Another guess. Another nod.

"Carl understood that I needed to find control of something. He suggested I go to the UP to get away from clan politics. Control myself and my life up there. I don't think he meant for me to be a bear for ten months."

Yeah, probably not. "And now?" she pressed.

He shrugged. "Now I will have to submit to Carl. Or not."

Great. Male dominance taken to animal extreme. Not something she wanted to contemplate. But that was tomorrow's problem after he fixed Vic. Meanwhile, she still had to keep him talking. "So back in Alaska, people figured out you could shift. Not just my brother, but the doctor. And the guards."

"Yes."

"And that means your CO, too."

"He said no one would tell. He certainly couldn't put it in a report. Who would believe it? But he expedited the paperwork for me to leave the military. Didn't like having me under his command."

And they were back to how Vic had destroyed his life. "So my brother's stupidity cost you your military career."

"Yes." A wealth of fury in that word. But a moment later, he started to relax back against the seat. As if he were consciously releasing each muscle one by one. "Maybe it was time for me to leave. My grizzly had been changing. The mountain was too close."

It sounded like rationalization. Or the beginning of acceptance. She couldn't tell and maybe he wasn't sure either. She opened her mouth to ask, but he held up his hand to stop her.

"I don't have an answer," he said. "Mount Denali is just a mountain. But it had a wildness to it that my grizzly liked very much. It made him more aggressive. Harder to contain."

That wasn't what she'd wanted to ask, but she'd go with it. "The mountain made it harder for you to stay human?"

"Harder to keep from ripping your brother's throat out for not listening to me."

She heard that. Except whenever she felt that way about Vic, it was an exaggeration. She was pretty sure Simon couldn't say the same.

"Then you come home, pissed off and suddenly without a career, and everything's different. This Carl wants you to submit, but you've got anger issues. So off you go to UP to get your head on straight only to shift to bear and stay there. For ten months. And then I show up. Have I got that right?"

"Yes." The word was clipped and angry, but he didn't elaborate. Good because when he took that tone, he scared the shit out of her. Fortunately, he made no moves. He just sat there and brooded as the miles sped by.

She judged it prudent to let him be for a bit, but an hour later they had to stop for gas. He'd been pretty cooperative so far, but he hadn't exactly promised to help Vic. In fact, even at his most uncommunicative, he'd said he'd be no help to her brother at all. But the gas tank wasn't going to refill itself, so she had to take the risk.

"I need to get gas," she said by way of opening. Typically, he didn't comment so she was forced to ask the question bluntly. "Can I trust you to stay with me? That you'll go to Detroit and see if you can help Vic?"

"I cannot help him. I'm sorry."

"Vic says you can." Then she held up her hand rather than rehash the same argument. "Just say you'll come with me to see him. Please." She hated that she had to beg the man, but what other choice did she have? When he didn't immediately answer, she tried for a light joke. "Besides, what else have you got to do?"

"I have been out of touch for ten months," he said. "There is a great deal I should do."

Like have a dominance fight with his alpha? No way was she letting that happen before he saw Vic.

"But you can take a day or so, right? See Vic while you remember how to be a guy?"

She held her breath while he seemed to think about it. And while she waited, they passed a freeway sign. There was an exit coming up with gas and fast food. She'd managed to snag a piece of pizza before it was gone, but she'd kill for a strong cup of coffee. This was the perfect place to stop, but only if he promised not to run.

"Simon—"

"I cannot read yet," he said, his gaze dropping to his hands. "Numbers have come back, but the words aren't there."

"So you need time to remember. I can help you, if you like."

He took a deep breath, his nostrils expanding as if he were pulling in her scent. "I would like your help."

"Deal." Relieved, she headed toward the exit. "I'll help you remember how to read. You see if you can help my brother."

His lips pulled back into a dark smile. "I will kick Vic's ass for worrying you with this lie."

She'd take it.

CHAPTER 5

Simon stopped answering questions somewhere in mid-Michigan. He was more interested in separating parts of his personality and body into categories. For the animal, all was one in a gooey disorganized mess. The man hated that. Overwhelming emotions were steadily pushed down into the bear and his cage. Certainly, he missed the bear's contentment with sunshine and green trees, but that loss was miniscule compared to the steady quieting of confusion. Bears did not travel at eighty miles per hour down a freeway, so even though the man understood cars, the animal felt nervous with it. Pushing that away helped the man take control. As did focusing on freeway signs and the symbols they contained.

By the time they hit Lansing, he recognized the golden arches of McDonald's and the green splatter of lines that was the Starbucks mermaid. Other memories were coming back, too. He spent twenty miles remembering how a car worked from the headlights through the tailpipe and every part within and around the engine. Which meant that numbers made complete sense to him. Letters couldn't be that far behind, right?

His companion, however, remained a mystery. A female human with that intriguing nutty, pungent scent. She was drooping with fatigue and they still had several hours to go, but he didn't have the mental skill to probe into that mystery. So his mind went elsewhere. He had been ten months unaware of the world. The man in him itched to focus on something other than the fact that he could not read.

So he turned on her radio and tuned it to the news, but listening was a struggle. The newscaster's voice was too different from Alyssa's, and he had to concentrate very hard. And still little made sense until Alyssa reacted. Her body tightened and her mouth flattened into a hard line.

Which was when he decided to ask her questions.

"What is he talking about?"

"The Detroit Flu." She glanced over at him. "It's some hideous virus that hit the city a couple weeks ago. There have been two outbreaks so far. I got it the first time and was a little cranky for a while." Her lips twisted into a mocking smile. "Well, crankier than my normal." Then her expression sobered. "Vic got it in the last outbreak. That was a few days ago. And he…and well, you saw what happened. That was the video."

Simon shook his head. "That video was not real."

"I shot it myself—"

"He fooled you. That was makeup. Prosthetics. Vic can be very dramatic."

"Sure, he can. But he wasn't faking that." Her fingers tightened on the steering wheel. "I saw the change. I saw his body go from normal to that." She turned to look hard straight into his eyes. "I saw it."

He believed her. There was too much fear in her for her to think anything else. And with her absolute conviction, he began to doubt. "Show me the video again."

She pulled her phone out of her pocket and thumbed it on. A moment later, he watched as Vic screamed while staring at an arm thick with fur. Simon let the video play through. Then he played it again, stopping and starting as he tried to find evidence of trickery.

It took him a long time, and he came up empty. There were thousands of possibilities, but none that he could prove to her. So he kept silent and tried to think. Something was teasing at his memory. Something about hybrids and half-shifters, but that made no sense. No one could half shift.

"Does it smell bad when that happens?" he asked.

She shot him a startled look. "He reeks. Like the worst thing I've ever smelled. Why? What does that mean?"

Simon shook his head. He didn't know. He had no idea why he'd even asked the question. It was a memory from after he'd left the military but before he'd gone to the UP. Those few weeks when he was always angry, most times drunk, and a few times asleep. A very few times, which was another reason he went bear for so long. The animal had no trouble sleeping.

"It's like I dreamed something about this," he said. "But I can't remember it."

"Well try!" she snapped.

He didn't react to her temper. He understood she was desperate to help her brother. And he was equally annoyed with himself that he couldn't grab hold of the memory. But that was what happened with alcohol. He'd been trying to drown out the pain of losing his place in the military. No part of him had wanted to remember anything.

"We should listen to more news," he finally said. "Maybe there is more information."

There wasn't except for a brief statement that there had been only two new cases of the flu since this morning. The CDC hoped that this time the outbreak was contained. Weather news followed, then ads. Nothing relevant, though it gave Simon time to practice listening to other people, other voices. He also spent a great deal of time watching Alyssa.

Her mouth remained tight and flat. The brief flare of hope when he'd asked about Vic's smell had died into a heavy determination. Her entire body seemed weighted down, into her seat, on the steering wheel, and even her chin angled down.

She didn't start rubbing her fingernail back and forth over the wheel until they reached the outskirts of Detroit. Back and forth in a way that indicated anxiety. He knew it could not be him that was the cause of her nervousness. She had been more relaxed in central Michigan. Therefore, it was the approach to Detroit and what awaited them here.

"Are you afraid of Vic?" he asked. "Do you think he will be violent?" In his experience, violence was a female's biggest threat.

"No, he wouldn't hurt me." She spoke the words slowly and without conviction. "Not on purpose. It's this...um...flu or whatever. It makes him crazy."

"What does that mean? Did he hit you?" He'd intended to speak with the same measured tempo he used as a man, but his bear surged inside him making his breath forceful and the words sharp.

She shifted her grip on the wheel, her fingers tightening as she seemed to twist against the plastic. "He didn't touch me, but he broke a shelf."

"That frightened you?"

She shot him a glare. "That terrified us both. His arm had changed and he started screaming that he was becoming a bear. He kept saying I had to find you. That you knew what to do." She shuddered. "I had to Taser him."

It took Simon a moment to remember what a Taser was, and when the image of Vic being electrified filtered through his consciousness, he had a strange reaction to it. Both horror and satisfaction shot through him, and he remained silent as he analyzed the sensation. Meanwhile, Alyssa kept talking.

"Vic would never hurt me normally. He's a dick for sure, but he knows I'd make his life hell if he did. He's been living in the apartment above me ever since he got home. Been studying to get his general contractor's license, and I pay him to do repairs and stuff. There are lots of handyman jobs around the neighborhood, too, and he's good at talking to people. If he could just follow through on what he promises without getting in over his head, he'd be amazing. But you know Vic, he'd rather talk a good game than play one. The military helped with that, so he's better now." Her hands twisted again. "Or he was."

She stumbled into silence. He saw the way her throat worked as she swallowed and that her shoulders had risen higher. She was anxious, and that made him uncomfortable.

"You must be tired," he said, stating the one conclusion he knew was correct. "Would you like me to drive?"

She turned, her brows raised. "You think you can do it?"

"If you gave me directions. I still cannot read, but I remember how an engine works."

"Yeah. Not letting you get behind the wheel until you say you remember how to *drive*. Knowing how to change the oil isn't the same thing."

He had no argument for that, so he shifted to study their environment. Tight rows of houses, small brightly lit convenience stores, and sidewalks in varying states of disrepair. The land was alive with late spring and it sprang up as weeds between rocks and broken concrete. The trees were sparse and the air acrid as it filtered through the car vents.

"Besides, we're almost there," she said as she turned off the radio. A part of him had been listening to the steady flow of news, but she absorbed his attention more than anything on the radio.

It was always this way when coming back from grizzly to man. The first person he met was the one he fixated on the most. Like a touchstone from which all other meaning evolved. It usually lasted a few hours as he reoriented to the world. But he'd never been gone for ten months before. Who knew how long it would last this time.

It didn't help that Alyssa was so damned interesting. Normally he fixated on Amanda at the pizzeria, and there just wasn't much to her. But Alyssa had been a vibrant, fascinating girl when he'd visited two years ago. And now she was triply intriguing. Back then, she'd been busy with school and a job running a laundromat. The few nights she'd hung out with them, he'd found her funny and smart, two qualities he most liked in women. Sexy as hell, too, but as Vic's sister, he wasn't going there. Which meant he kept his hands to himself no matter where his fantasies had wandered.

Then he'd spent the next years listening to every Alyssa story Vic had. Night after night, especially in the boring tundra of Alaska, regaling him with stories of Alyssa saying something smart, Alyssa being brave, Alyssa getting in trouble with a boyfriend before kicking the bastard's ass. If he hadn't been interested in her before those months in Alaska, he sure as hell was afterward.

And now she was here with him. But she was different than he remembered and very different than the sassy, vibrant sister Vic told stories about. Now she was tense, focused, and with a dark edge to her humor. That ought to make her less appealing, but it made her more so. Life had tempered her girlish charm into steel. And nothing appealed to both bear and man like a beautiful woman who could stand up to him. Who could dig out a bullet from his side and force-cajole him into coming down to Detroit. Her choices were foolhardy, to be sure, but he had to admire the chutzpah. More than admire, his bear was ready to declare her a mate, and that was a kettle of worms he dared not open.

Meanwhile, Alyssa drove into the parking lot of a three-story apartment building. Though the blacktop was cracked with weeds, there was a brand-new carport, and she pulled into the first space. "He built that," she said, a note of pride in her voice. "Kept him in beer and babes for a month."

"Only a month?" he asked.

She shot him a dry look. "He's living here rent-free."

"You own the building?"

She flashed him a smile. "Bought it a few years ago for a song. Detroit real estate being what it is." Then she turned to the squat rectangle structure with a fond smile. "It's ugly, but it's all mine. Laundromat on the first floor, apartments on two and three." Then she gestured to the brightly lit interior. "I used to work here."

He nodded. "I remember."

"So when old Mr. Delgado wanted to sell, I sweet-talked him into selling everything to me."

He'd bet everything that she had negotiated like a tigress and that they'd both loved every second of it. He would have said just that, but his senses were locking in to the city. The noise was constant, the lights dizzying even in this poorly maintained neighborhood, and the smells made his stomach churn. His bear didn't like any of it, grumbling in his mental cage, but the man sorted through the sounds. Cars, trucks. Music from down the street. A couple arguing closer by, but not a threat. Both man and beast hated the poisonous city smells, but it wasn't as bad as he'd feared.

Alyssa pushed through the front of the laundromat. The space was clean, the machines well maintained though aging, and the scent of chewy brownies and caramel popcorn wafted out in a sweet puff. He heard someone inside munching and words from someone else.

"Put that away," said a young man. "You're going to be high as a kite while you walk home."

"But it's so good," muttered a woman.

Simon stepped inside and saw a young black man lounging against a counter, his frame thin, but the muscles already bulging. His face was all good-natured cheer as he shook his head at a middle-aged woman in a muumuu that hung on her moderate frame. She was a large woman who'd recently lost weight, and she shoved another handful of popcorn into her mouth before firmly shutting the lid on a brown tin. Right next to her, a dryer was going with a dizzying array of colors tumbling around inside.

"Lyssa! Good to see you," the woman called. "I been sharing my popcorn with Malik here."

The boy raised his clean hands and shook his head. "I ain't touched a crumb. That's all you, Ms. Turley."

"Have the migraines been bad lately?" Alyssa asked as the dryer dinged and slowed.

"Plumb awful," the woman responded as she popped the tin open again and grabbed another handful. "I could barely see to come here tonight."

"Then you sit down and rest. Malik—"

"I'll fold up your dresses nice and neat for you, Ms. Turley," the boy said as he crossed to the dryer and began pulling out muumuus in a blinding array of colors and designs. Apparently, he'd done this a lot because he didn't even blink when he shook out some very large underwear.

"Well, thank you boy. Don't mind if—"

"And I think you should put this away for now," Alyssa interrupted as she neatly grabbed the popcorn tin and set it out of the woman's reach. "Save it for tomorrow."

Which is when Simon finally remembered that scent. Cannabis on the popcorn and a baggie filled with brownies. And also from Ms. Turley's pores. Lord, just standing near her was giving his bear a contact high.

Meanwhile, Alyssa stepped behind the counter, obviously checking on things while Malik finished with the woman's laundry. A few minutes later, the lady was carrying a basket of muumuus and brownies out the door.

"Be careful walking home, Ms. Turley," Malik called.

"I will," she called back in an exuberant singsong. "I surely will."

The door shut behind her, but Simon listened to her tuneless humming as she walked away. Then his attention was taken by Malik, who had straightened to his full height as he looked at Alyssa. "Been a busy night down the street. About average here."

Alyssa nodded as she shut the cash register. "Looks good," she finally said. "Any other problems?"

"No, ma'am." The response was as sharp as a salute and Alyssa patted his arm.

"Then keep on keeping on. We'll be downstairs."

The boy nodded, still standing straight as an arrow as she walked through to the back of the laundromat. Simon followed a step behind watching everything as they stepped into the main hallway of the apartment building. There were only two apartments on this floor. The laundromat took up the rest. When he thought she'd go to one of the doors, she surprised him. She headed to the back staircase and down to the basement level.

"Who's the pot dealer? Malik? You?" he asked.

"It's legal now or mostly, so don't give me any attitude."

At the moment, the attitude was all hers. He was just gathering facts. "You're not a legal dispensary."

She shot him a look. "And I'm not dealing. Neither is Malik." She jerked her chin toward the street. "It's two doors down. About half my business comes from people starting laundry here then wandering down there."

He thought about it and understood the economics of the situation. He also didn't have any moral outrage. It was a complicated world and people did what they needed to get by. Besides, there was more than enough for him to process when they pushed into the basement floor where metal cages surrounded storage. Apartment numbers were written on small signs attached to each padlocked door, protecting boxes and old furniture in a slightly musty display.

All except one cage with the number one on it. In it was a cot and a very angry brother. Vic stood as soon as they entered, a look of fury on his face.

"What the fuck, Alyssa? You didn't have to keep me locked up."

She stepped onto the concrete floor and Simon slipped in beside her. She moved forward quickly, but stopped just short of his reach. "How do you feel?"

Four words but they held a wealth of meaning. Simon couldn't understand all the undercurrents, but he guessed she was equal parts afraid of her brother and afraid for him.

"I'm fine, Lys. Really, I am." Then his gaze caught Simon's and relief cascaded through his features. Vic was a large man with hard, ropy muscles, but his face was as expressive as the most innocent of children. Every emotion flashed on his features and shocked relief screamed loud enough that even Simon could see it. "You came. I wasn't sure you would."

"You risked your sister's life in sending her to me."

Both Alyssa and Vic jolted at that. Vic opened his mouth to speak, but Simon didn't give them the chance.

"And now that she knows what I am, my life is at risk. Many alphas would kill for such a transgression." It was an exaggeration, but it wasn't a lie. Fortunately, Carl—the new leader of the Gladwin bear clan—was known to be rational. Some even called him progressive, and among shifters, that was a rarity.

"I didn't know, Simon." Vic gripped the chain-link fence around his cage. "But you're the only one who can help me. I'm changing into a monster." His voice had tightened with fear, but Simon ignored it.

"You risked my life and hers for a lie." He stepped right up to the fence. "You are not my friend." He glanced over at Alyssa. "And he is a terrible brother." With a nod to her, Simon completed his turn and began walking back to the stairs. Behind him, Vic called out.

"Wait! Simon, I'm not lying." He rattled the edge of the cage and cursed. "Damn it, Alyssa, let me out! Simon!"

He heard the rattle of keys as Alyssa unlocked the cage. Her voice shook as she spoke. "Is he right, Vic? Is this all some kind of stunt?"

"No!" Vic's answer was vehement, but it was Alyssa's cry of surprise that had Simon spinning around. He caught sight of Alyssa flying backward into the next cage, propelled by the force of Vic pushing his cage open. Even more surprising, the metal frame of the door banged backward hard enough to bend, and the clang was deafening.

That was a surprise to everyone. Vic paused a moment, his eyes widening as his sister caught herself against the opposite cage and pulled herself upright. But then his attention spun back to Simon.

"Come back here!" Vic bellowed, the cry deeper than a moment before. And a scent pervaded the area. Thick, oily, and nauseating. It was nothing Simon had ever smelled before, and the word "wrong" screamed in his head.

Simon stepped back down the stairs, using the one second he had to analyze the situation. His conclusion was very simple. Something was wrong and it centered on Vic who was barreling forward, his hands clenched into fists and his face pinched tight.

"Stop right now!" Simon ordered, his voice reverberating in the concrete and metal space.

Vic didn't stop. He grabbed Simon's arms with unnatural strength. "Listen to me!" he growled, his breath foul.

Simon reacted immediately. He broke Vic's hold and slammed the man back. But Vic was larger, and the solidity of his frame made it like pushing a brick wall. The man went nowhere, but at least Simon was free.

Simon ducked around to the side, his nostrils flaring. The smell was awful and it made every part of him rebel, especially his grizzly. Inside his mind, the bear fought to get out, but Simon refused. He'd been animal for too long lately. Another shift would likely be his last. He'd never come back to being a man. And even if he could, he was in the basement of a laundromat in Detroit. Someone would shoot him long before he regained control. Therefore, his grizzly remained locked away.

No problem. He had bested Vic before as a man. He would do so again now. He just had to be logical.

He ducked to the side though there wasn't a lot of room between cages. Step one: Begin with reason.

"I'm listening, Vic. Why did you want me here?"

"You have to help me!" the man bellowed. He was still going for a grappling hold, his arms spread and his hands extended like claws. Easy to avoid assuming Simon kept well out of reach. Then Alyssa's voice cut through the room.

"Vic, calm down. He's right here."

Vic swung his head around, the movement including shoulders and torso. It looked like a bear pulling his massive body to the side more than a man twisting. "Don't talk to me, you bitch. You did this to me."

Hell. Alyssa's face tightened, her expression flattening down as she set her feet. "Calm down. I did what you wanted. I brought him here."

Vic wasn't listening. Instead, he was lumbering toward his sister and Simon watched with detached surprise as the man's profile seemed to elongate. Maybe. It was hard to tell and no time to evaluate. But it raised enough of a question that Simon accepted the grim reality of what he had to do. If Vic was indeed turning into a bear—and his rational mind could barely fathom the concept—then Simon had to force the full change. He had to see it for himself to understand what was going on and prove that this wasn't some elaborate, incomprehensible hoax. And the only way to do that was to push the man into a blind fury.

But first he had to get Vic's attention.

"I'm over here, you idiot," he taunted. "You want my help? Come and take it."

Vic swung back, but Alyssa didn't keep quiet. "Don't be a fool, Simon. He's dangerous."

Maybe. Maybe not. But she sure as hell couldn't defend herself from her brother. Not at his current size and strength.

"Look at me, moron," he taunted. And when Vic turned, Simon struck. Two quick jabs to the face, hard enough to snap Vic's head back. Also hard enough to make Simon's hand pound. The bones of Vic's face were hard as hell. And not shaped right.

Vic roared and charged, still going for the grappling hold. His friend had always been more of a wrestler than a boxer. Simon danced around, punching as hard as he could in rapid fire. His blows weren't meant to take Vic down. The only safe space in this tight basement was inside Vic's cage. He had to maneuver them there. That meant quick jabs and fast feet as he backed into the cage. Vic would follow because that's what angry bears did. The plan was to get Vic inside the cage, then dance around to get himself out.

That was the plan and it started to work. But he hadn't counted on the smell. Worse than a dozen terrified skunks because at least those scents were natural. This smelled like industrial waste mixed with decaying flesh. And every time he took a breath, he wanted to gag. It destroyed his timing, shorted out his oxygen, and definitely gave Vic the upper hand.

"Simon, get back! Get out of the way!"

Alyssa's voice rang with command, but Simon had no intention of obeying. He had a plan that was working if only he could keep from choking on the stench. And all the while, Vic's body seemed to grow bigger and a little faster. Every time Simon connected, the impact seemed to strike against harder and harder flesh. Like pounding a wall that only got stronger the more times you hit it. Or perhaps his own hands were swelling. Had he damaged them?

Jab, jab, jab. Pause. Jab, jab, jab.

He set up a rhythm, pacing everything to an internal metronome. He even measured his breathing and picked out his targets with mathematical precision. The only random element in his attack was where he put his feet. In and out of reach, forward and back, stronger, slower, all at random and according to whatever opportunities Vic gave him.

When he couldn't punch Vic in the direction he wanted, Simon slipped into that location and lured the man forward. And step by smelly step, he drew Vic into the cage.

At least Alyssa was safely outside the cage. Now all he had to do was dance around his bloodied friend and get out. Except he hadn't expected Vic to change. True shifters change in a kind of glow. They suck temperature from the air, pull life from the ground, some seem to take the power out of the wind. Everyone was different, but they all had a soft yellow shimmer as the body changed from one state to another, often too fast for the human eye to catch. But back when he was a kid, he'd filmed himself changing just to watch it frame by frame.

Vic did none of that. His change was instantaneous, and though there might have been a dip in temperature, Simon was too busy scrambling backward to really notice.

Vic became huge. Like grizzly bear huge, but as a man. And he had thick fur on his torso and arms, bear claws for hands, and a large mouth. And the stench was horrendous.

Simon gasped in shock as he scrambled backward, but he was inside the cage. There wasn't anywhere to go and he banged backward into the cot. The impact caused him to suck in air, and that set off his gag reflex. He started choking, fighting to keep from vomiting while Vic roared forward. Simon's mind was still reeling, unable to process what had happened. That was not a normal shift. Vic wasn't a bear but he sure as hell wasn't human, either. And while his mind stuttered and his breath choked off, Vic attacked.

Simon rolled, able to do that much despite the way his body rebelled. Inside his mind, his own grizzly surged. It needed to fight and it wanted to kill. He held it back by sheer will. He could not shift here. Not against Vic, not with Alyssa just a few feet away. It was too dangerous for all of them.

But that meant it was him against a monster double his size inside an eight-foot cage.

CHAPTER 6

Alyssa couldn't stop screaming. At least not inside her head. It truth, her one and only scream had drawn in enough of the stench that she'd gagged. Holy hell, that…thing stunk. And that thing was her brother.

That was horrifying enough, but now Simon was trapped inside the cage with it. No way could he fight. He was scrambling and choking just like she was. Even Malik stumbled the moment his feet hit the floor, a gun lax in his hand as he gagged from the stench.

"Don't shoot," Alyssa managed to wheeze. It was too dangerous with Simon in there. Malik was a great shot, but she couldn't risk he'd hit the wrong man. And she sure as hell didn't want to clip the right one and just make it more angry. "I have…plan."

And she did. Sort of. But her mind was still screaming from the sight of her brother turned monster. He was the size of a bear with fur and claws. And he was in a killing frenzy. He was roaring as he lunged for Simon who just barely managed to roll aside, his own breath ragged from the stench.

Her brother turned and swung thick hairy arms at Simon, but he was off balance. It took her a moment to realize that his pants were hobbling him. The jeans were too tight and hadn't ripped like the tee had. The seams on the legs were splitting and the button had popped, loosening the waist. But the groin had to be squeezing Vic's balls hard enough to make him sing soprano. It sure as hell was hampering his movements, which was the only reason Simon was still alive.

Vic's roar came out again, this time higher in pitch. He tore at the denim, ripping it easily with his claws and drawing enough blood to make Alyssa whimper. Whatever this thing was, her brother was inside it. She didn't want it bleeding out.

"Get out of there!" Alyssa screeched at Simon. It was a stupid thing to say. She could see that he was trying, but Vic was flailing at his jeans with big movements in a tiny space. One wrong step, and Simon could be knocked unconscious.

At least he wasn't gagging anymore. He definitely had a green cast to his skin, but probably no more than she. And his eyes were narrowed in concentration.

Oh God, was he going to kill Vic? He'd been brutal as he punched her brother, but there hadn't seemed to be much damage. Blows, yes. Blood, no. And Vic had been pissed, but she'd seen more brutal fights between ten-year-old boys, so she hadn't interfered.

But this was different. This was a dangerous fight with a monster. She didn't want him to kill Vic, but what could he do? She scrambled sideways, grabbing the stun gun from the nearby table. That was her plan. It wasn't the kind that could send out darts. It was just a handheld model that she'd have to slam into his furry gut. But maybe if she could get Vic to come at her, she could zap him before he ripped her to pieces.

It was a long shot, but all she had. She held the weapon in shaking hands. It charged with a satisfying crackle, but damn she had no idea if it would take down someone as big as him.

"Vic, you bastard, turn your hairy ass around!"

Nothing. Her brother was still ripping in fury at the tattered remains of his jeans. Then the last seam gave way, and she knew she had seconds before he turned on Simon. Good. She was ready.

Except the minute Vic looked up, Simon tackled him. He sprang forward from the crushed cot and knocked Vic backward. They landed in a crash against the side of the cage, but this was exactly what Vic had wanted. He loved to wrestle and he gripped Simon like the man was a stubborn tick.

"Do it!" Simon bellowed. "Now!"

"Do what?" Run in there? Vic was on the bottom, Simon on top. No way was she going to be able to get through to her brother. And with the way they were fighting, rolling against the side of the cage, she'd be lucky if she wasn't flattened.

Except now Vic was digging in, his claws ripping into Simon's back. And as much as Simon fought, throwing punches like a madman, there was no room and no leverage.

"The cage!"

Shoot the cage? Oh duh! It was metal and Vic was plastered hard against it. Sure she'd get Simon, but Vic would take the worst of it.

Without overthinking, she dashed to the side of the cage where Vic's back was pressed hard against it. That's what Simon was doing. Pinning the larger creature against the metal. She couldn't be a 100 percent sure she'd get the prongs into her brother, but she sure as hell would electrify the cage.

"Get clear!" she screamed.

Not possible. He was gripping hard and now she smelled blood. And then the monster opened his mouth to bite. She saw sharp white teeth in a long jaw. No way could she let that happen.

She slammed the Taser against the metal and let it crackle.

Vic roared as his back arched. His arms flew open—or maybe Simon just sprang free—and then Simon began to punch Vic in the face. Over and over.

It was awful. The Taser just kept going. Vic kept roaring, his massive body jerking in spastic contortions. And Simon didn't stop. He slammed his fists into Vic's jaw over and over. Too fast for much current to get him, but he screamed with every blow as if it were painful. Or he was furious. Or insane.

She didn't know. She couldn't tell. And maybe she was screaming and crying, too, as blood and spittle flew.

The Taser cut out and she dropped limply to the ground, her entire body shaking. Simon was standing and his blows kept coming. Over and over, the beat unrelenting. The monster stopped bellowing. His arms had dropped to the ground and his shoulders moved only in time with every blow.

Wham. Wham. Wham.

The sound was wet with every impact, and Simon grunted with every blow.

"Stop," she whispered. "Stop." She hadn't the breath to scream it.

Wham. Wham. Wham.

"He's down," Malik said from beside her, his voice a thousand times stronger than hers. "Stop. He's down."

Wham. Wham. Wham.

Simon didn't hear them and one look at his face showed a monster in human form. His jaw was tight, his brows narrowed, and his nostrils flared. There was fury in every moment and the blood came from his hands as much as Vic's face.

"Simon!" she cried. "Stop!"

Wham. Wham. Wham.

She rolled forward, gripped the side of the cage and screamed as loud as she could.

"Simon!"

His head snapped up, and his fist froze midair. He stood there, his breath coming in heaving pants and his body taut with sweat, blood, and raw fury.

"Stop!"

No movement. Just his breath and his eyes burning into hers. Dark green, red flushing through the white. And his breath as rhythmic as his blows had been. Harsh sounds, but with a regular beat. Inhale. Exhale. Inhale. Exhale.

"Simon," she said, her voice no longer a scream. Now she spoke with the bite of command. "Come out of there now."

Would he respond to the command? Did she want him to? If he did, then he'd be on the outside with her. Vic would be safe, but would she?

She shoved that thought away. Her brother was the monster. Simon had been protecting her.

She softened her tone again until it was almost conversational. "You need to come out so we can lock him in."

She didn't know if he could understand her. He was still poised there with his fist raised. But after two full breaths, he slowly lowered it. His hands went to his sides and his shoulders dropped down as he straightened to his full height. It took him a moment to twist and walk in a stiff gait out the cage door. Then he stepped aside as she closed and locked it. The door was bent, the entire chain-link fencing was twisted, but she managed to get the thing shut and the padlock in place.

And all the while, Simon stood beside her, his breath harsh, still at that steady beat. It was Malik who broke the silence. Malik the scrawny kid who was a dead shot and had been no help whatsoever. At least he hadn't vomited.

Hell. She'd had the thought too soon. The moment the padlock clanged in place, Malik stumbled to the side. He rushed to the garbage can and lost the contents of his stomach. She could hardly blame him. The stench in here was awful. And yet she did. She'd hired him to protect her and her business, but he'd been useless. What good was a dead shot when she'd told him not to do it? Which made it her fault, not his.

Simon had saved her. But what had he done to her brother? The monster was immobile, its face bloody and body collapsed like a discarded rag doll. A huge, furry, disgusting rag doll.

"Is he dead?" she whispered.

"He's breathing," Simon said, his tone flat. "He'll probably heal when he reverts to human."

She spun to look at him. "He's a shifter, then. He was right."

"No." Simon's dark green eyes burned into hers. "He's a monster." Then he turned and walked to the stairs.

She was going to call him back. She was going to demand he explain what he meant. Her brother might look like a monster, but he was sick. And Simon was here to fix that. Vic was an irresponsible doofus who was just starting to get his act together. Simon had to save him.

Except the gouges of dark red on Simon's back told a different story. Her brother had done that with massive claws. And had his nose been a snout? And he'd been about to bite Simon with a mouth filled with cutting teeth. Not a molar in there as far as she could remember. She didn't want to look back to see.

So she focused on Simon. She had to say something to him. She had to get him to help fix this. He was their Hail Mary pass and he was leaving.

"Help us," she said. Not a command. Not even a prayer. Just a simple plea from the heart.

He paused with a foot on the stairs. "I can't," he said. Then he left.

CHAPTER 7

Simon walked steadily outside. He needed fresh air on his face and the smell of trees. He needed clean water gurgling nearby. But most of all, he needed away from Alyssa with her chocolate-brown eyes and her tight jaw. Her shoulders were broad for a woman, but they fit her perfectly as she Tasered her brother in one breath and then begged him for help in the next. No frail flower her, but also not a woman filled with pride. She would do whatever was needed to save her brother.

He admired her for that. But that didn't mean he could help her.

He stopped walking in the parking lot. The air here wasn't remotely clean and the stagnant pools of water nearby smelled of urban waste. How did people live like this? Fortunately, the pollution did have one good side effect. His grizzly that had been clawing to spring free, now quieted with a nauseated grumble. It didn't want out in this urban wasteland. It needed the silence in the UP and the cool darkness of a sky lit only by stars. Here, every neon light, every honking horn reminded him that being a man was not so great a thing.

Unfortunately, he didn't have a choice. He had no way to get back to the UP just yet. At least not until he remembered how to access his money without being able to read. Or failing that, jack a car and drive.

So he stood in the middle of the parking lot and glared at the nearby stop sign. He knew what it was by shape and placement. Knew, too, that it read "stop." But the shifting white lines made no sense to him unless it was the bend and curve of a very white, very strange plant. Which, of course, it wasn't.

"Thinking about walking back to the UP?" Alyssa asked.

He hadn't heard her come outside and her voice should have startled him. Instead, it helped him breathe. He could understand her words and when her scent hit him, he inhaled deeply.

"I have money. I could get a flight home." It was a lie. His bear was too close to the surface to subject it to the inside of a small plane. What if it went berserk and tore out the side?

She sighed. A quick tight sound that was as much animal as human. It was the sound of a creature changing direction. And when he turned to look at her, she offered him a can of beer.

"Here," she said. "It's Vic's, but no way am I letting him have this right now."

"Alcohol would be bad for him in his condition." Whatever monster was inside Vic, it was stirred by fury. Anything that dropped his inhibitions would be like adding fuel to the fire. "It is also prohibited for me in this protocol."

She cocked her head to the side like a bird inspecting a possible meal. "Awful big words there, Corporal Gold. You could just say you don't like the brand." She set the can on the trunk of her car.

"I don't remember if I like that kind of beer. I do remember that

I have things that I must do before it is safe for anyone to be around me."

She nodded. "Things like remember how to read?"

"Yes. Also, I must sleep and wake as a man." He looked out past her car to the steady march of houses, some in disrepair, some sporting flowers and fresh paint. This neighborhood wasn't thriving, but it wasn't lost yet. "You know what I am, but you don't understand what it means. You don't know that I walk a razor-thin line between beast and man." He gestured to the landscape. "If I become a bear here, how will I survive? And who will I hurt in the process?"

Her eyes widened and she swallowed. Then with a shaking hand, she grabbed the can of beer and popped the top, grimacing as she took a slug. "Vic has shit taste in beer," she said after a moment.

Simon felt his lips lift into a smile. "That is something I remember." He looked closer at the brand name on the can. "Vic likes his beer cheap."

"And plentiful." She drank some more. He found himself fascinated by the curve of her neck and the steady bob of her Adam's apple. Female necks were not alluring to him. They were simply the column on which the head was placed. And yet, watching hers held distinct appeal. He could not figure out what he liked the most. The delicate curve, the swanlike stretch, or perhaps it was the smooth landscape of skin broken by a mole just under her jawline. It all interested him.

And then she stopped drinking. He was saddened by that until she thumbed on her phone and spoke into the receiver. "It's me. I'm outside. Bring me some brownies."

Her face was animated as she spoke and he was man enough now to appreciate the fullness of her lips and the crinkle beside her eyes when she smiled. She set down her phone then returned his gaze. The arch of her brow lifted her expression into quizzical and his smile widened. But when he spoke, he kept his tone neutral.

"Alcohol is not allowed in this protocol," he said. "Cannabis is equally prohibited."

"You're not the only one standing here, Simon."

He nodded in acknowledgment, but she waved the gesture aside.

"Besides, these are my brownies. Just sugar, flour, butter, and five times the normal amount of chocolate."

He arched his brows. "That is a lot of chocolate."

"Desperate times, desperate measures."

They stood in silence while Malik brought out a plate of brownies. He set it down on the hood of the trunk with jittery movements and a nervous manner. As if he wasn't sure who to be more worried about: his boss Alyssa or the monster caged downstairs. She didn't help him. Just watched the boy with steady eyes as he delivered the dessert, seemed like he wanted to talk, but then thought better of it. A moment later, he nodded to them and went back inside.

Alyssa didn't speak until the door had shut behind him.

"You can't help Vic," she said. Her tone was flat but he didn't detect any acrimony in it. Just a statement of fact.

"I have never seen or heard of anything like what happened in there." Just the memory of it made his bear shudder in horror. "I have no answers for you."

"But you knew about the smell. Back in the car, you asked about the smell."

He had. But he still couldn't place that memory. And he sure as hell had never smelled something like that. "I have no answers," he repeated.

She nodded as she reached for a brownie. "Know anyone who would?"

"I can ask my alpha, but he is in Gladwin and our clan has a policy of staying far away from the Detroit bears." He shrugged half in apology. "Most believe urban shifters are crazy, bears even more so. At least dogs and cats can exist in a city. Grizzlies cannot."

She sighed, though it might have been because she was taking a bite of her brownie. There had been a definite note of delight in the sound. A moment later, she proved that her mind was quick in picking up the ramifications of what he'd said.

"So there are cat-, dog-, and bear-shifters. You're a bear and you're tied to the Gladwins. There are other shifters—bears included—here in Detroit, you're just not friendly with them."

He nodded. Then at her gesture, he took hold of a brownie. It was cool to the touch as if it had been in the refrigerator, but the way it smelled was pure human delight. "Vic was turning into a bear," he said, his mind cataloging the clues. "I'm sure of it. There was no part of him that looked lupine or feline."

She stared at him a moment, her expression vaguely horrified. But she didn't speak. Instead, she took another large bite of her brownie. He mirrored her motions, putting sugar and chocolate in his mouth as if it were a sacred act. Perhaps she had the right of it, he thought, as the taste exploded on his tongue. Rich chocolate and sugar had his human body clicking into focus. He remembered other tastes, other delights, all of them unique to man.

"This is good," he said as he took another bite. "Perhaps I will add it to the protocol."

She looked at him with an amused smirk. "I'm honored. My humble brownies in the mighty protocol."

He frowned, running over her words in his head. He heard the sarcasm, but it wasn't heavy. More like a wry comment as if to say, "So long as there's a silver lining."

Such practicality threw him, and he examined her even closer. She was busy licking brownie bits off her fingers and finishing off her beer. Normal actions, and yet in this situation, it seemed very strange to him.

"Why aren't you hysterical?" he asked.

She set down her beer, her expression steady. "Would hysterics help?"

"Of course not. They never help. But they would be a normal reaction to"—he gestured toward the basement and her brother—"the situation."

She shook her head. "If it's not useful, then I don't do it. But if you want to melt down, be my guest."

He leaned against her car and folded his arms as he faced her. She was watching him with a studied casualness. As if she couldn't care less what he was about to say and yet the animal in him recognized the taut attention she gave him. Everything might look smooth and friendly on the outside, but inside she was as focused as any predator in the animal kingdom. And that made his bear sit up and take note.

"When I left the army, I was an angry mess," he said. "I knew it was time, but I was still furious."

She arched a brow. Obviously, this was not what she expected him to say. "So?" she prompted when he went silent. "What happened?"

"I fought my alpha, stayed drunk, and lashed out at anyone who came close. Eventually I went to the UP where I turned into a bear and stayed that way for ten months until a pushy woman shot me and dragged me to Detroit."

Her eyes widened but her mouth stayed stubbornly closed.

"And now, I am struggling to remember the basics of being a man. How to act, how to move, how to fucking read." The curse slipped out and it told him how close to the ragged edge he was. His mind might be in control, but the beast—and all his fury—were frighteningly close to the surface.

He slammed his jaw shut and glared at her. This was her fault. He'd been happy as a bear. And failing that, he'd have been content in his cabin as he waited for his human side to recall the details of human survival. Here in Detroit, he was completely lost. And totally vulnerable.

"You're getting it," she said. "You've got your protocol and everything. It'll just take time."

He snorted. She did not understand his point, so he decided to make it excruciatingly clear. "Don't you think that one of us should be modeling normal human behavior?"

She grimaced. "There's nothing normal about this situation. So why should I react in a normal way?"

Because it was human? Because she was his touchstone right now and if she acted bizarrely, then how would he know how to act? Because he wanted her to be normal so he could understand her, and right now she was more mysterious to him than the stop sign he couldn't read and the brother he couldn't save.

And while he struggled with his thoughts, she reached out a hand. It was small and feminine, the nails close cut and without polish. When she touched his arm, he felt it all the way through to his spine. Warmth. Comfort. Human connection. It rocked him back on his heels with how wonderful it felt.

"We just need to help Vic. Then I'll take you back to the UP. I swear."

"I don't know how to help Vic," he said, and even he heard the plaintive note in his voice. He wanted to help. He wanted to because then she might touch him again. She'd withdrawn her hand the moment he snapped at her and he cursed his temper and the frustration that lay beneath it. "I am at sea in the human world right now."

"So let me help."

And here they were full circle. He was lost and she was not a reliable guide. He stared at her a long moment, wondering what he should say. And then he saw it. It was a small tic. Something he would never have noticed except that he was watching her so closely. But the more he looked, the larger the thing seemed.

She was breathing in quick tight pants. Like a rabbit on alert, her entire body was still, but her nostrils flared and contracted in quick succession, and it spoke of panic kept barely at bay. Her gaze might be steady, her chin lifted in defiance, but her breath told the true story.

And oddly, the knowledge that she was frightened reassured him. So he relaxed against her car and smiled. Her brows narrowed.

"What?" she demanded.

"I understand now and that makes me feel more in control."

"You understand what? My brother?" She couldn't disguise the note of hope in her voice.

"No," he said gently. "That you are afraid, though you hide it. And that tells me that you are used to being in charge, used to hiding your fear as you tell others what to do." He dipped his chin at her. "It is the mark of a good leader."

"Awesome. Now—"

"But there is a danger, too."

She sighed, then arched a brow. "Do tell."

"You act like a lieutenant in a war zone without the time off to rest. I think you are always on guard, always issuing orders, always under siege."

"So? This is Detroit. It's not so bad in this neighborhood, but it's not so great either."

"So how long have you fought to control everyone and everything? How long before you break?" He gestured back toward the basement without looking at it. "Things are very bad, Alyssa. You cannot manage as you always have. I think you know that."

"And what would you suggest I do instead?" Her voice held a heavy layer of disdain, but he ignored it.

"I think you should act as normal people would."

Her laugh came out short and derisive. "I don't do hysterics."

"Then what else would be normal?"

"Booze," she said as she slugged the last of her beer. "Brownies," she said when she was done.

"And babes," he finished for her, only now realizing that she was echoing Vic's favorite saying. He could remember dozens of times when his best friend had said just those words, just that way. And when he locked eyes with Alyssa, he felt her memory of it, too. How many times had she heard it? How many times had she harassed Vic about having no ambition in his life, no drive beyond those three things? She'd certainly done it a lot when he'd visited so long ago.

And now they'd said it to each other and the echo of the old Vic was her undoing. Her eyes abruptly teared up, her breath that had been short, now choked off with a sob. And her shoulders that had been so strong beneath a lifted chin suddenly caved in.

She slammed a fist against her mouth as she tried to hold back her emotions. He reacted on instinct, his grizzly surging forward before his mind even processed what was happening. A grizzly nuzzled his distressed mate. A grizzly licked her face and petted her fur. And a grizzly pressed his face to hers and purred in a gruff kind of way.

So he did that to her. He pulled her close and stroked her hair. It was still in that tight bun, so he tugged it free and burrowed his fingers into the mass. He pressed his cheek to hers and chuffed as if the sound were perfectly normal. And he held her while she clutched his shirt and cried as if her world were crumbling.

Her sobs came from the gut, pulled from deep inside and harsh to hear. There were no cries in those guttural sounds. No feminine keening or delicate snuffles. This was pain held deep. It was a hard knot that seemed to tear out of her and to fall on his shirt as she clutched him.

It lasted a long time, but his grizzly was always patient. It didn't measure time the way a man did. It only knew that the female was in pain, so he kept nuzzling and petting until the pain was gone. Until the sobs eased and her body shuddered against him.

In time, he realized she was speaking words. Two of them repeated over and over.

"I'm sorry. I'm sorry. I'm sorry."

That made no sense to either man or bear, so Simon simply nuzzled her some more and let the grizzly continue chuffing as he stroked her hair.

"I'm sorry," she said one last time as her clenched body finally eased. She still gripped his shirt in two fists, but her body wasn't jerking against him. So he stopped petting her and simply waited with her head cupped in one hand and the other resting against her back.

Then she eased back. Barely an inch, but it was enough

for her to exhale another sentence. "I've made a mess of your shirt."

"I have others."

She pulled back farther and her fists eased. Then she wiped her eyes with the palms of her hand. "Um, hold on."

She didn't look up at him, but shoved a hand into her jeans pocket. Then she came up with her car fob. The locks clicked open and then a second later, the trunk unlatched. He moved the pan of brownies to the roof of the car before they could topple while she grabbed tissues from the backseat.

"Your go bag," she said from behind the Kleenex. "It's in the trunk."

Right. So he could change his shirt.

He stripped out of the wet tee, folded it into a small square, then unzipped his bag. He moved by rote, his attention fully centered on her though he did not look directly at her. She was blowing her nose and throwing the tissues away. Then she did something else in the backseat of her car, though he had no idea what.

It was busywork. Something to do so that she would not have to look at him. He gave her the privacy to settle herself while he pulled out another T-shirt and pushed the dirty one into its place in the bag. A moment later, he straightened and pulled on the new shirt.

But when his head emerged, it was to see her looking at him with a steady, liquid brown gaze. Her eyes were still rimmed with red, but her expression was wistful and she extended to him a bottle of water. He took it gratefully, opening it with a swift twist, and slugging half the contents. When he finished, she was still watching him. Then she lifted a shoulder in a half shrug.

"I used to imagine what it would be like for you to hold me," she said.

He frowned. That was not what he'd expected her to say.

"Surely you knew," she continued. "I had the most horrible crush on you. Back when you visited."

"You are Vic's sister. I was staying in your house. I could never make a move on you."

She sighed. "I know. And you have no idea how much that pissed me off."

He looked at her and saw nostalgia in her face. It was in the tilt of her head and the swollen fullness of her lips. "I would go to bed and imagine you kissing me. And then I'd pretend all sorts of other things until we finally fell asleep in each other's arms. Some nights, I would just skip to that part. Others…" She flashed him a quick grin. "Well, other nights, sleep wasn't the featured activity."

"I always thought you were beautiful."

She snorted and brushed a hand across her face. "You never thought that. I heard you talking. You guys were all about big boobs and big butts." She gestured gruffly to her body. "I'm average at best."

"That was Vic, and I wasn't talking about your body."

She grimaced. "Thanks," she drawled, clearly not feeling complimented.

"You never let Vic get away with his bullshit. Your mother, our CO, even the cop who pulled him over for speeding—they all let Vic get away with nonsense. I never understood it. But you nailed him for it every time."

"That's being smart. It had nothing to do with beauty."

"In my world, smart is beautiful. The best kind of beauty. But if you want more, I can tell you that I find your body perfect in every way. It's strong with muscles that know how to work. Your skin is creamy smooth and your breasts are just the right size. I dreamed about you, too. But as with anything I can't have, I put away those dreams and refused to think about them again."

She jerked at his words, obviously surprised. "Why can't you have me? Because I'm Vic's sister?"

"Because I am a beast."

He turned away from her then. Zipped up his go bag and pulled it from the trunk. He reached up to close it, but she was there before him, pushing the metal down with a loud slam.

"A beast as in brutal to women? Or a beast like what I saw in the UP?"

"I am a grizzly bear–shifter, and you have no idea what that means."

She shook her head. "But you guys have wives, right? You had parents, a family."

"Many shifters mate, and my parents were raised in the shifter community, so they knew the risks." Then he touched her cheek, turning her to look directly into his eyes. "Why do you think I went to the UP? To a place where there are miles without people."

"You like the cold?"

"Because even among shifters, I'm considered too dangerous to mate. The bear is very, very strong in me." He let those words hang in the air. Saw the meaning hit her in her widened eyes and the sharp intake of her breath. Then she jerked away from his touch, her gaze going back to the apartment complex and her problems there.

"I don't even know why we're talking about this."

He didn't either, but he had never fully understood the subtleties behind human communication.

"I brought you here so you could help my brother," she continued.

"I can't."

"So you keep saying, but you know more than anyone else. You know he's a…he's like you. Sort of."

He thought about that. Vic had shifted into a partial bear. It had been patchwork and smelly, but there were similarities. Which meant if anyone understood what was happening with Vic, it would be the shifter community.

"I've been out of touch for ten months. Perhaps the Detroit bears know something."

"Great. How do I contact them?"

He looked at her. "You can't. It must be me. And it must be in person."

She frowned at him. "Is this a bear territory thing?"

He snorted. "It is a gangland Detroit thing."

CHAPTER 8

Alyssa blinked, her mind too dull and her emotions too wrung out to fully process what he'd just said. Still, she gave it her best, echoing what she thought she'd heard.

"Bear-shifters are a Detroit gang?"

"The Griz, I believe." He rolled his eyes. "Really obvious name, but no one asked me."

She wasn't very familiar with Detroit gangs, but the Griz were near enough to her neighborhood that she was aware of them. They did the usual: drugs, guns, booze, and really loud music. They certainly weren't the worst gang in Detroit. The idea that bear-shifters could be living that close to her was enough to make her world tilt. Again. And in a day filled with new information and horrible surprises, she really couldn't handle any more.

"Steady there." Simon's words were barely audible over the rushing in her ears. What penetrated her foggy brain was the sturdy grip of his hand on her elbow and the way he wrapped a strong arm around her waist.

She sank into him, letting her body sag while she breathed deep of his woodsy scent mixed with Irish Spring. Would that smell always make her knees weak and her head spin?

"Have you had anything to eat today besides beer and brownies?"

Honestly, she couldn't remember.

"Never mind," he said, his voice gruff. "I remember that you had a diet cola and a piece of my pizza ten hours ago."

And a granola bar she'd picked up at a gas station.

"That granola doesn't count," he said, somehow reading her mind. "It smelled like petrified gravel. Couldn't have tasted much better."

It hadn't.

"So where's your bedroom?" He was walking her back toward the laundromat.

"Inside." Apparently forming that answer took all the strength left in her body. While she was busy telling herself to stand up and walk on her own, damn it, the world decided to veer into more dizzying circles. *Oh hell.* She was going down.

Except she wasn't. When her legs gave in, he swung her up in his arms. She tried to resist. She tightened her hands and managed to keep her head from flopping backward. But her vision was crazy fuzzed out and her head felt three times too large. All she ended up doing was dropping herself onto his shoulder while he balanced her in his arms.

"I got you. Go ahead. Close your eyes. You've had a full few days so it's okay to check out for a bit."

Like her body was giving her any choice? She closed her eyes and let his scent fill her thoughts completely. Kind of like dropping back into her fantasies when she'd kept a bar of Irish Spring in her bedside table just to help her remember. Meanwhile, she noticed that he wasn't even winded as he took steady steps back toward the apartment. She wasn't a lightweight by any stretch of the imagination, and oh wow, it was awesome to be cradled in his arms as if she were the tiniest Barbie doll.

And yeah, fantasy land. She felt her core go molten at the feel of living out one of her dreams, and she might have nuzzled a little against his neck.

He stepped into the laundromat, barely even jostling her as he managed both her and the door. Then she heard Malik gasp in surprise.

"She's fine," Simon said, stopping anything Malik might have asked. "But she needs to sleep for a while. Where's her bedroom?"

"Um, it's across the hall. This way."

They'd need her key. It was in her jeans pocket, but no way was she going to wiggle around to get it. She was far too content riding in Simon's arms to change anything. Except that eventually they made it to her apartment door. Simon seemed to tuck his head down against hers. She heard him make a strange sound. Like a chuff of some sort. And then she sighed.

"You need my key to get in," she murmured.

"Yes."

"Set me down."

"Can you stand on your own?"

No. Yes. Maybe. She groaned. He was crouching down, gently setting her feet on the floor. "I am not a woman who faints," she said to no one in particular. She kept an arm wrapped around Simon's broad shoulders as she dug into her jeans pocket with the other.

"No," Simon answered. "You're a woman who drives without

sleep up to the UP and back to save her brother. But even Wonder Woman has limits."

It took concentration to bring her key out of her pocket. Even more to shove it toward the lock. She didn't get close. Malik took it from her and managed to get the door open. Then when she took an unsteady step inside, the world abruptly upended again.

Simon swept her back into his arms and was walking in his steady, measured pace through her apartment.

"Where—" he began, but apparently Malik was leading.

A moment later, Simon had crossed through her apartment and into her bedroom. She flushed when she realized she hadn't made her bed and that there was dirty laundry—specifically dirty underwear—in full view beside her dresser. Her brother had called in a panic, and she'd rushed out without taking the time for her morning rituals. Ones that included making her bed and drinking a thick mug of coffee.

But if Simon saw her red lace thong next to the matching push-up bra, he made no comment. Instead, he lay her on her bed. She had to let go of his shoulders. She had to stop drawing his scent deep into her lungs. She had to do a ton of things that she didn't want to do, like face the fact that she'd just let a virtual stranger carry her through her place of business and into her apartment. And now he was stripping off her boots.

"Head for the button of my jeans," she rumbled, "and I'll hurt you."

"Sure, you will," Simon said, sarcasm in his tone. Then he turned to Malik. "I've got her. You can go back to work."

"Yeah. Um, boss?"

"I'm fine," she mumbled. "Go on."

"Okay. Um, just call if you need something."

"I will."

Her left boot hit the floor, and then he started working on the right. She was lying bonelessly on the bed as she stared at the ceiling. She ought to feel mortified. She did feel mortified. But mostly she felt overwhelmed.

"I need to face my problems," she said. It was part of her morning litany and included things like take concrete steps toward her goals and allow no one to distract her from her purpose. "I need—"

"To give yourself a break." He dropped her other boot on the floor, then went for the button of her jeans. She gasped and put her hand on his forearm, but she didn't stop him. "You'll be more comfortable with these off," he said.

Of course she would. She'd be more comfortable naked with him inside her, too. But that wasn't exactly on the agenda. "I got it," she said, hoping it was true. She felt like even that small effort took a thousand times more energy than it should. "And no man goes there without my asking."

He chuckled. "You forget that I'm a shifter. I can smell things, Alyssa." He leaned down close to her neck and he rubbed his nose across her skin. And oh my God, did that feel good. "I know you're aroused. So am I."

Her breath caught and she froze. Was he about to seduce her? Now? She was equal parts appalled and excited.

"But neither of us is in any condition to act on this." He pressed his lips to her skin and she felt the stroke of his tongue. "Only an animal would take you now when you are too tired to resist."

He was half animal though. And he wasn't moving away from her neck. The edge of his teeth scraped along the underside of her jaw. She shivered and her nipples tightened to unbearable points. And oh did she want to give in. She had the excuse ready-made. She wasn't in her right mind. She'd had a beer on an empty stomach. She could justify anything if only he pressed her a little further. If his lips went from her neck to her cleavage and to her aching, hungry breasts. Or perhaps to the open wet place between her thighs.

If only.

He drew back. "I'm going to sleep on your couch. If you need anything, just call me."

She needed him to force her to do something that made no sense. She needed him to take what she was willing to give, but couldn't admit to. She needed him to take the lead because she was too embarrassed and horny and overwhelmed to do it herself.

As if reading her mind, he stroked a finger across her lips. Heat trailed and her mouth opened.

"Except that, Alyssa. Anything but that."

Then he stepped back and away. He was gone, presumably to settle down on her couch like a freaking priest or something. She was just deciding if she was pissed or grateful when he abruptly came back in. She was startled enough that she lifted her head as he held up her gun before setting it on her bedside table.

"This is for you," he said. "In case I don't wake up right."

Well that was scary sounding. She forced herself to push up on her elbows. "You mean, in case you wake up as a bear. In my living room."

"Yes." No hesitation, just a flat acknowledgment. "And if that happens, shoot to kill. I'll be too far gone to save."

Her mind stuttered to a halt. "I'm not going to shoot you!" Again.

"You won't be shooting me. You'll be shooting a feral grizzly."

"But—"

He held up his hand. "Shoot to kill, Alyssa. I'm not kidding."

He wasn't. She could see it in his eyes. And wasn't that a total buzzkill.

"Promise me."

She shook her head.

"Promise or I won't stick around. I won't be here to help out tomorrow with Vic. Or go see the Griz. Promise or I'll start walking back to the UP right now."

"You won't get two blocks without being jumped."

He arched a brow. "Then my problem is solved."

He couldn't possibly be that suicidal. Didn't animals have a self-preservation thing? But that was the problem, wasn't it? She wasn't talking to his animal side right then. He was all thinking human and his mind was made up. If she didn't promise to shoot him, then he'd leave just to ensure her safety.

She groaned. "You're a bigger pain in the ass than my brother. And that's saying something."

He grunted in a kind of acknowledgment. And when she didn't say anything more, he repeated his demand.

"Promise or—"

"I promise. I'll shoot your furry ass if you dare go grizzly in my apartment. Do you know how long it took me to decorate this place?" She added a glare of fury just for good measure.

"It's beautifully decorated," he said. "Every pink ruffle and bow is sacred. I'd kill myself if I ever hurt a single one."

He was teasing her. Her apartment was *not* decorated in pink bows or ruffles. Though there might be a rose undertone to the paint and a few white accents in the furniture. But there weren't any bows and he damn well knew it.

She collapsed backward on her pillow. "My place bought with my money where I live alone. Be grateful you're not sleeping on pink unicorn pillows with sparkly bling accents."

He didn't answer. In fact, he was silent so long that she lifted her head to look. He was right where he'd been a moment before, standing near her doorway, but this time with a soft smile on his face.

"What?" she demanded.

"I'm glad you're feeling better, Alyssa. We'll figure out what to do in the morning. I promise."

No mockery in his words. In fact, the genuine warmth had her tearing up again. When had she ever had someone help her in this nightmare of a life? Someone who wasn't her employee or her flaky-as-shit brother?

"Go to sleep, Simon," she said. She didn't trust her voice to say anything else. And she sure as hell wasn't going to burst into tears again.

"Good night, Alyssa." He backed out of her room, shutting the bedroom door firmly behind him. Then she heard him in her living room, presumably settling in on her couch. And she heard a grumble. A very loud one that included a snort.

She was pushing out of bed when she heard him speak, his voice carrying into her bedroom.

"Just make sure I'm really furry when you shoot me and it's not this synthetic disaster of a blanket!"

She had to think a moment, then she stifled her laugh. Her only blanket had been a gift from her brother before he'd gone on his first deployment. It was a fake fur monstrosity that collected static like a miswired charger and using it felt like being buried under a thick carpet. But it was warm, and her brother had given it to her, so it was the blanket that sat on the couch for every winter in Michigan.

And now it would be wrapped around Simon.

"Don't worry," she called back. "Your real fur is way thinner and patchy, too. I'll be able to tell the difference." Then she laughed, loud and long at his outraged grunt of a response.

CHAPTER 9

Simon woke early, and he woke human.

Part of him was disappointed by that. Grizzly emotions were easy. He wouldn't care that his best friend had turned into a monster or that he'd gone to sleep with the taste of Alyssa's lust on his tongue. He'd be completely consumed with eating and rutting and have little understanding of the consequences of those actions.

Grizzly life was easy, but it couldn't happen in Detroit. So he rolled off the couch and sniffed the air. He smelled cannabis and popcorn, and he heard the rumble of cars outside, which did not quiet the rumble of Alyssa's snores.

She was deep asleep and he was pleased. She needed the rest and he needed the quiet time to talk to Vic. Still, it was strangely hard for him to leave her apartment. His grizzly preferred to rest near the female, watching over her sleep and protecting her home.

But the man was in charge and though watching Alyssa sleep held appeal, she'd thank him more if he figured out what was wrong with

Vic. So he dressed quickly and headed down into the foul-smelling basement.

Vic had barely moved during the night. They'd left him unconscious as he sprawled against the now warped side of the cage. Sometime during the night, he'd rolled onto his side, but nothing more. And the echoing rumble of snores was pure Vic. Simon had fallen asleep to that rumble hundreds of times on deployment. Hell, it was almost soothing.

He walked over to Vic, taking his time to study his friend in detail. The monster was mostly naked, so beneath the blood, he saw patches of fur and the sharp claws on his pawlike hands. Thanks to the beating Simon had given Vic, the man's face was swollen and disfigured, but the elongated nose was still obvious as were the sharp-cutting teeth that seemed grizzly-sized.

And that smell. God, it wasn't as thick as it had been last night, but it was BO at its worst. Simon wondered if it might be a defense mechanism. Hard to kill the monster while puking up your guts from nausea. That's why he hadn't bothered to eat breakfast before coming down here. He didn't want it coming back up from the awful *wrong* smell that surrounded Vic.

When he had inspected his friend's body enough, he squatted down as close as he could to Vic's ear. He wasn't going inside the cage right now. That was much too dangerous, but hopefully he wouldn't need to. Instead, he pitched his voice low and soothing.

"Vic. Vic, buddy. Time to wake up."

He had to call a few more times, but eventually the snoring stopped as Vic snuffled and drifted up from sleep. Then came the low moan as pain must have hit. Honestly, there wasn't much of

Vic's entire body that had escaped damage. But hopefully, they could fix that soon.

"Don't open your eyes," he said. In truth, only one eye could be opened. The other looked swollen shut. "I know you hurt, but we're in a situation and I need you to keep your head."

Vic was military, so he knew to hold it together. At least for the moment. Sure enough, the man stilled but his nostrils flared. He was awake and starting to use his senses. Which meant Simon had to get him distracted before memory kicked in.

"I need you to remember something, okay? It sounds stupid but it's really important. Remember that bar we went to in Anchorage? You couldn't decide between the redhead with the big boobs or the blonde with the big butt. Remember that?"

Was there a shift to Vic's mouth? Was he smiling a little?

"Do you remember which one you picked? And what was her name? Amber? Betty?"

Vic's mouth started to move, but it wasn't formed right for human speech. He'd be able to do it, but it would be a struggle at first. Simon didn't want him that aware just yet, so he rushed to stop him.

"Don't talk. Not yet. I need you remembering. What was her name? I'll just call her Red." He thought his friend had gone with the boobs, but he honestly wasn't sure. "I need you to think back on that night. Do you remember what you did with her? She took you into the ladies' room, I know that." That bar had two ladies' rooms. One for the regular female customers—of which there were few—and another on the second floor for the prostitutes to use. The stalls were larger, the perfume heavier, and there was a bouncer posted right outside just in case the johns got a little too aggressive. In return, management got a cut of the girl's price.

Suddenly he snapped his fingers.

"No wait! I remember. You picked both. Boobs first then butt. Said it was the hottest time you'd ever had. Then you came back to the table, we finished another pitcher of beer, and you went back in for seconds. Do you remember that?"

There was definitely a smile on Vic's face now. And though he really didn't want to look, he glanced down long enough to see that Vic's boner was growing.

"Yeah, you remember. But it was the brunette who was most important. You tagged her last. Said she did something special to you. It was in the way she touched you. Do you remember that? What did she touch first, Vic? I need you to picture that moment. What exactly did she do to you? And then what did you do to her? The details are important, Vic. Every single detail. As if you were putting it on film. I want you to run through every single—"

His voice cut off because he could see it was working. The air near Vic got cold and there was a pale glow around his body. It started at his groin—no shock there—but rapidly expanded to Vic's entire body. The fur receded. The bones shifted and resettled. Swelling faded along with the claws, and though the skin remained bloody in patches, Vic's face eventually returned to normal.

Vic was a man again.

"Yeah, Vic. You got it now," he said, his voice muted. His best friend was a shifter. No doubt about it now that he'd seen it up close. But what the hell had he shifted into? "You can open your eyes now, Vic. Whenever you're ready."

The man's brown eyes blinked open. He took in his surroundings first, then locked in on Simon. It took two tries for him to speak, but eventually he did, his voice coming out rusty and thick.

"What happened?"

"What do you remember?"

Vic's eyes narrowed on the cage walls and the bent door. "I was locked in here. You and Alyssa came down and she wouldn't let me out of the damned cage." His voice tightened and he pushed up on his elbows.

"Easy there. You need to stay calm."

"Calm?" Vic mocked. "Calm? Look at this cage. What the fuck happened?"

Simon didn't answer. He wanted to see how much his friend remembered. And true to form, Vic started answering his own question.

"I was so mad. And you were saying…You said…" His eyes widened as he looked at the bent door. "I got out and you were giving me shit. And I got…"

"What? You got what? Say it." Simon invested his words with the bite of command.

"I got really pissed."

"Yeah. Then—"

"Holy shit!" Vic suddenly scrambled backward. He landed on the cot with a clang and his eyes shot wide with terror. "Holy shit!" he bellowed again, obviously replaying everything in his memory. He looked at his arms and legs. He realized now that he was naked except for the tattered remains of his jeans. "What the fuck?"

"Stay calm, Vic. Adrenaline only makes it worse. Panic fuels the shift."

Too late. BO flooded the air. Though it was noxious and nauseating, Simon didn't move. He needed to remain a calm center for his friend or they'd never get through this.

Meanwhile, Vic's nostrils flared. "Oh fuck, that's me! That's—"

"Yeah. It sucks. Now get it together." He straightened to a stand. "That's an order!" he barked.

The tone worked. Vic's gaze locked on Simon's and he breathed hard. In and out, the sound rasping through his throat. But as the seconds ticked by, the pulse in Vic's throat visibly eased. The harsh breathing slowed. And best of all, the stench eased off.

Vic got it together.

"What is happening to me?" He slowly stood to face Simon. "What am I becoming?"

Simon pursed his lips. "You're not becoming anything. The change has already happened to you, Vic. At least I think it's done." He was trying to focus on the positive here, though God knew he was making a big guess.

Vic leaned forward. "What?"

"I think your change is over. Now it's just a matter of getting control of it." He took a breath, then immediately regretted it for the smell. "You're a shifter now. You change when you're pissed off. You want to remain human? You stay calm."

"So I'm a bear? Like you?"

No sense in lying. "You're…your own thing, Vic. I've never seen the like before, but it's not impossible to deal with. Every adolescent shifter goes through this to some degree."

"Like this?" Vic asked. "The stink? The fur? The…" He tugged at the frayed denim. "The clothes?"

"Everything but the stink. That's all you."

"But…" He collapsed back on the cot, and Simon held his breath wondering if the flimsy thing would break. Even as a human, Vic was a big man. Fortunately, the cot was sturdier than it looked. "I don't understand. Is this how it happened to you? Just...you know, out of the blue?"

"Was it really out of the blue? What were you feeling before-hand? Why'd you have Alyssa come to me? What made you think of me?"

Vic rubbed a hand over his face, but he didn't speak. He just slumped there in defeat. Simon waited a long time, but in the end, he slipped his fingers through the chain link and gripped it tight.

"You need to talk to me, Vic. You asked me to help and I'm here, but—"

"I'm trying to remember!" Vic snapped. Except it was more like a growl as his head shot up and his mouth pulled back to show his teeth. It was an animal's reaction to being threatened, and they both recognized it. Simon just waited. Hell, his shifter friends had done a ton worse as teens, but it frightened Vic enough that his eyes widened with panic.

Anger, shock, panic, which led to more anger. It was a cycle Simon knew well. As did every shifter. But it was a cycle that had to stop.

"Keep it together," he growled, his own animal surging forward.

"I'm trying!"

Then Simon abruptly shot his finger forward in a determined point. "Don't you dare stink this place up again!" It felt like an awkward gesture. He'd never wagged his finger at anyone in his life. But it was something Vic's mother had done to him, or so he'd once told Simon. Simon mimicked it and prayed that his friend was conditioned to quiet down at that gesture.

It worked.

Vic tucked in his jaw and stared at the floor, but it didn't last long.

A moment later his gaze shot up and there was a pinched look to his brows. Worse, there was a rising stench in the air. "I can't stop it!"

"Yes, you can," Simon said. He was running out of ways to tell Vic the same thing. And then Alyssa's voice cut through the air.

"You weren't born able to speak, Vic. You weren't potty trained and didn't know your hand from your ass, but you learned. You formed words, used the toilet, and got control of when your hand and your ass interact."

Both men shot looks at Alyssa as she strode into the basement. Simon noted that her eyes seemed clear and her shoulders determined. Her hair was back in that tight bun and her expression was hard. But inside, he guessed she was cut to pieces by what her brother had become. Meanwhile, Vic groaned.

"Don't be a bitch, Lys. My hand and my ass are always in perfect sync."

She rolled her eyes, but Simon could see relief in the gesture. Vic couldn't be a monster while he was cracking jokes, right? And even better, the stink seemed to be clearing. A little. Which meant the anger cycle was broken and he had a chance to speak to Vic's rational mind.

"She's right that it's a new body function just like walking and talking. You have to learn how to control it just like you learned—"

"Potty training," Vic grumbled. "I got it. So when I start getting angry, I need to—"

"Think of the redhead."

Vic's brows narrowed. "I thought it was the brunette. You know, the one who took her time."

Simon held up his hand to stop his friend from saying anything more. He enjoyed a good sexual exploit as much as! any man, but he'd never thought of it as a spectator sport. "I just needed you to remember the details of being a man. The body, the feel, the...everything of being a man. That's what shifted you back to human. And by the way, that's what healed your injuries."

Vic touched his cheek, pressing in to the cheekbones. "You beat the crap out of me."

"You deserved it." It was a lie. Vic hadn't been in control. All Simon had needed to do was incapacitate him, not beat him senseless. The only one who had kept it together last night was Alyssa and he admired the hell out of her for that.

Meanwhile Vic shrugged. "Yeah." He looked at his sister. "Sorry about..." He gestured to the damaged cage. "Everything."

"You can fix the cage as your apology. You got yourself under control now?"

Vic groaned. "You're always giving me more work as an apology."

"'Cause you're always screwing up."

"This wasn't my fault!"

"And yet you're still responsible for your actions. You still have to face the consequences."

He growled at his sister. "You're still a bitch."

"And you still stink."

That pulled up him short, and his nostrils flared. So did Simon's as he tried to compare the air quality to what it had been a moment before. Vic reacted first.

"I do not. That's old stink."

Alyssa arched a brow. "So you've got it together?"

He held up his hands palms turned outward. "I'm sure."

"Then I guess you can learn." She stepped forward and quickly unlocked the cage, swinging the door wide. "Go take a shower and get some clothes on. We've got things to do."

"What things?" Vic asked, belatedly realizing he was standing naked in front of his sister. He tried to casually cover his important bits, but the whole thing looked awkward.

Simon took pity on the man. "We'll discuss that when you're showered. Go on. I'm going to figure out a way to fumigate this basement."

Vic took the escape and fled while the two of them watched his bobbing black ass climb the stairs. But the moment he disappeared upstairs, Alyssa turned to him.

"You think he's okay to be wandering around?"

He arched a brow. "You're the one who let him out, not me."

She shrugged, a guilty flush to her cheeks. "You said he could get control, and then he did. And I hated seeing him in here." She sighed, but her gaze didn't soften. "Now I want to know if I was being impulsive. Does Vic belong in a cage?"

Difficult question and all he had were guesses. But to suggest that Vic should remain in a cage was to say that every young shifter belonged locked up because they might lose their temper. It didn't work that way. Easy enough to stay calm when you were holed up in a basement watching TV. The only way to learn control was to test it. Out in the real world.

"I think I need to stick close to him just in case."

She nodded. "Fair enough."

"But now I need more answers. Were there any symptoms before he started changing? Was he especially surly? Did he get sick or have a fever?"

"Yeah. I already told you he had the Detroit Flu about three days ago."

"Tell me again." As they spoke, he found a couple big fans and one little one. Alyssa helped, opening the appropriate storage areas with her key. Then it was a matter of judging how to best get air flowing through the basement.

"Two outbreaks. I caught the first. Vic the second. Hospitals were overrun with people spiking fevers. A lot of the old and young died. The CDC was called in, but mostly it was just an ugly bug. I felt crappy for days."

"How many people got it?"

"Seemed like everyone. All at once."

"And what did the CDC conclude?"

She snorted. "What does the government ever decide? Nothing. Or at least nothing that they're telling us. But further investigation is warranted." Her last sentence was done in a mocking accent and he couldn't help but agree. "Well, if everyone got it, then it couldn't have done this or everyone would be running around with fur." Unless Vic had some preexisting genetic condition that the virus triggered. Maybe only an unlucky few were changed. "You and Vic are half siblings, aren't you?"

She nodded. "Yeah. Same mother, but our dads were different."

So Alyssa might not have the same genetic predisposition to going furry that Vic did. Maybe. Damn, he hated guessing. "We need more information."

"Which is why we're going to visit the Griz."

He shook his head. "Not *we*. It has to be—"

She held up her hand. "You can't leave Vic alone. And if Vic is going with you, then I'm going as back up. If my brother loses it, you need someone to help you." She held up the Taser with a strained smile. "Have weapon, will electrocute."

"This is not a good idea," he said, mentally scrambling for a valid argument.

"You remember how to read yet?"

He glanced at a magazine on the top of an open storage box. Though the hot babe cover was clear enough, the printed letters meant nothing to him. Yet.

"No," he bit out.

"You'll get there," she said gently. "I'll start teaching you as soon as we finish with the Griz."

"I know, but—"

"And you got any way to get around Detroit without me or my car?"

He had his nose. But in the soup of urban smells, picking out the scent of grizzly-shifters would be tough. He could wander for days without getting anything.

"No, but—"

"So stop fighting it. I'm coming."

"It's dangerous."

She snorted. "So is running a cash business in this neighborhood. And yet here I still stand."

He glared at her. "I don't like it."

She chuckled, a warm sound that was soothing even as her words irritated him. "Oh my," she cried in a mock southern drawl. "Someone doesn't like my choices. Whatever will I do?"

He had no answer to that, so he flicked on the fans. The fetid air started moving. If nothing else, at least he remembered how electrical fans worked. He was sure that would help enormously as he faced a criminal gang of grizzly bear-shifters...not.

CHAPTER 10

Alyssa tried not to let her anxiety show. She didn't like driving in this area of town. Hell, she didn't like driving in any place she didn't know the people and the streets like the back of her hand. What she did know about this neighborhood was it hugged the Bernd Creek, one of the tributaries into the River Rouge, and it was not a nice place to raise kids. It was also weird as hell to drive at twenty miles per hour while Simon and Vic stuck their noses out the open windows like dogs. They were trying to be subtle about it, but in this neighborhood, even her beat-up Chevy stood out.

"Which direction, Simon?" She tried to keep her voice low and soothing—more for her brother than herself—but every part of her screamed, *Leave now.*

"Feeling anxious?" Simon asked, his voice low. Then he kept talking before she could answer. "It's a low-level psychic thing some shifters can do. A subtle territorial thing. I remember it being strong in the Griz leader." He touched her arm in a slow stroke. "If you're feeling it, then we're getting close."

"I feel it in most of Detroit."

"Nah, you don't," Vic said from the backseat. "Not this prickling scalp anxiety."

Simon turned his startled gaze onto Vic. "You can feel that?"

"Like a zillion paper cuts all over my skin."

"Let me know when it feels like barbed wire."

Vic rolled his eyes and drawled, "Oh goody."

Simon turned back to the window. "It's a special sensitivity, Vic. That's a good thing."

"Tell that to my skin."

Simon didn't answer as he squeezed Alyssa's arm.

"What?" she asked.

"Huh?" He looked back at her.

She arched a brow, but he was obviously clueless. He clearly didn't even realize he had squeezed her. Or stroked her. Or any of the hundreds of ways that he had been touching her today. There wasn't anything overtly sexual in any of it. If there had been, she would have slammed him against a wall. She did not want a repeat of last night. Not when she'd sobbed on his shirt or let him carry her to bed. And nothing like what she would have let him do if he'd pushed last night in bed.

She was not having sex with Simon. It was a ridiculous thought despite her fantasies. Vic was in trouble, there were dangerous gangs involved, and only a moron would throw sex into the middle of that.

And yet every time he touched her skin, her entire body followed the stroke or squeeze. Her mind zeroed in on the sensations, her breath hitched, and her skin tingled. Like full-on tingles followed by heat. Not just on her skin, but inside deep where her womanly hormones were getting all revved up.

She hated it.

And yet, part of her sank into the feelings. How long had it been since she'd gotten revved up about anyone? Exactly two years, eight months, and a handful of days. That was when Simon had last visited with Vic. And that's when her fantasies of the hot army engineer had taken over her nighttime imagination.

"This is not the time or place," she grumbled under her breath. Too bad neither Simon nor her libido listened. He continued to touch her arm, and she continued to allow it.

Then suddenly he jerked her arm and pointed.

"There," he said.

"Oh hell," Vic moaned. "We've gone beyond barbed wire to axes and machetes on my skin."

Simon looked back at her brother. "It'll ease over time. Or when the leader decides he wants to talk to you."

"Peachy," Vic growled between clenched teeth.

Alyssa slowed the car down, taking her time as she drove past a converted storefront. It looked like it used to be an Ace Hardware, since no one had ever bothered to bring down the old signage. But black curtains covered the four large glass windows and a single poster by the door declared it to be "Kuma Dojo" with a grizzly bear silhouette as its logo. Pretty obvious to her, but even without all that, she would've known they'd found the right place. The smell was rank even on the street. Like Vic at his worst. And that psychic stay-the-hell-away had her knuckles white as she clenched the steering wheel.

"Drop me off here," Simon said. "Come back in an hour."

God, she wanted to. Not the leaving him behind part, but anything that got her the hell away from that dojo. Instead, she parked her car right across the street from the dark curtained doorway. Simon hopped out, but then so did she and Vic.

"We're just going in there to talk," she said as much to herself as anyone else. "That's not dangerous. That's normal civilized conversation."

"Except they're animals," Simon said. And then he shook his head. "You're an idiot for following," he said to her, but then focused on Vic. "And you keep it together or I'll rip your head off myself. Got it?"

Vic didn't answer. His skin was gray and his mouth pinched tight with pain. It had to be those axes and machetes he'd been talking about. But even with that, he was still following with one determined step after another.

Alyssa didn't know whether to be enormously proud of her brother or terrified for their stupidity. Both, probably. Nevertheless, they all walked together across the street. Until Simon held up his hand.

"Stay behind me, no matter what. And when I say run, you run. Hard."

She nodded and Vic did, too. Honestly, she wanted to be strong here, to back Simon up however he needed. But every step closer to the building had her knees weakening and her heart fluttering at panicked levels. She was really afraid that if he told her to run, she'd take the excuse and bolt. And she wouldn't stop until she was in Canada.

In this she was unexpectedly helped by the stench in the air. Hard to run when she was gagging for breath. She glanced at her brother who was shaking his head.

"It's not from me," he said, as he showed her his bare and very humanlike hands.

"No," said Simon as he put his hand on the door. "It's from inside." Then he hauled the glass door open and went in.

They followed a step behind, pushing through the dark curtain just as Simon had. But Alyssa never got farther than a half step before she felt Simon's hand press flat on her belly.

"Run," he said, his voice low and urgent. "Now."

CHAPTER 11

As a teen, Simon had seen his share of shifter battles. There was even a shifter summer camp that had an area designed for that. And yes, there were secret shifter fight clubs that every teen searched for but fortunately few found.

None compared to what he saw right now.

A single, moderately-sized grizzly bear stood backed into a corner. It was dark brown with black patches and matted with blood. His face was a swollen mass, and his right thigh had taken enough tearing strikes that it looked like ground meat. Blood flowed everywhere, but the creature was still fighting. It should have been roaring with the way its mouth was open and his teeth gleamed white and wet, but it didn't have the breath. It saved its strength for swiping with broad strokes in front of him, keeping the four...monsters...back.

Four who looked like Vic at his worst and a stench that matched. They were going in for the kill, encroaching step by step with murderous intent. And lest he think that the others in the room were going to help the pure shifter, the other nine, all in human form, were watching with looks that varied between glee and nausea.

This was a gang murder, plain and simple. And he'd walked Alyssa in seconds before it happened. And double hell, she wasn't leaving despite the fact that he'd just tried to shove her outside without drawing undue attention to them.

And now it was too late. Alyssa made a sound of defiance. It wasn't even a word, but she refused to budge, and nothing caught a male shifter's attention faster than a female refusing to obey. It signaled to everyone that she was a fair target since she'd just refused a male's protection.

The sound did little to distract the attackers, but it certainly caught the onlookers' attention. Multiple eyes swiveled in Alyssa's direction; Simon had to capture their attention quick or risk whatever they had in mind for her.

"We're just visiting," he said loud enough for everyone to hear. "Do you mind pausing in the…um…illegal activity over there while we're here? We don't mean to interrupt, but now that we've seen it, it would be best if it didn't cross any lines." It was a sound, logical argument that reminded everyone that they were humans subject to the rule of law.

It didn't work.

A stupidly large man stood up. Thick shoulders, broad nose, and dark yellow teeth in his pale Caucasian face. He was the Griz alpha, and his name was Nanook as a nod to his Inuit ancestor Nanook of the North. Also, he was the only known shifter who was part polar bear.

And he was really pissed off.

"How did you get in here?" he demanded.

It was that booming question that saved the shifter in the corner. At that tone everyone in the room—including the four attacking...hybrids?—turned to glare at Simon.

"We walked in," Alyssa snapped. "Through the door. Which was unlocked."

Hell, this wasn't the time for her to talk. But he already knew she attacked whenever she was scared. Big grizzly bear roars at her in the UP? She shoots it. Big alpha makes threatening noises here? She responds with a smart-ass comment and she probably had her hand on her gun.

She was going to die—or worse—if he didn't take control fast.

"Quiet!" he snapped, investing his word with the bite of command, and was eternally grateful that she was smart enough to obey. Then he answered the question that Nanook had really meant.

"I'm Simon Gold, one of the Gladwin grizzlies. I've been here before and we spoke, so I'm welcome here." That was the real question: How did he get past the psychic "no trespassing" vibes? Answer: He was bold enough to defy them because he knew that he was welcome.

"He isn't," Nanook said, jutting his chin at Vic. And then came the psychic blast that Nanook was best known for. It was like a physical blow to every nerve ending in a man's body. The first and only time that Simon had felt it, he had gone down on his ass and trembled like a child for twenty minutes.

Vic was no better. He dropped like a stone, but he wasn't trembling. No, he was full-on monster by the time he hit the floor. His mouth peeled back and fur came out. He'd been smart enough to wear sweats that expanded with him and his flip-flops fell away, so he wasn't screaming in pain from his clothing, though the T-shirt was stretched thin. What was really impressive though, was that his friend didn't flop on the floor like a beached fish. That had been what Simon had done two years before. No, Vic rolled jerkily to his feet where he faced Nanook on all fours and with his teeth flashing.

And the four other monsters abandoned the bloody grizzly to advance on Vic.

Shit.

"Stay there," Simon ordered to everyone, Vic included. "We're not here to cause problems. We just need some information."

Nanook snorted. "I just bet you do. Wondering what that is?" He gestured toward Vic.

Simon echoed the gesture only at the other four who were literally salivating to get to Vic. "You obviously know more than we do. We came here respectfully to ask if you'd explain."

"Want me to explain?" the man bellowed. "It's the fucking dogs, that's who! They've done this to us!" He advanced forward, his manner barely controlled aggression and Simon felt his insides grow tight. His grizzly was primed and ready, aching to burst free, but that would be disastrous. No way could his grizzly win in a fight. Not against everyone here. Not while still protecting Alyssa.

So he kept his voice calm, trying to pitch the tones to be soothing and deferential. "How did the dogs do this?"

"They do everything!" Nanook bellowed, obviously warming to a favorite theme. "See this?" He hauled over the nearest monster. "This was Jayden. He was a damned good mechanic. Now he's this. All the time." He shoved Jayden away who came up snarling. The only reason he didn't attack was because Nanook growled him down. Then he pointed to the others in turn. "Billy. Tyler. And that last one, she was Tiana."

Simon did a double take. That one was female? God it was hard to tell. Neither human nor beast, they were each a sick combination of twisted limbs and partial shifts. "They just changed?"

"It was the fever," Nanook growled. "Most get better. Some died. Then there are a few…" His voice trailed away as he looked at Vic. "Come here, boy. I can keep you from killing your family."

Simon felt Alyssa stiffen, but he didn't have time to fight her. His attention was firmly fixed on Vic as the man visibly trembled. That huge psychic blast was a once-a-day kind of deal for Nanook, but there was still power in his words. A kind of subliminal compulsion akin to the "stay away" message. But this time, his order was all, *Come here. Be part of my pack.*

And Vic had to decide that on his own.

Vic straightened, still in his monster form, but he was soon standing on his two feet.

"Vic, no!" Alyssa cried, but before she could do more, Simon grabbed her arm and hauled her back.

"Don't interfere," he growled.

"He can't—"

"He's alone right now," Simon said, stretching for the logic behind the decision. "He's not shifter and he's not human." God, it hurt to say it and it would kill him to think of his best friend as part of Nanook's brutal gang, but there was logic to this choice. "Sometimes being with your own kind is worth it."

Despite his restraint, Alyssa managed to grab one of Vic's furred arms. "Vic, don't. We'll figure—"

"Silence, bitch!" Nanook bellowed.

Alyssa rounded on the alpha, all flashing eyes and angry words. She would fight for her brother no matter what, and it would be the death of her. "My brother doesn't neeee—" Her last word ended on a squeak of alarm. It wasn't anything Simon or Nanook did. It was Vic rounding on her with a hiss.

Simon stepped in front of her. He would protect her.

Fortunately, Vic pulled himself back. And still in his monster form, he looked at Nanook. "I control myself." His words were slightly slurred. He hadn't mastered the technique of speaking while in this body. But the fact that he stood tall and faced off with a powerful alpha showed just how far the man had progressed.

Meanwhile, Nanook didn't take kindly to being disobeyed. He pointed a finger at Vic and blasted the man. Over and over. Simon didn't feel it. It wasn't aimed at him. But he could see the strain on Nanook's face, the throbbing in his temple, and everyone heard the alpha's harsh breath. But while Vic visibly swayed under the assault, he stood firm. And he managed three words.

"Not. Joining. Gang."

Which is when the four other monsters broke through their restraints. As one they leapt forward. Simon had been tracking them, knew the moment Nanook's control of them shattered. But even so, it was four against one.

He jumped in between, blocking the nearest two with swift blows to the face. One of the bastard's teeth cut the hell out of his hand, but that was the least of his problems. The other two were headed straight for Vic who was still doing the death stare with Nanook. He was completely defenseless.

Bam! Bam!

Alyssa had pulled out her gun and was using it to great effect. He had time to see that she'd gone for disabling shots to the legs, but he already knew that wasn't going to work. These four were feral. There was no gleam of intelligence in their eyes, just pure animal fury. They needed to be put down and fast.

His grizzly strained to get out, but it was too soon for him. He couldn't risk going mad himself, so he held it back. He used its fury to fight, but not its claws and mass. Two of the monsters had centered on him. They didn't work together, but they were ferocious and oblivious to pain. He got one with a swift kick to the knee that took it to the floor, but it didn't lay there and whimper like a normal man. Instead it just kept coming. It crawled forward using claws and tried to bite his feet. He kicked it back twice, and the second time got it hard in the face. Its head snapped back, but it still kept coming.

Fortunately, he had help. The wounded grizzly was doing what he could attacking from behind. But he was unsteady from that leg wound. And all the while, Simon was weaving and blocking the other monster. He couldn't find an opening to take it down. Certainly not while dancing around the one on the floor.

Meanwhile, Alyssa kept shooting. She must have figured out that wounding shots weren't going to work because a moment later, she fired and one of them flew backward, his face missing.

"Back off!" she screamed. "Or that'll be you!"

Again, it didn't work. Worse, Simon saw Vic go down on one knee as if crumpling under a great weight. Nanook was pressing him psychically, and there was nothing Simon could do to help. His friend just slowly bent down until first one then the other knee thudded to the floor. But all the while, he kept speaking. First it was, "No. Gang." But eventually, it was just a whispered, "No, no, no, no," repeated with every breath.

Simon felt fire blister across his chest and shoulder, and he cursed under his breath. He'd been too focused on the others and misjudged the monster in front of him. And while he was still recovering from the claw slice, the bastard on the floor got his shin.

Damn, damn, damn! His grizzly roared in his mind, and he considered letting it out. He'd loosened his boots before even coming in here, and it would take a second to pop his jeans, but it wasn't worth the risk. He might save Vic and Alyssa only to force them to put him down when he forgot how to go back to human. It was just too soon.

So he pushed his grizzly back and tried to finish the fight in the fastest way possible. Hand to hand was too slow since it was two on one. Which meant he had to rely on Alyssa, especially since another shot rang out and the other monster went down. That left the two on him. Worse, the other grizzly went down. Blood loss, probably. He needed to shift back to human but there wasn't time or space to worry about him.

Which meant he had one good option: Trust that Alyssa could read his mind and shoot the last monsters in just the right way at the right time.

Did he risk it? He didn't have the breath to call to her. His only choice was to dive out of the way to give Alyssa the shot. If she wasn't paying attention, she'd be completely vulnerable to attack. There'd be no time to reverse to save her.

Who was he kidding? Alyssa was always paying attention.

And with that thought, he took the chance. He let the nearest monster lean into the attack, then Simon dove completely to the side. He rolled with the movement then jumped up the second he—

Bam! Bam! Bambam!

Damn, she was good. The other two went down, bullets in their brain. Even better, Vic was starting to stand. His face was set—still in its monster form—but his eyes were clear and his claws were clenched into fists. A man fought with closed fists. An animal fought with paws spread wide. That showed clear as day that Vic was keeping control of his beast. He was stronger than Nanook, at least psychically, and Simon couldn't be more proud.

But one look at the alpha showed that the bastard wasn't used to losing.

Simon tried to break the psychic stare down. "We didn't come to fight, Nanook. Or to enlist. We just want to talk." No effect. Only one other way to appeal to his rationality. "We acknowledge your dominance, Nanook."

That caught the man's attention. He broke off his attack on Vic who visibly stumbled but remained upright.

Nanook's lips peeled back. "You attacked my men."

Alyssa's voice rang out loud and clear. "They attacked us!"

Nanook's eyes didn't even flicker. The air was getting cooler as he drew in energy for a shift. Those soft sweatpants wouldn't restrict him and the bastard was already barefoot. *Hell.*

Simon quickly started toeing off his boots. "We didn't mean any disrespect."

"You brought that thing in here! You attacked my men!"

Not logical. Not rational. Damn it, Nanook had lost his thinking mind, which meant there was only one way this could go: bad.

All around the room the others were stripping out of jeans, pulling off shirts, and kicking off flip-fops. Damn it, he was the only shifter moron in boots.

Then Vic spoke, his words clear despite his misshapen mouth. "Shoot him!"

"Don't shoot!" Simon ordered. "They'll mob us if you do." And in a shifter mob, everybody got hurt. Angry bears swiped at anything that moved and Alyssa, as the only plain human, wouldn't stand a chance. Especially since there was no way the three of them—four if he counted the wounded bear—could manage the ten…no eleven shifters in the room. Which meant they had one chance. One horrible, irrational, stupid chance. But it was the only hope he had of keeping Alyssa alive.

He shoved down his jeans.

Alyssa gasped. "What are you doing?"

"I challenge you, Nanook. It's clear you're crazy." He glanced at the others. "How can you follow someone that irrational?"

He knew the answer to that. Intimidation and brute force worked wonders. Especially since Nanook had that whole psychic blast thing. Fortunately, the bastard had burned that skill out on Vic. He hoped.

Nanook's mouth curled into a cold smile. "And when you're dead, I'll enjoy your woman."

Alyssa's voice rang out. "Fat chance, bastard."

Simon pulled off his shirt. "Vic, get her out of here."

"We're not leaving you," Vic said. His speech was getting clearer.

"I can't win," he growled as he tossed the last bit of clothing aside. "He's a fucking grolar."

"What?"

A grolar was a grizzly–polar bear mix. That meant that shifted, the bastard had at least a 150 pounds on Simon. But it didn't matter. It was too late. A naked Nanook gestured to his people. Four of them moved to block the exit, which meant that now no one was going anywhere. Not until the battle was done.

One last thing to do before shifting. He turned and looked at

Alyssa. It was stupid, illogical, and there was no time. He should be focused on Nanook, but he needed to see her face one last time.

God, she looked so beautiful. It was the fierceness he admired the most. Her eyes were wide with fear, but her stand was solid and her pistol remained steady in her hand. She was not a woman who lost her head. And definitely not a woman who ran.

"Simon," she began.

"Save your bullets for the ones on you. I'll do the rest." It was a wild claim. He had no chance here. He'd never been a smart fighter, just a full-out wild one. And raw strength never won out against intelligence. Not in a fight to the death.

He wanted to say more. He wanted a moment to memorize her face, to smell her scent. Something. But there was no time. Without warning, his grizzly surged to the fore. Survival instinct, probably, because Nanook attacked without sound.

Simon dove to the side, shifting midleap. His mind stepped aside and the animal came to the fore. His claws slipped on the hard concrete. This was not fighting in the woods as he was used to. This was the urban jungle and he had no weapon or protection in this open concrete space.

Nevertheless, he spun and faced a bear fully a third larger than him. Nanook had light golden brown fur and dark narrow eyes, plus sharp claws in paws that looked broader than a human head. And his jaw opened wide to expose teeth that could easily crush a man's spine. Or even a grizzly's.

Simon roared and he reared up. Fortunately, he wasn't stupid enough to attack. Not at his lesser weight.

The whole goal of a bear attack was to grab hold and get access to the neck. The back of the neck, the jaw, anything that a bear's mouth could crush. Failing that, a good bite that holds could toss a lesser weighted opponent to the side. Maybe expose throat or belly to a well-placed claw.

Nanook went for a brute-force attack. He reared up and pushed forward. Simon had no choice but to meet and grapple.

There was no way to win this, he thought over and over, even as he struggled for a solution. He lost ground in the grappling, as would always happen with an opponent so much larger. Nanook twisted him around and his teeth dug in. Simon adjusted, rolling with the move and using his more flexible body to escape, but it was a losing battle. He'd landed no blows on Nanook and though the bigger bear seemed winded, he showed no signs of stopping.

He felt the rage build inside his grizzly. A dark, feral possession that started to black out his thinking mind. This was the core of his animal, but it would not save him. Though vicious, the grizzly alone could not prevail.

Which left him with a single choice. He could merge his human mind with the animal. Not a distancing, with one in the forefront and the other completely detached, but a complete joining where man and animal survived as one. He never did that because his priorities got screwed up. His human rationality changed in bad ways. Like the time as a teen when he'd nearly killed his best friend. Since then, he simply flipped back and forth, like difference faces of the same coin. Grizzly. Human. Never both at once.

But it was his only hope.

So he did it. And he prayed his friends and his sanity survived.

CHAPTER 12

Alyssa had always been a fan of Animal Planet. It comforted her to know that nature had a cycle, that animals were predictable, and that even large predators could be viewed from a distance as the magnificent creatures they were.

This was something entirely different: this was two huge bears fighting to the death in a cinderblock building. And if things went really south, there could be eight more of those things all aimed at her and Vic.

She didn't care. She only had eyes for Simon. His grizzly form was beautiful. Golden brown fur with dark accents. Paws that could tear a tree in half. But it was his ears that she liked the most. They were round and cute on a very scary face. When he roared, she looked at his ears and remembered that he was a friend. A very sexy, uber logical friend.

She winced as the two beasts collided. Big grappling bodies. It was very Animal Planet, complete with growling and chewing. But Nanook was larger, and even she could see that Simon couldn't win in a contest of straining of muscles. But that's how bears fought and she wasn't surprised when Nanook got better leverage and threw Simon aside. Unless that was Simon escaping?

She didn't know, and it was all so loud and terrifying. She needed to think of a way to escape with Vic. She ought to be doing it now when everyone's eyes were glued to the fight. But she couldn't look away, either. That was Simon there, fighting for his life, and her heart pounded with every grunt and growl. And at the sight of dark blood slicking down his golden fur.

Shitshitshitshit. If she shot Nanook, they'd have every shifter in the place going for them. At least right now it was one on one. And no way would she think that one shot would take down that monstrosity.

And then something changed.

She didn't even notice it at first, but she was watching Simon closely. Hell, she was breathing as he breathed, gritting her teeth as he growled, and clenching her toes as he paced in the concrete space. So when he slowed his movements and his breath, she noticed. And when his head feinted left and right, her own neck tightened at the same time. What was he doing?

His eyes narrowed as he looked around the room. It was like she could feel the man thinking. Except up until this moment, he'd looked and felt just like she'd seen on TV. Just like any other grizzly bear caught on camera in the wild.

But that was her mistake. He was a shifter and now she saw the intelligence in him. And for the first time since the fight began, she felt a stirring of hope. Simon was smart. If ever a smaller creature could defeat a larger one, then now was the time.

She swallowed and murmured to her brother. "You okay?"

"No. But I'm ready."

That was all she needed to know. He was sane and with her. And looking very human, which was both reassuring and disappointing. He was probably way more powerful in monster form. So now they just had to wait for whatever Simon had planned. Except right now, he didn't seem to be doing anything but dancing around. He moved faster than Nanook, but neither was exactly fast. They were too huge.

Simon ducked around a support column and then waited. It looked like he was trying to hide behind it, which was ridiculous. Everyone could see him. But every time that Nanook moved to get at him, he just slipped to the other side. And that's when the strategy became obvious.

Nanook was not a patient attacker. He was getting pissed. His breath was loud and harsh, and his grumbles had turned into angry growls. Enough to terrify her, but Simon didn't seem fazed. Neither did he care that he looked like a scared monkey ducking back and forth behind the large concrete post.

And then suddenly, Nanook lunged. The motion was quick, startling her enough that she squeaked in alarm. Simon had been leaning in, reaching forward with a paw as if to strike, but Nanook caught him and wrapped him in a grappling hold.

Except that what he really caught was the concrete column. And better yet, Simon had ducked his head to the other side just as Nanook lunged. That meant that when the big one tried to chew on Simon's neck, all he got was concrete post.

"Yeah!" her brother cheered, and Alyssa agreed with the sentiment, but the thing was far from over.

Simon had his opening. He lunged forward with his jaws wide.

He grabbed hold of Nanook's dirty white neck and bit down. Nanook roared his fury and pulled back, but Simon kept his jaws firm. And with both sets of arms wrapped around a cement pole, Nanook couldn't take Simon with him.

God, the result was simple logic, but her entire body reeled at the sight.

Even though Simon had his jaws locked deep in Nanook's neck, the grolar shifted his grip and pushed away from the cement pole. Simon bit down harder and blood began to spray in every direction. Nanook bellowed, then tore himself free. But the hole in his neck was huge. Alyssa could see exposed tendons and blood spilling onto his dirty white fur, but it wasn't gushing and he didn't look like he was dying. Which meant that Simon better have another trick up his sleeve.

Or maybe not. He started the same ducking back and forth around the column. And he was making a sound that she'd never heard on any nature channel. It was high pitched and almost warbling. Clearly a taunting laugh and she could practically see the steam coming out of Nanook's ears.

But the big grolar wasn't completely stupid. He wasn't going in for the same kind of attack. Instead, he dropped his head, bunched his shoulders, and rammed forward…straight into the cement column. If he couldn't bite around the post, he was going to take the obstruction down.

The building shuddered and everyone looked up with worry. No way was that column going to hold for another assault. And if it went down, so did part of the roof.

Simon scrambled backward, but even he looked up to the ceiling. In fact, the only one who wasn't looking up was Nanook because he was backing up to do it again.

And then the eeriest moment of the entire day happened. Simon looked directly at her. It was like he was calculating in his grizzly mind exactly how many impacts the post could take and what were her risks standing about twenty feet away.

Then he jerked his head at the door. It was a clear indication that she should flee, but she wasn't the only one who saw it. The others did, too. And quite a few moved to stand between her and the door. Probably because if the building started coming down, they wanted to be the first ones out.

And that was all the time Simon had as Nanook started roaring forward again. But in this, Simon startled her. He bolted around the post then ran full tilt at Nanook. The two were like rams except when they met shoulder to shoulder, Simon took the brunt of it. He shuddered backward, slipping on the concrete floor and going down on his butt then side. And even worse, he appeared to be stunned. He just lay there not moving.

"Get up!" Alyssa screamed. "Get up!"

No effect. Except on Nanook, who began lumbering forward, his mouth gaping open in anticipation. The others cheered, egging him on with bloodthirsty cries. She tried to tune them out, but the words were graphic, ugly, and all about ripping out Simon's throat.

"Simon!" she screamed again, and this time she saw him twitch. His ear cocked toward her then fell back. Maybe. She couldn't be sure. And his breath never changed. "Damn it, get up!" she screamed again.

Nothing. And then Nanook attacked.

He'd been rushing forward on all fours, his mouth open and aimed for Simon's exposed throat. There might even have been a bit of a bounce there as he came down beside the prostrate grizzly.

Alyssa couldn't tell with her eyes tearing up and her throat raw from screaming.

And then something happened that she couldn't at first understand. As Nanook went in to bite, Simon rolled slightly onto his back. She thought at first that Nanook's jaws were that strong. That he'd rolled Simon over. But a moment later, she realized the truth.

Simon had been playing dead. He'd been waiting to roll over at just the right moment so he could swipe straight at Nanook's neck. His claws here huge and sharp, and given the open wound, Nanook was vulnerable. Simon's claws caught, pierced, and ripped across.

Blood gushed, pumping strong into the air and across the floor. Nanook tried to bite down. He was still moving. Or falling. Either way, Simon couldn't get out from under him. And he didn't stop the attack.

Simon pulled up his back feet and began raking at Nanook's belly. Other scents joined the coppery taste of blood in the air. And with Nanook's head and shoulder now down next to his mouth, Simon took a big bite. He was growling deep in his throat, the sound vicious as he bit down and shook his head like a dog. He was tearing pieces of fur and muscle away both above and below, and the mess was shocking.

Alyssa looked away, but what she saw around her wasn't comforting. All those naked shifters standing between her and the door began to shimmer. Some went slowly, others fast, but in the end, she wasn't standing with a bunch of naked guys. Now she was surrounded by grizzlies. Big, mean, unhappy ones that shifted from foot to foot and grumbled low in their throat.

She caught Vic's gaze, but there was nothing either of them could do. She might have been able to shoot her way past the four humans between her and the door. But now they were bears and they nudged her deeper into the center of the room.

First it was hot breath on the back of her neck. Soon it was shoves against her legs or back. She honestly couldn't tell if it was because they needed more room back there or because they wanted to eat her. Either way, she scrambled forward, as did Vic. And the only place to look then was back at Simon.

He was on his feet now, his jaws and claws systematically ripping apart Nanook. And all around them, the bears started grumbling. They shuffled and growled. Their breaths came in big bellows and their teeth showed yellow white.

Simon didn't notice. He was covered in blood as his jaws bit down and cracked off a couple ribs. Alyssa flinched at the sound, her heart hammering in her throat. The tension was climbing in the room, and she and her brother were in the middle of it. Finally, she couldn't take it anymore.

"Simon! Damn it, Simon!"

Her words echoed sharply in the room only because her voice was higher pitched than anyone else's. The bears were loud, and she didn't think anyone could hear her much less the grizzly with its snout deep in blood. But Simon did hear.

She saw his ears twitch and his head came up. His head swiveled back and forth as he took in the room. His nostrils flared as he stood over the carcass. And then he released a roar that took Alyssa to a knee. It echoed in the space and the sound seemed to beat her down. Her brother fared little better. He stumbled beside her, but he regained his balance and remained upright beside her. Protecting her, she guessed, but she was the one with the gun.

But who the hell did she aim it at? Simon? He was an adult grizzly growling over a kill. And his roar told everyone in the room that it was his. His food. His kill. His territory.

But it was eight to one here. They could overrun him in a second. And probably flatten her and Vic in the process.

The nearest bear lumbered forward. It was big and all black. She realized belatedly that it didn't have a grizzly hump, but it was still huge. And it opened his mouth in a sound that Alyssa couldn't hear in all the noise. But she heard Simon.

He turned straight on the black bear and roared back, hard and angry. The sound ripped at Alyssa's insides. God, she couldn't stand to see another fight. Not here. Not now when there wasn't room to flee.

Except when Simon's roar stopped, the black bear didn't attack. And he certainly didn't rear up on his hind legs. Instead, he flopped over onto his side. A full-out plop that exposed his neck.

Submission?

Holy crap, that's exactly what it was. The black bear was submitting to Simon who stood there staring at it with nostrils flared and his mouth dripping with blood.

Alyssa wanted to speak. She wanted to bellow that the bear was submitting and Simon didn't need to attack it. But her voice was frozen in her throat. It was terror, pure and simple. She just didn't want to draw attention to herself and she damned herself for being a coward.

Then Simon stepped over the edge of the carcass. He was coming toward her, though his eyes were on the bears nearest her. He didn't even give the black bear any acknowledgment that she could see. He just lumbered forward, closer and closer to her.

She shied backward, but there was nowhere to go. The grizzlies behind her were rocking back and forth on their feet while grumbling deep in their throats. What was Simon doing? And when the hell had she fallen to her knees? She was crouched now, huddled back against her brother. The gun was still in her hand, but the handle was slick with sweat and she didn't know if she could raise it. She was trembling from head to toe.

And still Simon lumbered forward.

She swallowed, trying to force herself to speak. She managed a bare whisper. "Simon, please." She didn't even know what she was asking him, but it was all she could get out.

He roared again. Straight at the bears behind her. He was so close, she could feel the heat of his breath. She could see the gore on his body and the way his roar made the fur tremble on his sides.

Then she heard it.

Thud. Thudthud.

All around her, the bears were dropping with heavy thumps onto the floor. One by one they sat and rolled over, exposing their necks. And this, too, was something she'd never seen on the nature channel. They weren't dogs. These were grizzlies and another black bear. But they all dropped, even Vic beside her though he went to his knee and not the floor.

"Tilt your head," he hissed at her.

"W-what?"

"Expose your neck! Submit to him!"

She wasn't a dog to roll over on command, but in this, she obeyed without hesitation. She submitted to Simon as he lumbered in a tight circle. He glared at everybody in the room, herself and Vic included. And when he had gone nearly full circle, he did it again. He roared.

At least this time she could cover her ears. His back was to her, so she could duck her head into her hands, though it clapped the hard butt of her pistol against her head. She didn't need to hear that terrifying sound again, but apparently the others did.

Because this time after the roar ended, there was dead silence in the room. No grumbles. Certainly no growls. Not even the huff of a breath. Every single bear was on his back and silent.

And it stayed that way as Simon continued to prowl. He walked in another slow circle that came too near her for comfort. Then again. Two times around, plus another roar. Then a third. Once he lumbered close to the carcass and bit off another rib. He crunched it in the silence while everyone else stayed frozen on the floor.

And when the rib was gone, Simon went back to prowling. To Alyssa's eyes, he seemed agitated and angry. That was understandable twenty minutes ago, but now? He needed to settle down. But the more he prowled, the more upset he seemed to get.

Another roar. God, by the end of the day she was going to be deaf. Two more circuits, and then she realized the truth.

He wasn't settling down. He was winding himself up. Had he lost himself in the bear? He had to remember who he was. He needed to shift back into a man. But it wasn't happening. Another roar convinced her of it.

And go figure. She wasn't deaf, but she was freaking tired of flinching every time he took a deep breath. So she stood up.

She was surprised that her legs had any strength. But she could remain terrified only so long before she just got annoyed.

"What are you doing?" her brother hissed, but she waved him to silence. She didn't want to say that she had no idea.

She straightened her shoulders and waited until Simon had lumbered back around to face her. His face was matted fur and gore, so she focused on his ears. Those cute rounded ears. One of them was covered in blood, but the other still showed golden brown. So she looked at that and pitched her voice low and soothing.

"You win, Simon. You're the big bad here."

He growled at her, low and threatening. She almost dropped right then and there. Not just to her knees but all the way down. Instead, she stiffened her legs and faced him down.

"You're the powerhouse, Simon. Everyone has submitted to you. Everyone. You won."

His growl deepened and she smiled. Holy moly, she must be insane, but that sound was just like the grumble her father made when waking up. A grumble and snort mixed together. It was kind of cute.

"What do you need, Simon? What do you need to feel safe?" She gestured behind him at the carcass. "Do you need to eat some more?" God, she prayed not, but she understood the animal need to eat his kill.

He chuffed, the sound not so angry as frustrated.

"No one is challenging you, so you're safe from them."

She watched to see if he would look around at the bears on the floor. He did, but only with the briefest turn of his head. A moment later, his gaze was back on her.

"He wants you," Vic said. "Holy God, he wants you."

"What?"

"You're the only female here," he said. "You know. Kill. Eat. *Mate.*"

The thought sent shudders of terror down her spine. She was not mating with a gore-covered grizzly. But Simon the man? Hadn't she nearly done that last night?

She swallowed. "You have to shift back, Simon. You want me? You can have me as a *man*." She didn't think twice about what she was offering. She was talking to a grizzly bear, after all. But God, she wanted to bed Simon the man. She'd wanted it every night for more than two years.

She stood there in front, her knees quavering but locked solid as Simon moved forward. For such a big creature, he seemed to walk with precision. Every paw was placed exactly where it needed to be. And every sharp tooth was exposed as he approached.

Did he think she was challenging him? Should she show him her neck? She didn't know and the back-and-forth in her panicked brain was making her sick. What should she do?

She held her ground and spoke again, her voice as strong and loud as she could make it.

"I want a man, Simon. A man!"

He stalked closer. No other word for it. He approached her slightly from the side, then he adjusted to face her. She felt his breath on her face, smelled the scent of blood, but also, weirdly, Irish Spring. How that smell could cling to him here, she had no idea, but she caught the sweet smell or pretended she did. And finally, ultimately, she changed her focus from his ear to his eyes.

And then he widened his mouth a little farther.

She would have run then, but there was nowhere to go. This close, he was way faster than her. And besides, she didn't know if her legs would bend or just collapse. So she stood still while his wet pink tongue stretched out and caressed her arm.

A wet lick with a long tongue. Like a dog's kiss, she supposed, though she thought of it more as a grizzly caress.

She reached out her other hand. She wasn't going to pet him on the blood-soaked fur, but his ear was still clear as was a patch of fur behind it. So she scratched him there. She sunk her fingers into the soft fur and scratched.

He released a chuff that she took as a grizzly moan of delight. Then a moment later she drew back.

He quirked his head then pushed his ear forward. He didn't like that she'd pulled away, but in this she remained firm until he was butting his nose against her belly.

"As a man, Simon."

Then it happened. A brief shimmer in the air. A sudden sharp blast of heat. And then when she blinked again, he was changing right before her eyes. His body pulled together, the fur dropped away or disappeared. Suddenly there was a naked man on all fours in front of her and he was miraculously clean. The blood must have fallen away with the fur, though his nose showed traces as did his hands.

She dropped to her knees before him, the breath leaving her lungs in a *whoosh*. This was Simon before her, trembling and naked. She wrapped him in her arms as his breath came in short tight pants.

"I got you," she said over and over. "I got you." And she kept saying it until the shaking eased. And then a moment later, he took a deep, slow breath. "Simon—" she began but he cut her off.

"Stay down. Stay quiet," he said, his words harsh.

Her head jerked back at his rough tone, but she didn't argue. And she didn't fight him when he grabbed her gun from the floor where she'd dropped it. His fingers fumbled with it for a moment, but eventually steadied. Then she waited in taut silence as he stood and faced all those grizzlies who were now rolling back to their feet.

CHAPTER 13

Simon's mind was a dark place of violence and possession. He owned these creatures now. He could do whatever he wanted to with them beginning with the woman. As soon as he could, he was going to mount her and impregnate her because she was beautiful and she was his. But first he had to make sure every lesser creature here gave him due reverence.

And that meant someone else had to die. It was just a question of who.

He looked at them as they came to their feet. A couple brown bear-shifters, the rest grizzlies. Some impressive in size, others just big. He glared at them all, then bellowed his first order.

"Human. Now."

He waited, watching to see who obeyed quickly, who struggled to change, and who he would kill first. He didn't need another dominance show. He was standing next to Nanook's carcass. But it never hurt to drive a point home.

None hesitated before the shift. One by one they turned from dark glorious fur to naked flesh of unimpressive bodies. None here matched his physique and none would dare look askance at him. If they tried, he would kill them, plain and simple. He also scanned the discarded clothes, noting that nearly every pile had a gun. If any man turned to dress, he would be the next to die.

Simon waited and watched, his mind and body unified in speed and intelligence. Splitting his mind into bear and human was stupid. It made it agonizingly difficult to switch between bodies and he constantly risked being trapped in one form or another.

Not now. Not when he was one being with one goal: dominate all he saw.

An old Hispanic man was the last to shift. Probably one of the weakest here. Perfect as the first cull. Simon could kill him as an example. Or maybe he should target the biggest one.

He walked over to a huge black man with broad shoulders and meaty fists. A scar cut across his jaw, stark and impressive given that he retained the mark even after shifting. That meant whatever had caused the wound had cut into the man's psyche as well. He had a hard jaw and narrowed eyes, and though his head was tilted in submission, he held it at the bare minimum angle.

"Who is your alpha?" he asked the man, his tone flat.

"You are," the man snapped in near military precision. But he'd been the only one to answer, and that was unacceptable.

He glared around the room and repeated the question.

"Who is your alpha?"

"You are!" every man rushed to answer.

"Whom do you obey?"

"You!"

Then he turned to the black man. "Why do you obey me?"

"Because you are."

Good answer, but there was little humility in the man's gaze. Lip service, then, because he smelled no terror coming off him. Nothing but the lingering scent of stale cigarette.

"I should kill you," he said casually.

The man's head jerked straight in surprise, but he didn't speak.

"Do you know why?"

"Because I am large and scary looking. Because I am the next logical challenger."

"Yes." Then Simon allowed his lips to curve. "I don't need to be a grizzly to kill you. I could do it right now with my bare hands."

Again the man stayed silent. So did almost everyone else. Everyone but Alyssa who whispered his name.

"Simon."

It was barely audible and not meant to distract. It was a plea or a prayer to God. Either way he whipped around and stalked toward her. In this group of dangerous, vicious creatures, she was the only one who dared challenge him. She was the one who looked him in the eye and he should kill her. But she was female and he meant to mount her. So she would not die yet, but he would punish her.

Once in front of her, he gripped her arm and hauled her to her feet. And when she was not sufficiently compliant, he jerked her against his body. She was dressed in tight jeans and a thin tee, and he was naked. And while he held her hard against his body, he rubbed himself up and down against her crotch. Let them see how big he was. Let him see what he would do to her.

She gasped in shock, her eyes going wide. Behind her, Vic shifted uncomfortably, but he didn't speak. If he did, he'd be the one to die. But Alyssa's brother kept his eyes down and his hands clenched. And best of all, Vic was completely and totally human looking now. No monster in sight.

So he focused on Alyssa.

"I told you to be quiet," he said against her ear.

He was gloriously erect now. Around her, it took nothing for him to be hard as a rock. He thought about bending her over here. He could show everyone that he possessed her. But he would be vulnerable while inside her. It was too soon for such a thing, more's the pity. Because he wanted her now with a hunger that burned in his belly.

Meanwhile, her expression softened. It was not the look he expected. He only understood submission or challenge. But her brows lifted and her mouth eased. And then she slowly lifted her hand to touch his cheek. Her skin was cool and her touch gentle.

He reared back in shock and though she stilled, she didn't cringe at the violence he felt churning inside him. She simply stood poised with her hand suspended in the air. And then she spoke, her voice barely audible even to him who stood a few inches away.

"Come back, Simon. Come back to who you really are."

He inhaled, his nostrils flaring. He scented fear from everyone around him including her. Good. But from her, he also scented arousal. He saw it, too, in the rapid pulse in her throat and the flush to her cheeks. But beyond those signs, she remained steady and focused.

"Do you remember why we're here?" she asked.

"Doesn't matter. I own them now." His gaze cut around the room, searching again for his target. Maybe the wounded one who'd been nearly killed by the monsters when they'd first walked in. He stalked over to the man who looked like a pale blond surfer with bloodshot eyes and shaking hands. The fight and the shift had taken everything out of him, not to mention the thigh wound, which had sealed in the change back to human but still looked like a raw jagged line.

"Who are you?" he demanded, his voice raw.

"Yours." His voice was higher than the black man's, but no less quick. It was the weary anger that simmered in the man's eyes that bothered Simon.

"Why were they trying to kill you?"

"Because I'm a cop, and I was asking questions."

Interesting. Part of him wanted to know more, but the rest was more concerned with obedience. "Who did you ask?"

"Nanook."

Simon's hand shot out, hard and sharp. He slapped the cop across the face and sent him reeling. He didn't need to kill him to show power. In this, all he required was his open palm, which was more insulting than a fist.

And again, he heard only one person react. Alyssa gasped and again, she whispered his name. But this time she added a plea.

"Simon, come back to me."

He ignored her and focused on the cop. "That's for questioning your alpha." But then the curious part of his mind pushed to know more. "What did you ask?"

If the cop refused to answer, he would be the one to die. But he didn't. He pushed himself upright from where he'd caught himself on support column, and his gaze flicked to Vic. "I asked what he knew about the Detroit Flu."

Flu? It took him a moment to even comprehend the word. But then he remembered. It was a tiny unseen enemy that destroyed from the inside. "Why?"

"Because some people who catch it turn into that." He didn't gesture at Vic. He pointed at the nearest of the dead monsters.

"You're a cop, not a doctor," he said, feeling his higher brain functions shift into analysis mode. It wasn't an automatic change. He had to decide to do it, but once he made the choice, the questions became easier.

"I'm a cop looking for answers. Nanook said the wolves did it."

"Wolves!" Simon snapped. Another enemy? He would destroy them.

The cop nodded. "But he blamed the wolves for everything. I wanted to know why specifically they were responsible."

"And what did Nanook say?"

"He said I asked too many questions."

"Cops usually do," he said, the tone almost casual. It was not a tone he was comfortable with, but it came out anyway. Which told him clearer than anything that he was losing control of himself. His minds were splitting apart again, the human finding humor in strange ways that the animal didn't understand.

This was bad. His goal was to dominate all, and if he couldn't control his own mind, then he would appear weak before the others.

So he stalked away, fury in his every moment. And again, he considered killing the cop. But before he could decide, he came back to Alyssa. To stand before her and glare. To see if he could intimidate her with just his stare.

He could not.

Worse, she lifted her chin in a show of defiance. "We came for information about the virus. To find out how to fix Vic."

"Vic is fine. He is mine now."

He hadn't missed that Vic had snapped a response along with

everyone else. Vic had acknowledged him as alpha and was therefore one of Simon's. The ownership went two ways, he thought now. They gave loyalty, Simon gave protection.

So he looked at Vic. "You are under control." It wasn't a question, but Vic answered anyway.

"Yes, sir!"

Simon liked the military response. He especially liked it from his friend who had served at his side so long ago.

"You will not lose control. You will not go monster unless I say so. Unless I order you to. Is that understood?"

"Yes, sir!"

He looked back to Alyssa. "Vic is fine."

"But are you?" she asked. There was no challenge in her tone, more of a soft concern. He felt emotion stir inside him. Whereas his mind didn't fully understand her question, his feelings responded to the warmth in her tone, the softness in her eyes, and most of all, the touch of her hand on his arm. He stared at her fingertips. Creamy brown, a shade darker than his fur. Shapely nails for a human and uncolored. Not sharp as might be serviceable as a weapon, but curved and pretty.

He did not understand pretty, and yet his body pulsed with desire. It liked pretty, and it liked her.

"Are you questioning me?" his tone was sharp and angry.

Her eyes narrowed. "I would never challenge you, Simon, but I will question you. Are you going to hit me, too?"

"Maybe." It was an honest answer. He really didn't know.

"I'm not going to react well to that."

He acknowledged that with a nod. As an alpha he could not expect his people to appreciate all his actions. Simply obey them.

Except, now that he thought about it, she had not sworn loyalty. Her voice had not been among those acknowledging him as alpha.

He touched her chin. He had meant to jerk her face up to his so that he could stare directly into her eyes. But instead of a harsh push, his fingers caressed. He urged her face toward his and she complied without hesitation. Not because she obeyed but because she wanted to challenge him silently. Because her eyes were her message. And from her hard, cold look, he saw what he had always known would be there.

She was an alpha, too.

Smaller, yes. And definitely weaker. But she was an alpha female with all the glorious challenge that entailed.

"You will submit to me," he said. Behind him, he heard a rustle. Movement that should be stopped, but his attention was on her and he would not waver.

"Not if you hit me."

His nostrils flared at the illogic of that response. Dominance was established physically. Except as he inhaled, her scent filled his mind. The lure and temptation of a female who was nearly as powerful as him.

"You will submit," he repeated. "I will not need to hit you."

"I will submit if and when you deserve me." Then she lifted a brow. It was a strange expression and one that he—again—needed to analyze using his higher brain function. It was neither challenge nor defeat. It wasn't a logical look, but it was an affectionate one. And from that place, he reasoned it was a good thing. Even more, he devised an appropriate response.

He smiled. And she did in turn.

"There you are," she murmured.

"Yes," he said, feeling that her words had made it so. He was still one creature—both man and bear—but she brought a second purpose to his life: to please her. It was as if his mind had climbed a step. First, establish dominance. Second, please the female. What would be third?

Before he could answer, a rustle interrupted his thoughts. He didn't know whether he smelled the scent of aggression first or heard the cock of a pistol. Either way, he reacted immediately.

He spun and fired the gun.

Two shots, direct to the chest.

A wiry white man slammed against the back wall, then slid down, dead. His pistol flopped to the floor.

Behind him Alyssa cried out. Simon had his hand out to keep her from moving. Everyone else simply stood, though the scent of fear spiked in the room. As did the smell of blood and gunpowder.

"Who was he?" Simon asked, his voice sharp and loud.

It was the cop who answered, his voice dry with satisfaction. "Nanook's beta. He ran the drug operation. Probably thought he'd take you out and step into alpha."

"A real leader would not be so stupid. He could not have survived as alpha." He glanced over to the big black man. "You would have killed him first."

The man's eyes widened in surprise, but he didn't deny it. "He killed my little brother. Was just waiting for the right opportunity."

Political maneuvering within the clan. Simon acknowledged it at the same moment his higher cortex began tabulating problems. He was now leader of an organization that had a history and a structure. The Griz had a role in the community: selling drugs and countless other things. He might be in charge, but that was simply a matter of appearance. And fear. He would need a lot more to effectively lead these people.

He turned to the cop. "Do you know about the drug organization? Who buys, who sells?"

The man straightened. "I'm on the gang side, not narcotics. But yeah. I know."

"Then seize it. Take it. Do whatever you have to, but end it." He watched carefully to see who objected, who appeared angry. There were a few, and he noted them. The others showed worry, but not anger. And a few were clearly pleased, including the big black man.

One however, flushed hot then cold. He was a handsome Caucasian with soft hands and a fondness for smoothing down his hair. Simon focused on him.

"What did you do for Nanook?"

The man froze for at least a heartbeat. But then he lifted his gaze to meet Simon's eyes. "I was his accountant."

Money man. *Nervous* money man. "Nanook owes money?"

"The Griz owe money. To the supplier."

"As the new alpha by challenge, Nanook's assets are mine. You will use those to pay off the debts. Will that cover it?"

The man's eyes widened. "Um, yes. I think so. If I can get access."

Simon's eyes narrowed. "You worked for Nanook. You would not have survived if you did not scare him in some way."

The accountant answered with a smirk appeared. "Yeah."

He turned back to the cop. "I will not prosecute my people. Will you work with him? End the drugs, give up the names of the suppliers, but no Griz goes to jail."

The cop nodded once, a quick, excited slash of his chin. "We'll want them to testify."

Simon shrugged. "They committed the crimes. They will admit to it in court or face my penalty."

The black man cleared his throat. It was a small sound, but Simon was listening very closely. He focused on the man.

"What is your fear?"

"A lot of change. And dangerous men do not like change."

"What did you do in the drug trade?"

"Nothing!" he snapped. And when Simon continued to stare, he shrugged. "I went along as protection. And 'cause I'm a medic. But I didn't touch any of the stuff."

Point of pride there. And he was a "medic," not a nurse or a doctor. "Military?" Simon asked.

"Army. Been out for a year."

"And you're here because you're a grizzly. You're part of this because of the fur." It wasn't a statement, but the answer was clear on his face. On most of their faces.

Shifters needed clans. It provided protection, community, and safety in the jungle—urban or otherwise. And though bears weren't as tight as dogs, they liked maintaining ties. Which meant that whether or not they supported the gang's activities, they would need to be part of this clan. And Nanook hadn't been one to let a lone shifter wander free. He would have demanded that they join up or die.

"I am the new alpha," he said, and the statement reverberated in the room as much as it did in his heart and soul. "I will protect you. I will lead you. And where I go, you will follow." Then he took a deep breath allowing the rightness of this to sink into his body and soul. Here was the third step in his mind: to lead. It was what he was born to do. "If you choose not to follow, you may leave with my blessing."

One last look around before he spoke in booming tones. "Who follows me?"

They answered as one. Not in words, but in a low growl that grew in volume until it became a roar. Even Vic joined in until the space pounded with the sound. And when it was done, Simon looked at them all and grinned.

He was their alpha, and they were his.

He took a moment to absorb their strength into his body, their support into his soul. And then he turned to Alyssa because she alone had stayed silent.

"Now it is your turn."

CHAPTER 14

Male bonding done right was a fearsome thing. It brought together all that heady testosterone into a force that echoed in the bones and stirred even the most timid to battle.

Alyssa wasn't timid by any means, but this man, this creature that was Simon stood like a god before these men. If he told them to die for him, she believed they would. And they had only just met him.

But what did she think of the man who had just killed not once but twice right before her eyes? She was a civilized woman and she hated such brutality. Except she had cheered when he'd killed Nanook. Her mind had stuttered into shocked awe when he had shot the drug dealer. And now, when he'd brought his men to a growling roar? Her heart had surrendered. Though she'd kept silent, her body had thrilled at the sound and her breath had whispered out in a sigh.

She was wet and willing for him, and the very thought shocked her to her core. She'd promised that he could have her, but at the time it had been simply a way to bring his mind back from the animal inside. Now she realized, she'd been lying to herself. If he asked, she was pretty sure she'd do whatever he wanted.

And that terrified her a hundred times more than the violence she'd just witnessed.

He was looking at her now. His body was strong and fiercely male, and he clearly gave no thought to his nakedness. Though, damn, it was hard to keep her eyes on his face. He spoke to her in a low undertone.

"I need to learn the details as fast as possible," he said. His gaze flickered, and she was startled to sense uncertainty despite his gruff tone. "Will you take notes?"

He still hadn't remembered how to read and he needed her help. "Of course." She pulled out her cell phone. She thumb-typed way faster than she wrote.

Then he looked at Vic. "I need a beta," he said to her brother.

Vic frowned. "I have no idea what that means."

"An XO. Will you serve me?"

"Yes, sir!" Vic straightened into a military salute that was crisp and so handsome on her brother. Every now and then he gave her a flash of the man he could be, and right here despite all the changes, she was seeing what she'd always hoped was in there.

"The bodies," Simon said with a gesture. "Talk to the cop. Figure out what's the best thing to do."

"On it." Wow, her brother even did a military turn as if he were on a parade ground. Meanwhile, the cop nodded to Simon and then Vic.

"My name's Ryan Kennedy. Detective."

"Vic Nelson. Simon's beta."

They shook hands awkwardly, but soon got to business by talking in low tones. Alyssa turned back to Simon, belatedly realizing that she was now the center of his attention. And he just stood there looking at her with an intensity that made her heart beat triple time.

"Simon?" she finally asked when the tension got too much for her.

His voice came out in a bare whisper. "Four steps. First, become dominant. Second, please the alpha female. Third, lead the clan." He paused as his eyes became brilliant green. "Fourth, lead wisely."

She didn't know what to say. Her mind was still spinning on how he could please the alpha female and the guess that he meant her. But that wasn't what he was asking her, and she struggled to catch up.

"My thoughts are simple: four steps."

"Dominance, female, leadership, wisdom. Got it." She didn't get it, but that's all she had at the moment.

His gaze traveled the room, pausing significantly on Nanook's carcass and the dead drug dealer. "You are the alpha female. Your role is wisdom. Only you can stop me before I go too far." She nodded, her gaze cutting back to Vic, but Simon grabbed her arm. "They've sworn loyalty. They can't disobey."

And since she was the only one who hadn't growled or roared, that left her. And what a sticky place that was. She was supposed to be the brakes on an unpredictable, violent man? No way. That was crazy and a sure way to die. She'd seen that enough just growing up in Detroit. And yet, the way he looked at her—dark and intense as if she was his only lifeline—had her aching to reassure him.

"I can tell you," she said in a whisper. "I can't make you listen."

He swallowed, and his gaze turned anguished. "I know." Then he glanced behind him at the body of the drug dealer. "I just killed a man."

"You just killed two."

"I don't regret Nanook. He demanded the challenge and would have killed me. The other—"

"Was about to shoot you. Same self-defense argument."

"Or entrapment. I knew where the guns were. I knew someone would grab one."

Surprise flashed through her body. While she'd been barely following what was happening, he'd been thinking at least two steps ahead. She'd always guessed Simon was smart. Now she realized he was probably the smartest man she'd ever met.

But rather than give away exactly how sexy that made him in her eyes, she looked down at her phone. "What do you need from me?"

"Just take notes."

She nodded. "Who do we start with first?"

He gestured to the huge, ebony-skinned man with the scar, and pretty soon she was tapping out details faster than even her thumbs could manage. Which meant she quickly gave up and switched to record. His name was Hank and he was very familiar with the details of Nanook's operation. He shared them easily while she gestured for Detective Kennedy to listen in.

Next step was to control the physical space. Apparently Nanook, who had no known relatives, lived right upstairs in what turned out to be a luxury man-cave of truly appalling leather and velvet taste. His only nod to style was that the painted picture of dogs playing poker was done as bears. Simon took one step inside, wrinkled his nose and said, "Get rid of it all."

Alyssa blinked and said, "Come again?"

Simon gestured to the huge open area that took up the entire second floor. "Sell or burn everything. Take the money as a legal defense fund for my people. Give all paper and electronic files to me."

She nodded slowly. It was a huge task and certainly one she was willing to do. But it was going to take some time and effort. A lot of—

"I'm hiring you, Alyssa. A thousand a week at first. More as we get settled."

A spark of greed kindled in her belly, and she arched a brow. "I have a business."

"That's why it's only a thousand at first. Because you'll be splitting your time."

Good thing she had things running like clockwork at the laundromat. "Triple it and you'll get me twenty-four/seven this week. We'll renegotiate next week."

"Deal."

And so began the most incredibly exhausting day of her life. It wasn't just that he needed her to write down everything he learned, but there were bodies to take care of and police statements to give. Nothing in the upper story could be dealt with until that was done.

All in all, it went pretty smoothly. Detective Kennedy smoothed things over and even recommended a good lawyer. Alyssa was able to check out the guy through her own contacts, and declared he was a good choice. Plus, it helped that Simon turned over all the records they could find regarding the drug and weapons business. Yes, Nanook had been into all sorts of nastiness.

Simon worked methodically. He would not be rushed and nothing distracted him. She had to admire such a steady and organized mind, but as the day wore on, she saw the toll it was taking on him. Though he never raised his voice, his words got more clipped, his orders became commands, and he rarely waited long enough to see if they were obeyed. Or even acknowledged. By the end of the day, there was no softness in him, not even for her. At least twice in the afternoon, he'd managed a whispered, "Thank you," to her. Now she didn't even see a gentleness in his eyes much less gratitude.

He was cold and impatient, and he turned up his nose at the pizza she'd had delivered. When she'd offered him a glass of tap water (he refused to touch anything Nanook had in his refrigerator), he'd slapped it out her hand like it was toxic waste.

It was midnight when she lost patience with him. Most of the men were gone, though Detective Kennedy was likely to be working at the precinct through the night along with Vic and the accountant whose name escaped her at the moment. Hank remained a silent witness to everything that went on while a steady parade of people wandered in, greeted Simon by showing him their neck, and then wandered out. They never shifted and they never said much of anything, but Simon would whisper to her after they'd left.

"Wolf."

"Cat."

"Human."

"Bear child."

She found out later that meant the child of a shifter but one who had never shifted. They still owed loyalty—to a point—but were rarely counted as part of the real clan. As far as she could tell, they were from all walks of life and had varying degrees of annoyance or respect at being called in to greet the new alpha. But it was the last label that finally tipped her into fury.

"Sycophant."

"That's Mrs. Garcia, and she's important in the neighborhood," she snapped. And when he just looked at her with a flat expression, she continued on her tirade, barely able to keep her voice low. "She owns the cleaning company who is bleaching everything tonight and her nephew is the one taking out the furniture. They're doing it as a personal favor to me." And because she'd promised them a big healthy check if it was finished by tomorrow at noon. "Plus her sister's kid runs a furniture store that can get you what you want wholesale."

"And she's important in your neighborhood," he repeated, as if that explained everything. He gestured to her notes. "Alyssa, I can smell the cannabis on her. She's the dealer two doors down your street."

"She's smart and honest—"

"I'm not making a value judgment," he said, his voice showing the first signs of strain since this began. "Just a notation that she'll turn on me if the situation doesn't benefit her. Am I wrong?"

No, he wasn't. But it still pissed her off. She'd been working without a break from the moment she'd gotten up this morning. And yeah, it was exactly what she'd promised to do, but damn it, she hadn't realized how difficult it would be to stand beside Simon and take orders like she was his servant or slave.

She wasn't. She was his assistant, obviously, but she was also something more. Or maybe she wanted to be more. And maybe this back-and-forth in her mind was the real reason she was upset. Because she hadn't thought it would be midnight, and he'd still be treating her like she was one step up from a computer note-taking app.

Rather than argue with him, she thumbed her phone shut. It was near dead anyway. "I think that's it for today."

His eyes narrowed, but not at her. He was looking at Mrs. Garcia as she started directing a small army of cleaners.

Alyssa spoke up. "She knows what she's doing. And she'll keep her mouth shut." Then before he could ask his next question, she answered it. "She also knows how to look for hidden caches better than anyone else I know. And she'll turn it over." When he still didn't respond, she lifted her chin. "You trust me? Because I trust her." Plus she might have told Mrs. Garcia that there were hidden cameras everywhere, which wasn't a complete lie. As far as she knew, Nanook had secret devices in the walls. She hadn't had a chance to look.

"What exactly does she do? *Exactly.*"

She winced. "She grows and distributes the weed. Has a huge hydroponics setup in her home run by her nephew who is a botanist of some kind. And a niece who cooks. The cleaning crew is legit—run by her daughter-in-law—but it's not the main source of family income. And I trust her." At least in this, she did. Mrs. Garcia would absolutely do what was in the best financial interest of her family. And that included not betraying Alyssa in this cleanup job.

"Very well," Simon said as he packed up Nanook's computer. Alyssa had already looked at it. It was mostly a porn repository, but there were some potentially important files. It would have gone to the precinct with all the other electronics, but this had been in a secret cubbyhole under a floorboard. Simon had found it simply by sniffing from about two feet away, curling his nose, and pointing.

Apparently, shifter noses were ultra-specific. Which is why he made one last reminder before leaving the place.

"Get rid of the appliances, too."

She knew. He wanted nothing that smelled of Nanook left anywhere. Which was why she'd also instructed Mrs. Garcia to double the amount of bleach they used. By noon tomorrow, the place was going to be cleaner than a surgical suite.

They descended the stairs to head home, but stopped when they reached Hank. He stood by the front door with his arms folded as he watched everything. She looked at him curiously, but he refused to budge.

"I'll watch," he said, his gaze shifting to Simon.

The two men stared at each other for a long steady moment before Simon nodded. That was it. Then he walked straight to her car and climbed in the passenger side. Apparently male communication didn't require a lot of words.

She had no choice but to get into the driver's seat and wearily chauffeur Simon back to her place while all the details of the day spun on a loop through her head. Deaths. Drugs. Police. Guns. It wasn't unusual for life in Detroit, but it sure was a lot for one day. And damn it, Simon didn't even look tired.

They didn't speak on the drive, but Simon couldn't seem to sit still. He spent the whole time popping open the computer before shutting it irritably again. Then he'd look out the window, shifting his large frame in her small car. Then he'd close his eyes only to grumble deep in his throat before starting it all over again. By the time they reached the apartment building, she was ready to scream at him. She'd done her fair share of babysitting. Cranky toddlers were not her forte. Neither were twitchy men who could go furry in the blink of an eye.

When he leapt out of her car before she'd put it in park, she let him go. She needed a moment of silence in the quiet confines of her car. Except a moment later, he pulled open her

car door with a huff. "Are you coming? You have to teach me
to read."

She looked at him blearily, seeing the way the light made his
brown hair look like a white halo around his shadowed face. She
didn't like the look. Neither did she care for the impatient demand
in his voice when he continued.

"You agreed to twenty-four/seven."

"Silly me."

"Next time, negotiate smarter."

She did not like that tone, but she couldn't argue with the sentiment. Then he leaned in and popped her seatbelt as if she were
a child. Next, he grabbed hold of her arm and pulled her out. She
barely had time to pull out her keys before he was manhandling her
away.

She let him get away with it for two steps. Far enough for her to
catch her balance and not get clipped by the car door as he slammed
it shut. But then she dug in her heels and jerked her arm back. It
didn't work. He was solid as a tree and all she managed was to give
herself bruises as he held on. But it was enough to get his attention
as he stepped around to glare down at her upturned face.

She spoke first, her exhaustion keeping her from minding her
tongue. "What the hell is wrong with you? You should be dropping
with exhaustion. Instead, you're acting like…like…" She threw up
her hand, this time managing to dislodge his grip. "Like a bear with
a sore paw."

He'd released her arm, but now he caught her chin. He lifted her
face up to his as he leaned in until they were nose to nose. She felt
the heated rush of his breath and the trembling restraint in his hand.
He wanted to grip her a lot tighter, but was holding back.

"You think this is the animal in me? This is me as an angry bear?" His voice was a low growl, but it was quickly rising in volume.

"I don't know—" she began, but he cut her off.

"Bears are simple creatures. They eat, fish, and sleep for months. They like honey and chasing a mate. But mostly, they like wandering the woods in clean air and watching the rabbits scurry away." He shook his head. "I'm not being a bear. This part of me is all human. Bears don't care about power structures or making money. The males don't hang together and they certainly don't swear loyalty. And they don't strategize on how to kill one another." He took a deep breath. "I chose to stop splitting myself in half. At the beginning of the fight, I chose to be both bear and human unified into one soul."

"But that's good, right?"

He shrugged, but the intensity in his gaze didn't ease. "We'll see. I am now an alpha. Bear and human combined. I lead, they follow. I use the power of the bear and the cunning of the man. Combined."

He held silent there, his eyes burning into her. He wanted her response, but she had nothing to say. Her mouth was dry and her heart was beating a thousand times a second. So she couldn't speak. She could only listen to the anguish in his words as he continued.

"That's what I did today, Alyssa. I figured out how to kill Nanook and how to consolidate his power under me. I left guns out so I could learn quickly who was the most impulsive and the biggest threat. I left them knowing someone was going to shoot at me while I was standing next to you." He arched his brow. "Is that a bear thing to do, Alyssa? Risk the alpha female's life for a power gain?"

She shuddered, not wanting to relive that moment. At the time, all she'd felt was a sudden tension as Simon had spun around and shot twice. She'd seen the dead man's gun go flying, knew it had been self-defense, but hadn't for a moment thought about where she'd been standing when the bullets started flying. All she'd known was that someone had been about to shoot Simon. But he was right. A fraction of an inch shift, and she would have taken the bullet instead of him.

The very idea left her skin clammy while nausea climbed in her throat. Then she heard Simon curse and suddenly she was upended. It was like a repeat of yesterday, only this time, she hadn't been sobbing on his shirt. This time she'd simply been thinking about the day and suddenly he was carrying her again.

She had the wherewithal to keep hold of her purse, but beyond that, her head dropped against his shoulder and she clenched her eyes shut. Her free hand wrapped around his shoulder and gripped tight.

It was stupid to take comfort in his strength. His heat made his scent even more heady and the steady shift of his body as he maneuvered through the dispensary to her apartment was lulling. But still, some part of her had to protest.

"I wasn't going to faint," she said against his neck. More like throw up, but she wasn't about to admit that.

"Did you get any of that pizza?"

No. The men had gobbled it all down. She'd managed a diet soda though, which was more than what he'd had.

They made it to her door and he set her on her feet. She didn't wobble, thank God. She also didn't protest when he pulled the keys from her unresisting fingers and unlocked her front door.

"Well, order another pizza now," he grumbled. "You have to eat."

Not after the way he'd curled his lip at the order this evening.

"There's lasagna in the freezer. We can microwave it faster than any delivery."

He stilled as he looked at her, his eyes lighting with surprise. "Really?"

She shrugged. "I don't just make brownies. There are chicken potpies, too. That's the Tupperware in the refrigerator."

"Which is faster?"

"Potpies."

He grabbed those while she dropped down onto her couch. Her head fell back, and she closed her eyes. She pretended she could still smell Irish Spring and feel his arms around her. And she didn't open them again until she heard him cursing.

When she looked, he was staring at the microwave, his finger hovering over the buttons. It took her a moment to figure out the problem, and then she remembered he couldn't read. "See the rows of white buttons?" she said. "Second one down on the left says 'Reheat.' That's what you need."

He traced his finger over and pressed. But after the microwave started, he remained there staring. He was right. He needed to remember how to read. Even the simplest tasks in life required literacy.

"First thing tomorrow," she said gently. "We'll start with the basic alphabet and—"

"No!" he said, spinning around with a snarl. "Now!"

She didn't argue with him. She could already tell he wasn't in a rational enough place for words. Which meant she had to look deeper at what was really going on in his head. Hadn't he told her that she was his wisdom? Perhaps it was time she tried it. She sat up straighter, talking out loud as she thought through what was going on.

"So the bear side is the simple one. Eats, sleeps, has sex."

"Yes." The word was half growl.

"And the human is the violent one. Analyzes, strategizes, implements."

"Yes." This time the word was snapped out, almost like a response to a military officer.

"So who feels pain? Guilt? Fear?"

"What?"

She straightened up off the couch, her entire body aching with the movement, but still needing to be close to him as she spoke. "It's what you said. Smoky the Bear lives a life of woodsy contentment. Mr. Human is more like Mr. Robot with the thinking and planning. Where do the difficult emotions go? Who has empathy, who feels remorse?"

He stared at her the same way he'd been looking at the microwave a moment ago: as if trying to decipher a secret code. But she was speaking plain English.

"Who feels bad, Simon?" She made it to his side and lay her palm flat on his chest. Through the thin T-shirt, she felt his muscles ripple, but he didn't move. He just kept staring at her, until she repeated the question. "Who feels bad?"

"I do." The words were rasped out, and she ached at the painful sound.

"You do," she echoed as she stepped closer. He didn't touch her. In fact, a quick glance told her that his hands were clenched into fists by his side. So she stroked him. First with her palm across his chest. Then with her other hand, caressing his jaw. "You're not just a bear and not just human. You're both, Simon. And that's a complicated place to be."

"No," he said, his eyes shutting tight. It wasn't a denial. It was more like defiance thrown into the wind. No, he didn't want to feel this way. No, he didn't want to live this way. No, he didn't want any of this.

Which is when she realized the truth. After all, he hadn't asked to become the Detroit bear alpha. He'd been Mr. Happy Grizzly in the UP when she'd shown up and shot him. Then he'd wanted to hole up in his cabin while he remembered who and what he was, but she'd dragged him down here. Then he'd had to fight Vic and Nanook, and suddenly he was alpha of a grizzly clan in a city that was perpetually teetering on the edge of destruction.

No wonder he was fighting this. Whatever life plans he'd had, they were certainly changed now.

"I'm sorry," she whispered, guilt descending hard into her soul. "You didn't want to come, but I just dragged you in." She dropped her head onto his chest. It had grown too heavy to support. "This is all my fault."

"No." The word was fierce this time. And she felt his arms circle around her, his palms flat across her back. "I could have refused at any point."

She snorted. "You did. I bowled over you."

He stilled. And then he pulled back, lifting her face with a tender nudge to her chin. "Do you seriously think you could have forced me? How? Were you going to carry me into your car? Did you put a gun to my head and make me fight Nanook?"

Maybe he was right, but that didn't ease her guilt. "I'm sorry," she whispered.

"I'm not," he returned. "Not about that. And not about this either."

She frowned. "Wha—"

He kissed her. Long and deep. First with his lips, then his tongue teased through the seam of her lips. He pushed inside and played with her while her breath grew short and her nipples tightened. Her knees weakened and she felt his penis hot and pulsing through his jeans. And she lifted her knee to coil her leg around him, opening herself up to him while drawing him tight.

The microwave dinged while they were entwined. Her kitchen filled with the scent of hot chicken potpie, but she wanted only the smell Irish Spring and him.

Then he pulled back, his eyes dark and but his lips curved in a self-satisfied smile. "You know what else bears have?"

She shook her head, too dazed and breathless to answer.

"Really good tongues." Then he cupped her face. His palm was so large that he could touch the length of her jaw while pushing his fingers into her hair. "I want to lick you while you come on my tongue. I want to mount you from behind while squeezing your breasts. And I want to feel your legs wrapped around me as I pound my release into you."

Her eyes widened at his words, but that was nothing compared to the contraction of her womb. Lord, she was practically orgasming just from his words.

"Alyssa?" he asked, and she had no brain to process his question.

"Hmm?" she responded as her eyes fastened on his mouth.

"What do you say to that?"

Her gaze finally lifted to his eyes. And once there, she smiled. "Okay."

His nostrils flared and his hands tightened for a moment. But beyond that, he remained absolutely still. Then she winked at him.

"How about now?"

CHAPTER 15

He made her eat first. Alyssa couldn't believe it. What man delayed sex for any reason? But he was adamant, and so she shoved too hot potpie into her mouth while her belly jumped and tightened in anticipation. He, on the other hand, took his time as he ate huge forkfuls of the meal. He coiled his tongue around his fork while he winked at her. Then he made noises of appreciation that she'd only heard when her brother watched porn with the volume dialed up.

"You're terrible!" she said after a particularly loud smack of his lips.

"You're not finished," he said, pointing with his fork at her plate. "And you're going to need all your strength."

She rolled her eyes. "Promises, promises," she taunted. "You're going to pump twice and be done. Then two minutes later, you'll be snoring and I'll be left high and dry."

He arched a brow at her. "Is that a challenge?"

"Hell, no. I'm just reminding you that you said some very specific things a few moments ago. I expect you to be a man of your word."

"I thought you wanted a man with a tongue."

"Can't I have both?" she asked before she popped the last bite into her mouth.

"You can tonight." Then he looked at her plate. "You done?"

She took her time licking her fingers, mimicking his erotic sounds as best she could. She didn't think it was working until she glanced at his hands. His expression remained flat, almost casual though his nostrils flared. But his hands kept spreading on his thighs before curling in and make deep imprints on his jeans. Open, then slowly curling into claws.

Oh yeah, she was getting to him.

Finally, she popped her last finger out of her mouth and wiped it on a paper towel. Then she smiled and sighed. "Yeah," she said trying to make it sound like a moan. "I guess I'm done—Eep!"

She was over his shoulder and being hauled into her bedroom. She started to laugh but that made the bounce on her full stomach too much. So she settled for gripping whatever part of him she could squeeze, starting with his trim waist and extending down to his taut butt. But she didn't get in more than a single fondle before he was flipping her back over before she dropped onto her bed with an "Umph!"

Laughing, she said, "Well, that was decisive of you."

He didn't answer as he stripped off his jeans and tee, leaving him naked and proudly erect. She flashed back to that afternoon and the feel of him hot and hard as he'd rubbed on her in front of all his men. At the time, she'd been flustered, aroused, and embarrassed, but not now. Right then, the memory made her skin burst with a flash fire of heat.

She sat up and put her hands to her T-shirt, planning to pull it off, but his hands were on hers before she could bare more than her belly button.

"I've got it," he said as he brushed her hands aside. She wouldn't have let go, but he also flicked his fingertips across her belly, which made her gasp. And in that moment of response, her fingers went lax and he slipped beneath her clothes.

Hot fingers, large hands, and a gentleness that had her skin trembling in response. He pulled up her tee while skimming across belly and breasts. Her nipples hardened but she didn't move. It was too exquisite to feel a man touching her so sweetly.

He pulled off her tee then unhooked her bra. She'd always hated that she was a full-figured gal. Breasts sent the wrong message in business and frankly, they got in the way whenever she worked out. But the way he looked at them bouncing there before him made all the annoyance disappear. He touched them reverently and the slow, tentative touch was more erotic than anything she'd ever felt before.

"Simon," she said on a groan.

"Lie back," he said as he nuzzled her neck. His five-o'clock shadow sensitized her skin and when he nudged her with his nose, she giggled. He pulled back in surprise, but she didn't let him go anywhere. She had her hands around his back, stroking up and down as she felt every muscle and tendon. Damn, he was one fine man.

"It's just nerves," she explained. "I haven't done this in a long while."

"Shhh," he said as she toppled backward onto her pillow. "This is the most natural thing in the world." And then he began to kiss her.

He started high, along her cheeks and lips. Then she felt him press kisses to her eyes before he nuzzled in her hairline. It was light and playful, but he was also very thorough. He seemed to need to touch and taste every inch of her. At first it was gentle and sweet. But soon her skin began to tingle and her breath grew short. He hadn't even touched her breasts yet and she was aching for him in the worst way. She tried to pull his face around to hers. She wanted to kiss him long and deep, but he was unwilling to move from where he was scraping his teeth along her jaw. He had no problem with the way her hands roved over his body and, God, she loved the feel of his skin hot and strong beneath her fingertips.

He was sucking lightly on her collarbone, slipping lower on her body. She stroked her fingers across his short buzz cut hair, liking the way it felt like velvet. Better yet was the way he hummed when she used her nails over his scalp. No other way to describe it except as a deep hum of approval that vibrated from his chest through hers.

Then hallelujah, he found her breasts. Lots of time here while he nipped or sucked at them. Her aching nipples got the attention they wanted and her breath stuttered while her knees fell open. Oh yes, he had a marvelous tongue. And oh God, she was going to melt or explode or just die from the pleasure of it all.

"Simon," she gasped. "I can't wait."

She unbuttoned her jeans with fumbling fingers and pushed them down. But he didn't let her up so she could strip them completely away, and he didn't rush what he was doing. No man had ever nuzzled her rib cage beneath her breasts. No man had ever rubbed the edge of his teeth along her less-than-flattering belly fat. But he did, and by the sounds he made in the back of his throat, he was well pleased with what he found.

By the time he put his lips to her mound, she'd lost all shame. She wanted him between her thighs now. He tugged her jeans past her knees, so she could finally work them off and kick them away. And then just when she thought he would fulfill his first promise to her, he pressed his fingers deep into the crevasse at the top of her thighs.

Her muscles there tensed in reaction, but then fell open with a flexibility she hadn't ever felt before. She wanted to ask what that was, but she hadn't the breath. And the need to have him touch her was overriding all other thoughts.

Thankfully, he did exactly that. He used his fingers and his tongue to work her open. He inhaled deeply and murmured his pleasure at her scent. And then he licked. Everywhere. Every way.

She came almost immediately. A detonation that had her hips lifting off the bed while her knees tightened around his broad shoulders. But that didn't stop him. While she was crying out in delight, he just kept licking. Deep inside, across her mound, and then with slow broad strokes across her clit.

Never had she guessed any man could be so steady, so unchanging in his attentions. He was going to lick her everywhere while she rode wave after wave of pleasure.

Insane. And amazing.

She gave herself up to it and to him.

"Turn over," he said when he had finished kissing her legs.

She hadn't the breath or the strength, but he was implacable.

"Turn over," he repeated as he rolled her onto her belly.

He kissed the back of her calves then licked the crease behind her knees. He spread her legs and nuzzled between her thighs. Then suddenly she felt the grip of his hands on her hips. It was so different from the steady strokes of his tongue that she was startled out of the haze of pleasure.

"Simon?" she whispered. She didn't have the strength for more.

Then she gasped as he hauled her hips up and set her on her knees. Her upper body was still collapsed on the mattress, but he didn't allow her to stay that way. He pulled her up and braced her hands. Then he set himself over her, his size only now really embedding itself on her thoughts. She nearly fit beneath him this way. He lay on her back and fondled her breasts, squeezing them before twisting her nipples.

She'd been in a lulled daze a moment before, so now his touch felt like lightning bolts to her breasts and nipples. And then she felt his penis push between her folds, thick and hot and so beautifully hard.

Yes. She'd wanted this for what felt like eons. *Yes, yes, yes.* Every panting breath was an echo of what her heart and mind was singing.

And still he fondled her breasts while she arched her back. She wanted him inside. So large. So hard. But first he had to—

He thrust and she cried out, startled because it was so quick. One minute he'd been teasing her, and then suddenly he was inside. Too big. There'd been a flash of pain, the steady stretch to accommodate. So big. She felt split open.

He started to draw out. He straightened off her back and his hands slid to her hips. Part of her thrilled at the possession. Most of her thrilled at it, but a tiny part of her brain was screaming. She'd needed him to do something first. He had to—

"Condom," she gasped. Then she repeated it louder. "Condom!"

He wasn't listening. His hands had tightened on her hips now, and he was thrusting inside. A steady pulse of penetration. In and in and in.

She started to struggle, but he held her fast. He couldn't release. She couldn't get pregnant!

"Simon! Stop!"

He didn't. He wasn't. So she became frantic.

She slammed forward and twisted. She grabbed his hand and tried to push him away. She had to stop this!

His hands tightened. God, he was so damn strong! She'd barely made it a few inches, and he made that up with his next thrust.

"*Stop!*" she bellowed.

He froze, completely embedded inside her. She was twisted around, trying to look at him. She saw him blink twice and focus. His breath was coming in heaving pants and his eyes burned with intensity. But he didn't speak, so she had to.

"You need a condom, Simon. I could get pregnant."

She watched his nostrils flare and knew her words had been a mistake. He wanted children.

She scrambled forward, and this time she managed to escape. He fell out of her, and she nearly moaned at the loss. But she used her momentum to lurch to her bedside table. She pulled it open and grabbed a foil packet. Spinning around she held it up between them.

"You have to wear a condom."

His penis was wet and dark as it bobbed between them. His breathing was the same as it was before, harsh and steady, and his eyes were the same intense stare of incomprehension.

He was being a bear, she realized. In a place so primal that it couldn't communicate, and it sure as hell didn't understand modern birth control. So it was up to her.

He was still kneeling on the bed, looking at her with dark, steady eyes. She ripped open the packet and pulled out the wet latex. She'd never done this before, but she knew the basics.

First, she stroked him, sliding her fingers across the wet head and thick stalk. He rumbled, low and deep, so she did it again though she added some pressure. He made the sound again, this time louder and she knew he was pleased.

Now came the awkward part. She kept stroking him with one hand while the other managed the condom.

His rumbling came at a higher pitch this time, the sound tighter and slightly annoyed. But she didn't let it stop her. She kept stroking him as she rolled the condom down. And then when it was done, she looked up into his eyes.

"Now it's okay." She touched his cheek and then went in for a kiss. His lips were tight, but she teased the seam of them with her tongue. And when they relaxed and opened, she invaded him. She pressed inside him and felt the shudder that went through his body.

And then suddenly, her knees were swept out from beneath her. She was abruptly dropped onto her back as he landed on all fours above her. No more kissing as he wordlessly looped her legs over his arms.

And then he widened her and thrust inside.

Impaled. Split open. Any of a thousand different words cut through her consciousness. But they all meant the same thing. She was completely vulnerable to him, wide open and barely able to move. While he did what he wanted.

He thrust into her. Deep strokes that she felt all the way to her back.

Steady pound as he pierced straight through her core.

An unrelenting beat as her body grew taut around his. As the thump of his body against hers had her legs tightening, her breath stuttering, and her body gripping him. Taking him. Sucking on him.

He went on and on as she arched and gripped. Thighs, belly, core. She tightened around him. Harder. Thicker. Stronger.

Her toes curled and her head dropped back.

And still he kept pounding.

Orgasm.

Waves of pleasure while she writhed around him.

He was the center, and she was the one spinning wildly around him.

Yes.

God, yes!

It went on forever while she pulsed and sighed. Pleasure so beautiful. Sweet waves that lapped at her while she remained anchored to him.

Had he come? He must have. His expression was blissful. And yes, she felt the pulses of his organ, but it was a minor thing compared to the pleasure that kept her heart and mind aglow.

And when she was completely boneless lying there, still impaled by him, he leaned down. It was a slow movement, so she saw it coming. She stretched forward, but hadn't the strength to meet him. So he came to her.

His lips to hers. His mouth on hers.

A kiss. A long, slow kiss with a tongue that was thorough in her mouth.

And when he was done, he pulled back. Not just away from her mouth, but from her body as well. He dropped back onto his calves and he stared at her. There was love in his eyes, but also a vague confusion. As if he didn't know what to do next.

"Still deep in the grizzly, aren't you?" she asked.

He didn't answer, so she took that as a yes.

"That's okay. I like your grizzly."

So she cleaned him up. She disposed of the condom and brought a wet towel to wipe his body of the sweat. He chuffed as she worked, clearly wanting to touch her. But she held his hand away, feeling both too tired and too energized to allow more sex play. It was a new feeling, this whisper in her heart. She didn't have to look too closely to understand it.

Tenderness. Affection.

Love.

She was in love with Simon. After less than two days, she'd tumbled headlong into love. With a bear.

If she weren't feeling so wonderful, she'd call herself an idiot. Instead, she tossed aside the washcloth and nudged Simon until he lay down in her bed. Then she burrowed beneath the covers and his arm so that they could spoon in their sleep.

Two breaths later, and she was out. The last thing she remembered was Simon pressing his lips to her neck for one last, sweet lick.

CHAPTER 16

Simon woke as a man, his grizzly mind tucked away, and his first thoughts were to take stock of his situation. His human body was warm and healthy, the sheets smelled of Alyssa, but his arms were empty. So he climbed out of bed and went in search of her.

He found her in the kitchen as she frowned at her phone, a news reporter's voice coming through the tiny device. She looked up as soon as he entered, and her expression softened in a way that thrilled both man and bear. Her eyes lightened and her lips curved. Best of all, she set down her mug and phone to cross to his side.

"Did I wake you?" she asked. "I tried to be quiet."

"I woke because you weren't with me," he answered. Then he drew her into his arms pressed his face to her hair. She smelled slightly nutty, but mostly of what they had done last night, and he couldn't resist nuzzling down to her neck to lick the skin beneath her ear.

She chuckled, then lifted her head. "You're talking again. That's a good sign."

He nodded and stayed in that place of holding her for a minute longer. Just a minute. But eventually, he had to explain. If not for her, then for them both. Because she needed to understand him if they were to continue together. But how to explain when he wasn't even sure of what had happened?

Eventually, he pulled back. "You must have questions."

"A zillion. But mostly it comes down to one." She touched his cheek and he loved how her eyes grew soft. "Who is the real you? Are you the growly bear? The Machiavellian leader? The vicious killer or the thorough lover?" Then her lips curved into a smile. "Or are you the man who held me all last night like he needed me in his arms?"

"I guess I'm all of them. I put walls between them because it's better that way. But sometimes…" He shook his head. "There's a dark place I can go, Alyssa. It's human violence coupled with a bear's ferocity. It's fury and deliberate destruction, and the last time I went there…" He shook his head.

"What?" She stroked his cheek. "Tell me."

"My best friend was teasing me about how I sucked in basketball." He shook his head. "Basketball. Can you believe it? I nearly killed him because I couldn't hit a jump shot." He snorted. "That's why I enlisted, you know. I figured if I was going to be a violent killing machine, I might as well do it in the army."

She pulled back from him, not in fear but in confusion. "I don't understand. You had a death challenge with your best friend? Over basketball?"

He touched her face, startled that he wanted to tell her this. He'd never told anyone. But he told her because he wanted her to understand. He needed her to know how amazing what she'd done was.

"It's a place where man and animal merge in the worst of both. We were teens and both shifters. It was spring, too, which always makes us hot." He closed his eyes, remembering every detail of the day. The smell of flowers and the sound of animals mating. They were outside on a basketball court, but in Gladwin, Michigan, the state park was right there and coming alive. He wasn't new to shifting, but he was still prey to all those teen hormones. And the girls were nearby watching, including an extra pretty one he'd been trying to impress.

"You don't have to tell me," Alyssa whispered as her hand stroked his shoulder.

"I do," he stressed. If she was to be his alpha female, she needed to know it all, including her part in all of this. "You have to know what happens. What I can do. What you did."

He felt her hand tighten as she said the words he hadn't been able to. "In case you go there again?"

He nodded, his gut twisting. "A shift in power is always dangerous. A new alpha will get more challenges—"

"Tell me what you need me to know."

His lips curved. She always cut straight to the point. "We started playing basketball, me and Jason. He laughed at my jump shot, which really did suck, and he said I couldn't sink one with him in my face. He said it really loud, and there were girls watching."

"You were a teen boy. That's what boys do."

"I know. And he was good, and I couldn't get past him. I couldn't sink the shot. I felt the grizzly coming out, but we were in public. I couldn't go bear and what would be the point? It wasn't like a bear can play basketball."

She snorted. "People would pay to see that." Her tone was light, and it frustrated him. She needed to take this seriously, but the fault was in himself. He couldn't express what he wanted to. But she was listening, so he tried again.

"So I merged the two. I'd never done it before but it was so easy. All the fury of the animal without the fur. All the intelligence of the man but without the restraint of morals or logic. I had a single goal—to sink that shot—and I didn't care what I did to accomplish it."

She stilled, but her voice remained gentle. "Teens are stupid. Boys most of all."

He couldn't argue, but he also couldn't hide from what he did. "I beat him up, Alyssa. I punched him and when he didn't go down, I hit him as fast and as hard as I could. He was down on the ground with broken bones, and the only reason I stopped—the only reason—was so I could stand up and sink my jump shot."

He looked at her, trying to see if she understood. She didn't. She just stared at him with a vague kind of confusion. "Okay," she said slowly. "That's horrible. And a lesson in why teenage boys can't be trusted with anything. But—"

"It was a basketball game, and I nearly killed him. What if it had been something different? What if he'd teased me that I couldn't get the girl? I wouldn't have stopped, Alyssa. In that place, I don't stop for anything even if it's murder or rape."

"That's a big leap, don't you think? From hitting your best friend—"

"I put him in the hospital. Also the three guys who tried to pull me off. They didn't have a chance against me. Not when I'm like that. And the only reason I stopped, Alyssa? The *only reason* is because I made the jump shot."

"I got that. You made your goal, so you stopped."

"And because the girl I wanted sucker punched me until I hit the ground."

She snorted. "Hooray for girl power."

"I've touched that place other times in my life. Once in Afghanistan when we were pinned down. The only reason I stopped then was because I was shot and unconscious. Once on leave when I was jumped by muggers in Turkey." He felt his jaw clench, but he forced the words out. "I killed them."

"They sound like reasonable choices, Simon."

He touched her cheek. "It's a scorched earth place in my head, Alyssa. When I go there, everybody dies."

"You didn't kill everyone yesterday."

"Because you stopped me. Because you pulled me out of it."

She shook her head. "Don't put that on me. I didn't do anything but..." Her voice trailed away as her cheeks flushed. Any other time he would have found the expression adorable. This time he just touched her fingers, stroking his thumb over her knuckles.

"You centered me. When I fought, Alyssa, it was to protect you. When I killed Nanook, it was to keep you alive. And when I risked your life against that drug dealer..." His voice cracked but he forced himself to continue. "It was to impress you."

She blinked. "That doesn't make sense."

"It's not a logical frame of mind." While she absorbed that, he told her the rest. "Then you stayed by my side as I cemented my position. And last night..." He took a deep breath, drawing in the scent of sex that still lingered in the room. "You understood what I needed, where I was without me having to explain. I needed to be an animal but not killing. I needed to be a man with a woman, and not playing power games."

Did she understand how important that was to him? That she could keep him within the bounds of decency? And she'd known what he needed without him explaining. He might be the scariest shifter around, but she held the power over him. And that made him vulnerable to her in ways that terrified him. It also gave him hope that he wasn't alone and that was the rarest gift of all.

Did she understand that? Did she know?

No, she didn't. Because all she did was stretch up on her toes and press a kiss to his lips. And when he would have deepened it, she pulled back. "I guess you answered my question. They're all you. Animal, man, determined, and sexy. It's all you."

"It's not. It's pieces of me—"

"It's you. Different moods, different needs, but they're all you."

Maybe. And maybe it didn't matter because whatever part of him dominated, they all centered on her.

He dropped his forehead to hers and breathed her scent again. He'd never tire of that. And he'd never forget it. "Come back to bed, Alyssa. We'll explore every aspect of—"

She kissed him, deep and so giving. He drank it all in, soaking up the passion that was Alyssa. And when he lifted her up in his arms, she wrapped her legs around him. He was naked and she wore yoga pants and a tank. She helped him strip it off her. And he pinned her against the wall while he suckled her breasts.

And when he would have plunged inside again, she gripped his ears. "Condom," she gasped.

This time he understood. He carried her into the bedroom and opened the bedside drawer. She helped him put it on while he stripped her pants away. And when she would have stroked him to completion, he pushed her backward on the bed. He spread her legs and pushed slowly inside.

He wasn't in that primal place anymore. He wasn't a beast mating in the woods. This time he was a man and he used his mind to make it good for her. He pressed his thumb to her clit and held it there. Then with every thrust, he added an extra stroke. A little more spice, he thought, until she was on fire.

And when she was gasping and clutching at him, he let his body take over. He stroked her one last time, loving the sound of her climax. And then he pounded into her. Harder and faster until his mind whited out and his body exploded.

He released into her so many times while her body greedily milked him for more. And when they were done, he pressed his lips to hers and nearly said the words out loud. They came to the tip of his tongue, but he held them back.

It was too soon to tell her. It put too much on her when they'd only known each other for a short time. And he didn't want to admit to feelings that meant he would center on her for the rest of his life. That was too scary a thing to say out loud.

So he held them back and stopped himself from even thinking the word, "love."

And this time when he woke up from his doze, she was still in his arms. She lay sleeping tucked up against him and he pressed his nose to her skin right below her ear. And he stayed there until she finally stirred. And even then, he held her, pressing kisses to her neck until she murmured.

"Is that my cell phone?"

It was. Out in the kitchen, her phone was buzzing.

"I'll get it," he said, but she was already out of bed and rushing naked into her kitchen. He followed because it was her. And because she was naked. He watched as she snatched up her phone and thumbed it on.

"Yeah? This is her. Yes, he's here. I'll tell him. Yes, I'll be sure to tell him." There were more words, each becoming more clipped than the last. And when she finally clicked off her phone, her expression was grim. "That was a Detective Phillips. He wants us to give our statements in an hour."

Simon frowned. "We already gave our statements to Kennedy."

She snorted. "Yeah, but Ryan's in the gang unit. Phillips is from vice. He wants to talk to us alone." Then she sighed. "We need a lawyer."

He nodded. "The Gladwins have one. I'll call…" His voice trailed away. Where was his phone? How did he call? "Damn it, I need to remember."

"It's in here," she said walking into her second bedroom. She'd converted it into an office with two desks, a corkboard covered with articles he couldn't read, and a complete computer setup. His laptop sat on the second desk and his cell was right beside it. Nanook's computer was still in her car. She grabbed his cell and tried to thumb it on, but it didn't work. "It's dead. I should have realized you needed to charge it."

Obviously, she was accustomed to thinking ahead for other people. "That was my responsibility," he said as he held out his hand. Except where was his charger?

"I've got one," she said, answering the question he hadn't asked out loud. She pulled one out of a drawer. "I upgraded last year, so you can have this."

He took it, taking a long frustrating moment to remember how to plug it in to his phone and then again into the wall socket.

"It's really dead," she said, "so it'll take a few to even start."

"I know how my phone works!" he snapped. Then at her raised eyebrows, he took a deep breath. Damn it, he wasn't used to being this ill equipped to handle his life. "I need to call Alan. He's the lawyer. But his number is in my phone and I can't read to recognize his name."

She nodded. "I've got that figured out, too." She tapped on her laptop, which came to life on a *Sesame Street* program. "It's just a matter of remembering things. I figure you start with the basics and build up until it comes back. It shouldn't take you long."

It shouldn't, but even a few minutes was too long to remember something he'd been doing since he was five. And they didn't have the time. They were supposed to go to the police station, but the cops would likely put them in separate rooms. She couldn't cover for his lacks. And without time to find a lawyer, who knew what kind of legal hot water he could land in? It was just too complicated and he wanted to slam his head against the wall until his stupid brain worked.

And just when his frustration was growing into epic proportions, Alyssa touched his arm. "Hey, you haven't eaten anything. Want some breakfast? Or at least coffee?"

"Coffee. Definitely coffee." That way he wouldn't just be stupid. He'd be alert and stupid.

"Coming up."

She went back into the kitchen and he followed like a damned puppy dog. He watched as she pulled down a coffee mug and poured. And he lingered as he took it from her so he could stroke her fingers and not think about the disaster lurking ahead.

"Drink," she said. "I'll make us some eggs."

"Thanks." He drew the mug to his lips and inhaled.

Taint.

The scent was subtle, akin to bacon sizzled too long, and it made him wrinkle his nose in disgust. But it had been a long time since he'd had coffee, and God knew he wanted the caffeine, so he took a sip despite the smell.

Nausea roiled in his gut and he spit out the brew straight into the sink. He dumped his mug, too, while Alyssa stared at him in shock. And then he backhanded the faucet to kick it on, but the spray held the same smell. Stronger even, and he slammed it off as quickly as he could.

"What's wrong?" Alyssa gasped.

"Did you drink that coffee?" he asked.

"Yeah. Some at least."

He grabbed her mug and sniffed. Sure enough, the same taint was there. He dumped it while she sputtered her protest.

"It's bad," he said. Then he pulled her over as he turned on the water again. "Smell that. Can't you sense it?"

She inhaled, but then shrugged as she straightened up. "It's Detroit. Who can tell what's in the water?"

"And you still drink it?"

She opened her mouth to argue, but then bit her lip. "I guess I didn't think about it."

He'd been a bear for the last ten months, but even he'd heard of the water disaster in Flint, Michigan. "No more water," he said. "You don't drink this at all."

"Um, okay. We've got a few more bottles of your special water. Is it okay to wash the dishes?" She looked to her bathroom. "And what about the shower? You've been here a couple days now. Are you just now noticing this?"

He pursed his lips. She had a point. "Hold on," he said as he crossed to the bathroom and flipped on the shower. It didn't take more than ten seconds for him to smell the taint in the steam. It was thick enough to make him choke as he turned it off. "That wasn't there yesterday," he said. "Whatever it is, it's new."

"Oh goody," she drawled as she plopped her hands on her hips. "Look, it's impossible to function without using the water. Are you sure—"

He cut her off. "I'm sure." He kept his voice firm, though inside he was questioning. The UP had beautiful water and besides, he'd been a bear. What did he know about crappy city water? Except he couldn't bring himself to change his mind. That water was bad. "We'll mention it to Kennedy—" He cut off his words as an electronic chime sounded from the office. And continued to sound, along with a steady buzz. He looked to the room with a frown.

"That's your phone," Alyssa said. "Sounds like you've missed a few calls."

He nodded but he didn't move. Damn it, he might remember how to answer the phone, but he couldn't read to figure out how to get his messages.

"I got it." She went back into her office and again, he followed her. "What's your phone code?"

Numbers he could remember, so he told her and within a moment, she was scrolling through his messages.

"Do you want the oldest or the newest?" Then before he could answer, she snorted. "They're both from a guy named Carl. I'm guessing he's that alpha you mentioned. He's left about a dozen—"

"Call him back."

Carl Carman was his alpha, or had been his alpha before he'd killed Nanook and taken over the Griz. Either way, Carl should have been his first phone call after he woke up. And after his fight with Nanook. And maybe first thing this morning. So it was no surprise when the man came on the phone practically vibrating with fury. Alyssa had put him on speaker, so Carl's voice filled the space with booming threat.

"What the hell, Simon! What the hell are you doing?"

"Hello, Carl," Simon said, his voice deepening at the sound of aggression. He deserved it, he knew, but that didn't stop his grizzly from growling deep inside him. "I've been busy."

"Busy? Busy taking over Detroit?"

"Yes." And fighting Vic and making love with Alyssa. And a host of other things that flashed through his mind.

"Don't you think you should have talked to me first?"

"There wasn't time. Nanook was trying to murder a cop. It was the only way to…" Keep Alyssa alive. "To calm things down."

"Violent overthrows don't usually quiet things down."

"It has for the moment." He hoped.

"Fine. You calling about the Detroit Flu? I've been watching the news and that video from the hospital looks awful familiar."

Simon frowned. "I haven't seen—"

"I have," Alyssa interrupted. "It was someone changing. Just like Vic."

"Who's that?" Carl abruptly demanded. "Identify yourself!"

"She's my assistant," Simon said, a growl coming through his tone loud and clear. He did not like anyone talking to Alyssa with any-thing but respect.

"Assistant? Just how long have you been in Detroit? You're sup-posed to check in with me once a month, and it's been—"

"Ten months. Yes, I know."

"Ten fucking months! What the hell were you doing?"

Simon thought about lying. The last thing he wanted to admit to anyone was that he'd been a bear all those months. That amount of animal time was unheard of. Anyone who lasted that long stayed furry. The fact that he'd come back was both unusual and grounds for a deeper inspection into his psyche. Humans didn't live wild without going native...and crazy. In fact, if Alyssa hadn't shot him, if it hadn't been a matter of survival, he probably wouldn't have ever come back to human. Which meant that it would have been Carl's job to hunt him and kill him.

"Simon? Don't you dare—"

"I was grizzly. The whole time."

Carl's curses echoed long and loud through the phone. "You can't do that, Simon."

"I certainly can't now. I'm alpha of the Griz."

"Yeah, lucky you," Carl drawled, clearly not sympathetic. "So if you're alpha now, you've got to deal with the Detroit Flu. I saw that video on the news. We had people changing like that. They were kidnapped and injected with some bad shit. Most died, but a few changed. Like what was on that video."

Simon's head snapped up. "They were kidnapped?"

"Yeah. We've got a serum. It's not a cure, but it slows down the process. Enough for someone to adjust. But you've got to stop who-ever is injecting people with that shit."

Alyssa was shaking her head and at Simon's nod, she spoke up. "It can't be an injection. There's too many people getting sick. It's been happening all over Detroit."

Which is when Simon put it together. "It's in the water," he said. "That's what I smelled." He looked at Alyssa. "You said there were two outbreaks. That means two times when someone tainted the water."

"But you smelled it this morning. You just noticed it this morning," Alyssa said.

Simon nodded, his gut twisting with horror. "Yeah. Which means we're about to get a third outbreak of the Detroit Flu."

There was a long pause as everyone considered that possibility. The ramifications were hideous. And then Carl spoke up, his voice weary.

"Look, I don't understand this science stuff. I'll email you everything I've got. You've got to get it to somebody who can handle it. Do you know any shifter-aware doctors?"

"I just got here, Carl. And Nanook wasn't exactly the note-taking type."

Alyssa frowned. "Maybe Detective Kennedy would know?"

"You'll have to figure it out. With the quarantine, I can't get there to help."

"What?" Simon's voice was sharp, and he could hear Carl's sigh through the line.

"Jesus, turn on the news. The city was put into quarantine a couple hours ago. Nobody in or out. You got national guard blocking everything." Then he snorted. "You sure picked a great time to go grizzly in Detroit."

That was the understatement of the year. The city was going to go insane in short order, and shifters would be the most vulnerable to the chaos. Their animal natures were going to react to the tension and without a way to run off the excess emotions, there was going to be some ugly fights. And that's if they were lucky.

He looked at Alyssa. "Did you know about this?"

She nodded. "I was listening to the news when you got up. I was going to tell you, but we got distracted." Her cheeks heated at just how they'd gone off course. Fortunately, her words gave a difference explanation. "You were focused on the taint in the water."

"It has to be it," he said, though his doubts kept his voice quiet. "Nanook thought it was the wolves."

"Nanook thought everything was the wolves," Carl grumbled. "Look, I'll try to figure stuff out on this end. Can you get the info to the cop?"

Simon nodded. "We're headed there now."

"I'll check back in a couple hours."

"Yeah—"

"And Simon? Don't go grizzly again."

Simon bristled at the tone. He was in control, damn it, and he didn't need another bear telling him things he already knew. "You're not my alpha anymore," he said, his voice low and threatening. "You can't give me orders—"

"It wasn't an order, you moron, it was a damned plea. If you lose it, I'm the one who will have to shoot your ugly ass, quarantine or not. I got problems enough here and Becca's pregnant. I sure as hell am not going to miss the birth of my son just because you can't remember to keep your hair on the inside."

Simon frowned, struggling to process all that information at once. Not the fact that Carl would be his hunter, but that Carl had gotten his girlfriend pregnant. Or maybe they were married by now. And though it was the most inconsequential thing in the very long list of things he needed to know right then, somehow it hit him broadside. Marriages and births were incredibly important in the shifter community. Especially within his own clan. And Simon had missed all of that.

"You're having a son? Congratulations."

"Yeah," Carl's voice was gruff with clear pride. "Yeah, we found out a month ago. Tonya's pregnant, too, and Alan's so deep into father mode that I hardly get to see him anymore."

Tonya and Alan? God, what else had he missed?

"Congratulate them for me." He looked at the clock on the printer and used the time as an excuse. "We've got to get to the police station."

"Right." Carl's voice was all back to business, but before he signed off, he had one more suggestion to make, though it came out more as an order. "And Simon? Get yourself a girl."

"What?"

"You're on the edge. We both know it. The right woman grounds people like us. She'll keep your head in the right space."

Simon's jaw tightened, but he couldn't stop himself from looking up at Alyssa. Her gaze was fixed on the phone, very carefully avoiding his. So rather than acknowledge any of the sudden tension that was thickening the air, he chose to deflect. "I don't need dating advice from you," he growled.

"It's not dating advice!" Carl snapped. "It's a warning. Find a girl or I'll have to break quarantine to run you down. I don't want to do that, but I will. You can't go feral in a place like Detroit."

No, he couldn't. It would be too dangerous for everyone.

"Carl—" Simon began, but Alyssa cut him off.

"He's got me," she snapped. "And I'll keep him human."

Simon looked at her, seeing the determined jut to her chin. If anyone could keep him human, it would be her. And he couldn't deny the wave of raw pleasure that came from her words. She was his, and that thought flushed him with testosterone-filled pride. But it also wasn't true.

He was so strong a shifter, it was dangerous for him to have a human relationship. He could get too violent, too animal, or too damned focused. Regular humans could get hurt so easily. He didn't want to risk Alyssa like that. Though God only knew if he could give her up. He already thought of her as his alpha female.

But Carl didn't need to know that. And he wasn't ready to explain things to Alyssa yet. He needed her too much right then to push her away. But he had to tell her soon. She had to understand what she was risking.

"Send me that serum information," Simon said. "And a list of any shifter-friendly lawyers. And judges. And medical anything." At this point, he'd take a shifter-aware orderly.

"There aren't any," Carl growled. "Because all the sane ones don't live inside the city."

Sadly, he knew that was true. And with that, he thumbed off the connection. "Okay," he said as he avoided looking Alyssa in the eyes. "Play me all my messages, starting from the top."

CHAPTER 17

Alyssa gave all the files to Detective Kennedy, but his response wasn't encouraging. He was a gang cop. He had no legitimate reason to be talking to the CDC and didn't know anyone in authority who was shifter-aware. Worse, every cop was helping to contain the unrest as people began to feel the effects of the quarantine. The gangs were being especially violent, but so were bankers and soccer moms. And worse, by afternoon the news confirmed that a third wave of outbreaks was sweeping through the area. It was like the entire city was on edge and rather than pulling together, people were throwing knives at each other. Or bullets.

At least they'd managed to get a good lawyer. That was Kennedy's recommendation, too, and he turned out to be young, handsome, and sharp as tack. He was there when Alyssa gave her statement and he sat by Simon, too. Apparently, he'd been up all night as members of the Griz gave their statements and bartered their deals for turning state's evidence. It was a messy business and Alyssa did her best to keep up, but mostly, it was a *Law & Order* episode with too many people involved for her to keep straight. Plus, she'd never really liked that show because it always ended on a "life sucks" note.

Simon spent the whole day in that neutral expression place where his mind was a steel trap. Nothing escaped his notice, and no emotions leaked through. Similar to yesterday, he was a Spock-like machine as he answered questions, directed his people whenever possible, and didn't give her anything more than orders. Not a soft look, not a gentle caress, not even a whispered "thank you."

Years ago, she would have been hurt by his attitude. Now she just accepted it. After all, she understood what it was like to focus solely on getting stuff done. No distractions, no interference, and none of those pesky emotions clogging up the flow.

Great, except she'd just declared her love this morning. She'd said out loud that she was his. And no, she hadn't expected him to drop onto his knee and swear eternal devotion. They'd been on the phone. But she'd thought he'd give her some sort of reaction if only a kiss. Something to say, *I'm yours, too.*

It hadn't happened. He'd asked for updates on the cleaning crew and had her run through his email out loud with him. And when she was busy driving to the police station, he had her pull up a *Sesame Street* program on her phone so he could learn his alphabet. Instead of a declaration of love, she heard "C is for Cookie, that's good enough for me."

Don Juan, he was not.

And so they churned through the day. There were a thousand things to do at the Griz headquarters. And when Simon was closeted with Joey the accountant, Alyssa had to deal with a disaster at the laundry. People doing laundry were usually mellow. Especially ones who wandered down the street to get some pot. Not so today.

A fistfight broke out over use of a dryer, and now Malik was nursing a broken nose and a bad attitude.

She'd sent him home, but that meant she had to cover his shift, which made Simon even more frustrated. He had to confess to Joey that he couldn't read, and that meant one more person in on Simon's biggest vulnerability. That made them both jumpy, but there was nothing she could do about it. The streets were heating up, grocery stores being the biggest battlegrounds. Everyone wanted food now. And gas. And a way to blow off steam after two more "monster" videos appeared on the Internet.

It was enough for her to beg Vic to stay in his apartment. Especially once the news hit that a guy with a too full beard was shot on the street because someone thought he was a monster. Scary times for everyone. So why was she obsessing like a teenage girl about whether her boyfriend loved her?

"Hey, are you sure Simon said the water was bad?"

Alyssa looked up from repairing a broken washing machine to see her brother coming in the laundromat front door. He was dressed in shorts and a tank and drinking from a refillable sports bottle.

"Yeah. Said we shouldn't even shower in it."

She looked closer at him. He'd been working out, probably running through the nearby park, and as she watched, he squeezed the last of his drink into his mouth.

"Really? Tastes fine to me."

"Was that tap water?" she cried as she stood to face her brother.

"Yeah. Refilled at the drinking fountain." Then he curled a lip at her. "Don't get pissy. I needed to burn off some energy. I called Simon and since he didn't need me, I thought I'd go for a run." He sauntered around the busted washer and headed for the sink. Popping on the tap, he started refilling his bottle.

"You can't drink that!" She grabbed for the bottle, but he elbowed her out of the way.

"It's fine. Simon's hyper."

"Damn it, Vic, it's serious!" She reached again for the bottle but he knocked her back. She stumbled backward into a machine, which was bad enough, but he followed her with a hand on her throat.

"I like it," he hissed.

She stared at him, hardly daring to breathe. She was caught with the largest washing machine behind her and the hard length of her brother's bigger, stronger, and definitely bad-smelling body. It was the BO that came with the monster, and she didn't need the pinpricks of claws against her throat to see he was changing.

She had two choices. She could try and fight him, but he'd most likely take out her throat first. Or she could try to talk him down.

"Vic, what are you doing?" she rasped as calmly as she could. "Think."

He wasn't listening, and he wasn't thinking. He leaned forward, his breath harsh in her face. "I like the water." And then, out of spite, he turned the bottle upside down and squirted it in her face.

She sputtered while he laughed, and that gave her the opportunity. She pulled up her knee as hard as she could while simultaneously knocking aside his arm. The good news was that she nailed him hard.

He doubled over with wheezing gasps. The bad news was that he changed right there. Full-on monster, tearing his tee and stretching his shorts to breaking. He swiped at her, his jaw snapping loudly and too close to her face. The only thing that kept her from being disemboweled were his shoes. Too tight for his monster feet and he fell over while trying to walk.

Which is when it got immeasurably worse.

Ms. Turley came in. She was munching on a tin of cannabis-laced popcorn, but what she saw was Vic. And she started screaming and pointing.

"Run!" Alyssa screamed, but it didn't work. The woman probably couldn't hear her over her screeching. And then, Ms. Turley shifted as well. Right there in her muumuu, she suddenly sprouted fur and a muzzle. The screams became howls and her fingers became claws that dropped the popcorn in favor of swiping at Vic.

Vic spun, his nostrils flaring as he scented the new stench. He growled at the woman and she growled back.

"Stop it!" Alyssa screamed, but it was no use. The two were siting each other and whereas Vic was hobbled by his shoes, Ms. Turley had been in Crocs that were easily kicked aside. "Don't you dare!" she bellowed at the woman. And when that didn't work, she tried any of the other screams that had sometimes worked.

"Take it outside!"

"I'm calling the cops!"

"I don't fucking believe this!"

Holy shit. She was hysterical, and that wasn't going to stop her brother and a sweet old lady from attacking each other. Which is when she saw the fire extinguisher on the wall.

It was her only hope and she grabbed it like the lifeline it was. She popped the pin with fumbling fingers, then aimed and shot. She got Ms. Turley in the face and then she went for Vic. Both of them snarled at her and advanced, but she didn't stop. It wasn't exactly a water hose, but it was enough. Before long, the two were hissing and spitting on the slick floor. And while they were gasping for breath, she tried again to reach them.

"What the fuck is wrong with you, Vic? You had it under control! And Ms. Turley, aren't you hungry?" She scrambled around as fast as she could to grab the popcorn tin. Then she slid it across the floor straight into the woman's side.

Ms. Turley's nose started twitching and she looked over. A moment later, she was muzzle deep in the tin, eating without the use of her hands.

One down. One to go.

She glared at Vic who was wiping away the foam with hands, not claws. And that gave her hope.

"You in there Vic? You got it together yet?"

He didn't answer. At least not at first. She caught a flash from his eyes as he glared at her, but he didn't attack. Then he jerked himself around, flopping onto his ass as he grabbed at his shoes.

"Fucking things," he muttered before he kicked them off.

She feared he would leap up and attack then. He had mobility. But instead, he leaned back against the side of coin machine and released a heavy sigh while he stretched out his feet.

Alyssa blew out a breath. "Vic? You in there?"

"I'm never wearing shoes again."

She liked them. That was twice now that she'd managed to escape him because he was hobbled by his own shoes.

"You ready to listen?"

He scraped foam off his arm and chest then gave up the task as useless. "The water's bad," he said, his voice deadpan. "I drank a ton at the fountain and then refilled the bottle."

"You said you liked it."

"The monster likes it," he said. Then he looked up at her, his brown eyes wide and rimmed with red. "The monster likes it a lot." Then he turned to look at Ms. Turley. "She probably had it in her tea."

Yeah. Ms. Turley enjoyed a pot of her Chinese herbs every morning and another in the afternoon. Especially during allergy season when her migraines were the worst. That's why the woman bought the popcorn. She'd feel a headache coming on and reach for her tea and popcorn. Between the tea and the THC, she said her pains would dull enough that she could function.

"She's okay right now," Alyssa said. "I'm more worried about you."

Vic looked up. "It's like ants under my skin. Fire ants with pinchers. And yeah, I want to kill someone." He took a deep breath. "I want to hurt whoever did this to me and to an old pothead like Ms. Turley." He must have seen Alyssa tense because he shook his head. "I'm under control."

"Yeah?" she challenged.

"Yeah." Then he looked at Ms. Turley. "What are we going to do with her?"

Like she knew? But of course, she had the answer downstairs. "Let her finish the tin. That will quiet her enough to get her into one of the cages."

He nodded as he slowly stood up. She couldn't stop herself from tightening her grip on the fire extinguisher. If he went nuts again, it was her only defense. His eyes narrowed when he saw it, but then he sighed.

"I guess I should go in there with her."

God, part of her wanted to say yes. When he went monster, he scared the hell out of her. But she needed him in control. And locking him up wasn't going to give him the practice Simon said he needed. Which meant he had to make the choice himself.

"Do you feel like you're going to lose it again? I mean, you just drank the stuff. Is it getting worse?"

He went quiet, obviously considering. She watched him close his eyes and his fists. He took a deep breath and then curled his lips in a growl. But he didn't make any sound. Instead, he opened his hands and his eyes. "It's close, Alyssa. I don't want to hurt you. Or anybody."

"Then keep it together." She took a deep breath, reaching for logic. "Look, the first couple times we had to knock you unconscious. But yesterday and now? You ended it yourself."

He didn't answer. He was looking at his hand, his teeth grinding as claws popped out and fur sprouted. And then, a moment later, they faded back. Human hand. Smooth skin. Then he opened his hand and flipped it over to show his very human palm and wrist.

"It's amazing, isn't it? I mean, I'm kind of like Wolverine."

She nodded, a slightly hysterical chuckle building in her throat. "Well, you kind of look like a black Hugh Jackman. If I squint. Or am really drunk."

He snorted. "Please, I'm hotter than that guy any day."

"Yeah, right," she drawled. "Okay Mr. Clooney, help me get Ms. Turley downstairs."

The woman had finished the popcorn tin and was now lying back with a soft smile on her doglike face. Definitely not a bear monster here, but either way, she needed to be contained even if it was just to keep her apart until her human face returned. Fortunately, she'd eaten enough popcorn that she'd be high as a kite for hours. Which meant when Vic squatted down and pulled her arm over his shoulder, she did little beyond a soft whine.

"Come on, Ms. Turley," Vic said. "I've got brownies downstairs for you."

"Not the brownies she likes," Alyssa muttered. "That popcorn was the extra-large tin, you know. It usually lasts her a week."

"I might have one or two in my apartment," Vic said as he grunted under the woman's weight. "I get the feeling that I'm going to need more control in the future, not less."

She looked in her brother's eyes and saw a growing maturity there. She hated that he was a…a whatever he was now. She didn't like the risk or the uncertainty. But she couldn't deny that the change had helped him grow up. He was acting more adult every second.

"Don't know why you wanted pot to help you laze around the house doing nothing. You've been doing that since you were eight," Alyssa said.

"Only because you kept picking at me. Play Barbies with me or I'll cry. Waah waah."

"Bullshit," she retorted, smiling as they bickered all the way downstairs. It felt normal. She and Vic had sniped at each other from birth. The fact that it was happening now was reassurance that life could get back to normal. She hoped.

They locked up Ms. Turley with a bottled water and a blanket. Vic brought her a brownie and Alyssa found the woman's purse and pulled out her phone. Five minutes later, Ms. Turley was streaming a romantic comedy and munching on brownies. She'd probably fall asleep halfway through the movie and be fine by morning.

Or at least that's what Alyssa told herself. They went back

upstairs while Alyssa considered suggesting Vic eat a brownie. Anything to counteract the effects of the tap water. But the moment they stepped into the laundromat, they both drew up short. Simon stood in the door frowning at the foam that covered a third of the floor. Beside him loitered Joey the accountant, as he unsuccessfully tried to hide his smirk.

The moment she entered, Simon's gaze snapped up to hers. She felt her face heat in embarrassment and her belly flutter in lust. Clearly, she'd turned into a teenage girl. Fortunately, any tendency toward girlie giggles were rapidly killed as he scanned her from head to toe in the most clinically detached way possible.

"You're all right." It wasn't a question.

"Yeah." She cut a glance at Vic, but he was already grabbing the mop, his face hidden as he spoke.

"The water is tainted," Vic said, completely deadpan.

"I believe I told you that."

"Actually," Alyssa cut in. "I texted that to him, but now we know for sure." She sighed. "And we've got Ms. Turley locked up downstairs. She's not a threat. In fact, she's high as a kite and as happy as someone who looks very doglike can be."

"Wolf DNA," Joey said, his tone filled with disgust.

Simon didn't appear to hear the sneer as he nodded. "We believe that whatever is in the water activates shifter DNA. If you don't have enough, you just feel sick."

"You get the Detroit Flu."

He nodded. "If you have more, then it activates and you become a kind of hybrid." His gaze was on Vic who stiffened, but didn't comment.

She started to move a washing machine over so that Vic could mop up all the foam. "What if you're already a shifter?"

Surprisingly, it was Vic who answered, his gaze coming to rest Simon and Joey. "You get amped up, don't you? I mean, I'm already a…a hybrid, but this is like bad E. I feel like I could go ten rounds against Ali. And I really, really want to."

Simon watched her brother, his expression flat. And the longer he held Vic's gaze, the more her brother flushed. Then suddenly her screwup of a sibling straightened into military correct posture, his shoulders back and his head lifted.

"I was an idiot, sir! I won't disobey orders again."

"See that you don't. Now clean up this mess."

Alyssa thought that her brother would argue, but he nodded sharply. "Yes, sir!" This must have been how he was in the army, and she had to say that the look was good on him. Meanwhile, Simon turned to Joey who was inspecting the empty tin of popcorn.

"Thanks for the ride, Joey—"

"Your mate's a drug dealer and yet you want to shut down our operation. Don't you think that's a bit hypocritical?"

Alyssa stiffened. She'd already pegged Joey as one of those holier-than-thou pricks who sneered at the poor. He probably had roots in a slum worse than this neighborhood, until a little bit of money and education had pulled his family out of the gutter. But instead of extending a hand to help a neighbor or a cousin, they focused on how much better they were than anyone else. And that set her back up.

"I run a laundromat, asshole—" she began, but Simon was there before her, rounding on the smaller man and stepping so close into the guy's personal space that Alyssa feared another brawl.

And yet when he spoke, he kept his voice coldly matter of fact.

"She is not my mate," he began. "And do not equate cannabis with what Nanook sold. They are not the same."

"They're all—"

"And do not interrupt."

Joey shut his mouth, but it was pulled into a sullen pout.

"The time for discussion is past."

"And when exactly was that?" Joey challenged.

"You made your case this afternoon. I have considered it and found it lacking." His tone made it clear that he found Joey lacking as well. A sentiment that Alyssa cheered. "You may go now."

Joey took a step back, but he was shaking his head as he moved. "You're not in Hicksville anymore," he sneered. "This is a mistake."

"Then it is mine to make." Simon glared down at the smaller man. "I expect a progress report by eight a.m. tomorrow."

"Which you won't be able to read."

Simon arched a brow, but he didn't argue. He didn't have to. He was acting as a military commander and expected obedience. Problem was, Joey wasn't a recruit. And he sure as hell hadn't been taught when to keep his mouth shut.

"You're making a mistake," he repeated as he took a step toward the door. "And she," he added, gesturing to at her with a dismissive wave, "is a disaster waiting to happen." Then he curled his lip. "Just hope you're not around when it all goes boom."

And with that, he stepped outside and disappeared.

"Fucking poser," Alyssa muttered when he was far enough away not to hear. "Are you sure you need him?"

"Yes. And he is not wrong. The cannabis is dangerous."

"What?" Her voice was sharp and angry. She'd noted that he hadn't claimed her as his girlfriend. Hell, he'd all but said they were nothing to each other and that had hurt so bad it had temporarily stolen her breath. So she'd buried it under a tide of righteous indignation. "Don't you dare lecture me on the evils of marijuana, you asshole. Set aside the real medical benefits, I've never had a problem with someone who was high. Drunks, on the other hand? They get into bar fights, beat their wives, and drive into minivans of kids." She made a wild gesture out the window. "Besides, I don't sell it. I just don't criminalize those who do."

He listened to her tirade with that infuriatingly flat expression. And when she paused to take a breath, he spoke.

"With the tensions out there, the cannabis dealer is a target."

"So are grocery stores. In fact, they're worse. Do you know how many shootings there were today? Seven. Do you hear me? Seven."

His mouth flattened. "Then you are in even greater danger." He looked out the window at Mrs. Garcia's house. "Her business will threaten yours."

She took a breath to rip into him. Part of her knew that he was right, but she was still smarting from the way he'd dismissed her before. From the fact that he was taking the poser's side instead of hers. From any lack of softness from him at all when she'd been tied in knots waiting to see him again. But before she could let any of it fly, he held up his hand.

"This is your choice. You will do with it what you will. I am tired, though. May I rest on your couch?"

He was tired? She was practically falling over from the work she'd done in the last two days. And good God, what was wrong with her? She'd turned into a screeching adolescent shrew. Except she wasn't screeching, thank God. She was holding her words and her thoughts inside. And when he stared at her calmly, clearly waiting for an answer, she had the wherewithal to nod once. Then she dug her house keys out of her pocket and tossed them to him.

It wasn't until he had left the room for her apartment that she realized Nanook's apartment was furnished again. She'd gotten the basics in there—all new—and he'd said yesterday that he would stay there. As alpha, that was his home and he needed to stay there until his position was established.

So why was he here?

The teenage girl inside her was spouting all sorts of romantic nonsense as an answer, but she was an adult woman. She knew that if she'd been more than a hot screw, then there'd be more of a connection between them. More tenderness or communication or something that wasn't issuing orders and a polite request to sleep on her couch.

And yet, she didn't want to believe she was nothing to him. She couldn't.

So she abruptly walked to her desk and wrote up a sign that she taped to the door.

Closed until further notice.
    Don't drink the water. It's tainted.

It likely wouldn't help, but at least she'd made an effort. Then she locked the door and turned to her brother.

"Can you finish in here?"

Vic nodded, but he sighed as he looked at her. "Don't push Simon. He doesn't work like normal people."

"What does that mean?"

"It means that he hates drama. And girlfriend drama is the worst kind."

"Didn't you hear him? I'm not his girlfriend."

"I heard." Vic started pushing the mop again. "But I don't think you did."

She wanted to curse her brother out for that. She wanted to tell him that he didn't know shit about what was happening between her and Simon. But she held back her words. Because obviously she didn't know shit, either. And it was past time for her to find out.

CHAPTER 18

Simon fell onto the couch with a sigh. He wanted a beer. Hell, he wanted to get blind stinking drunk, but that was never a good idea for a shifter. And besides, if he wanted to wipe out his brain function, all he had to do was go grizzly. In fact, that's exactly what he'd done ten months ago, and where had that gotten him? Ten months older and now without the skills needed to survive in Detroit.

He spent a few minutes with his eyes closed, remembering the bliss of wandering the UP as a bear. For ten months he'd slept, ate, and searched for a mate. No other thoughts on his mind, no other complications in his life.

He longed for that simplicity again, even though part of him sneered at the sheer uselessness of it. The world didn't need more bears shagging in the woods. It needed smart men who could control a fracturing group of grizzly-shifters. But hell, it was hard, dangerous work, and he feared he wasn't up to the task. He wasn't leaving. Not by any stretch of the imagination, but the task ahead was daunting. And though he felt like he'd found his purpose in life—leading the Griz—that didn't mean he'd be any good at it.

He heard Alyssa come in, and he kept his eyes closed, pretending to be asleep. He'd felt her reaction when he'd said she wasn't his mate. He'd known she was hurt and confused by everything that was happening, and he felt an ache deep inside at that. It was one of the reasons he was waxing nostalgic about being a bear. Grizzlies didn't worry about other people's feelings. They didn't think ahead about how dangerous marrying a shifter would be for a woman. They simply mounted when the female was willing and wandered off when they weren't.

"Quit the bullshit," Alyssa said. "I know you're awake."

He slowly opened his eyes.

"Look," she continued, "I'm not going to jump you. I just want to talk."

He arched a brow. Jumping would be okay with him.

"And I know how those words strike horror in men, but I mean it. Things have gone really fast lately, and it's hard for me to keep up. I just want, you know, clarification on some things."

He didn't respond. She was running this show and so he waited until she found her way to saying whatever was on her mind.

"Aren't you going to say anything?" she asked.

He sighed. Women could be so damned illogical. "You haven't asked a question yet."

She blew out a breath. "Right." Her tone conceded his point, but she was clearly frustrated. "Look, are you one of those one-night stand guys? I didn't think you were, but if you are, then it's okay. You've had me. We both enjoyed it. I just need to know that we're done. We can move on."

His head was lying backward against the couch, but at her words he lifted it off the cushions to stare at her. He looked at her fierce stance with her hands on her hips and her chin lifted. He saw the sweet shape of her breasts and the flare of her hips. Her wonderful nutty scent filled his nostrils and the sound of her tight breaths reminded him of other sounds she made, other times when her legs had been wrapped around his hips as she climbed to orgasm. These were constants whenever he looked at her and even when his eyes were closed, he remembered them. He relived them. He loved them.

Damn it, how could she not know that?

But obviously, she didn't, so he spread his legs, making the bulge in his crotch obvious. And in case she was missing it, he gestured. "Alyssa, I want you. I'll always want you."

She jolted at that, and her gaze dropped to where he was now throbbing with want. And then her hands slid off her hips and but her chin didn't lower. If anything, it tipped up a notch.

"So we're just fuck buddies? I don't do that, you know. Not even for you." Her voice trembled with the words, but he couldn't tell if it was the force of her conviction or because she wondered how he'd react.

"Do you know what it's like being married to a shifter? The animal comes out sometimes at night. We don't control it. It just happens, and suddenly you're in bed with a grizzly bear." Her eyes widened at that, but honestly forced him to admit the truth. "It's rare, but among strong shifters like me, it happens."

He leaned forward onto his knees, the weight of what he was saying feeling like it was pushing down between his shoulder blades. But he kept his head raised so he could look her in the eye. "I'm now alpha to a group of crazy urban bear-shifters. What the hell kind of nutcase chooses to be a bear in the city? They have to blow off steam, so they get into a war with the wolves because the dogs have to blow off steam, too. And why not run drugs or guns, too? It's dangerous and we can scare the shit out of normals by going all big and bad." He shook his head. "It's suicide driven by shifter madness and I'm in charge of them now. And I'll stay there until someone is bigger and badder, and he kills me."

She dropped to her knees before him. "That's not going to happen."

"Of course, that's how it happens! That's how shifters work."

She shook her head. "I was talking with Ryan some. You know, Detective Kennedy. He was explaining things about shifters and stuff. There are a couple million of you in the US alone. You have families and clans. All walks of life, too, like doctors and lawyers. You can't just be killing each other willy-nilly without the rest of us knowing. I don't believe it."

He nodded. "When there are places to run. When we can let loose on the animal side."

She gripped his thighs and he felt his groin pulse at the feel. She was so close, he could have her flipped over, stripped, and then be inside her before she would think to cry out.

"You're the most controlled person I've ever known. Even when you're wild, when you can't even talk, you never hurt me. You were more considerate than any lover I've ever had."

His nostrils flared at the idea that she'd ever had someone other than him, but he ruthlessly strangled the thought. It was uncivilized, and he was being civil right now. Which is why he didn't throw her down on the floor and eat her until she came all over his tongue.

"My mother left us because my father went grizzly and ripped apart the living room. He was horny and trying to mount her." He closed his eyes as he remembered. Simon had come home in the middle of it all and was able to tackle his father, though doing it as a scrawny teenager wasn't going to save anyone. So he went grizzly, too, and when it was done, half the house was destroyed. "She took my sister with her, and I've never seen either of them again."

"My God."

"We already knew I was a shifter. That's why she left me behind." He shrugged. "I don't blame her. Life with two grizzlies in the house was horrible. And dangerous." That's when he'd first started thinking about the military.

"Bullshit," she snapped. "Any woman who leaves her kid like that is wrong. Just…wrong."

She didn't get it. "She was terrified for her life. With good reason."

Alyssa nodded slowly. "Maybe. But even if that's true, you're not your father. That's not who you are."

"No. I'm in a more dangerous situation." He gestured over her shoulder at the outside window. "Joey's going to attack me soon. I give it a few days at most."

"What?" The word was sharp and loud.

"I may not be able to read words, but faces are becoming clearer by the second. He thinks I'm an illiterate hick. He's waiting for the right time to kill me, take over, and run the drugs himself." Simon snorted. "He has an undergraduate degree in business. He thinks that's all he needs to run an urban grizzly clan." The boy's idiocy would get him killed, but that didn't mean there wouldn't be collateral damage. He couldn't save Vic. Vic was a hybrid and therefore in the thick of this. But Alyssa didn't have to be. She was as vanilla as Betty Crocker.

"So you'll take care of Joey," she said.

He touched her cheek, loving the feel of every part of her skin. The feel, the color, the hills and valleys, and even the flaws. Because they were all her. "There's always a Joey. Always a Nanook."

"And you'll always be Simon." She pressed her hand to the back of his. Her words were gentle and there was such faith in her eyes that it cut at him. His mother had once looked at him that way. And then she'd grabbed his sister and taken off.

"You don't know the monster I can become."

She snorted. "You mean like ripping apart a grolar in front of me? Or shooting a drug dealer twice in the heart? Or how about when you spread me open on the bed and went in without a condom? Tell me, Simon, are you ever going to be worse than that?"

"My father was."

"I'm not in a relationship with your father." He felt the tension in her words. The implied question: Were they in a relationship?

"I don't want that life for you," he said, and he struggled to keep his tone level. "I don't want you to be afraid of me. Or of the life I will lead as the Griz alpha."

She tilted her head to the side. "I don't remember giving you control over my life or my choices. You're not my alpha."

He looked at her and saw that she meant every word. She wanted to be with him. She trusted and believed in him despite everything she'd seen, everything he'd done. That simple faith cracked open every wall he'd erected in his life. Every barrier he put between himself and the rest of the world tumbled down. And all he was left with was a yearning that screamed through his body, that hollowed out his belly and ached in his throat.

He wanted her faith. He wanted her love. And he needed it with a hunger that didn't understand boundaries or her choices. It was the kind of need that destroyed a living room. Or a family.

And so he brought out his last argument. The last barrier to a life she would end up hating.

"Have you thought about children?" he asked. "Shifter kids are hard to raise. They're impulsive and wild, and that's even if they don't shift. If they do, well, many don't survive the first change. There are instinctive needs and they hit at random when the hormones start flowing."

"I live in gang territory in Detroit. Kids are always in danger. And dangerous to others."

"How many friends have you lost?"

Her gaze skittered away. "Too many."

"You want to risk that with your own kids?" He dropped his forehead to hers. "A shifter adolescent in gang territory Detroit. The complications of that are astronomical." He shuddered at the very thought.

"Kids are always hard. One way or another." She lifted up until they were nose to nose. "If we get there—when we get there—we'll have decisions to make. Maybe we go live in the UP."

"I'm alpha of the Griz. It's the purpose I've been searching for since I left the military. I'm here until I'm killed."

If she paled at his words, he didn't see it. But he heard her breath catch and her heartbeat sped up. But she kept her body still and her eyes steady. "That's bullshit, and you know it. Once things stabilize, you can go on vacations. Our kids can take weekends and run off their animal stuff. We can go to the UP and still manage things back here."

She was seeing all the upsides. All the possibilities, and a logical man would acknowledge them. But even as he nodded, accepting her words, his mind replayed the day his mother had left. The fear in her eyes and the screams of his sister who didn't want to go. His mother had been a strong woman, too. She'd loved his father and him, but the shifter life had driven her away to the point that she'd left the man she loved and her only son. She'd run away and he couldn't blame her for it. It wasn't her fault. It was the shifter's fault, and he and his father both carried the gene.

"I'm afraid I will destroy you," he whispered. "And that would destroy me."

She cupped his cheeks in both her hands. She pulled his face up to hers and she pressed her lips to his. He clung to her then. Just his lips, but oh he reached for her with them, wanted to draw her close forever. But other than his mouth, he held himself back.

"Simon," she whispered. "I don't destroy so easily."

True. It was one of the things he most loved about her. She was strong and determined. She ran a successful business in Detroit. And she'd whipped her brother into shape when he'd probably fought her the whole time. She was damned strong, but he couldn't risk it. He wouldn't risk her. She was too special to destroy.

"You're locked in your head, Simon," she said as she straddled his lap. "You're seeing only the bad side."

"Someone has to."

"Okay. So you saw it. You told me. And your mother was a bitch. But I'm not going to let her weakness destroy us. I'm just not."

He huffed out a breath. "You don't know what you're asking for."

"Yeah, I do." She pressed another kiss to his lips. "I'm asking for you."

He shook his head. "I can't, Alyssa. You don't understand what it means."

She must have understood the importance of what he said. She must have felt the tension in his body because she stilled. Then she straightened up until she could look directly into his eyes. "We don't have to decide anything tonight. It's late. We're both tired. If all we do is a repeat of yesterday, a coming together—"

He gripped her arms and tried to hold her back. But he didn't have the strength, so he tried to use words. "It's not like last night. Then I needed you to bring me back. To show me..." Love. "Tenderness. Gentleness."

"Yes," she said. "And—"

"And I don't need that now. I'm not in that place now."

She smiled. "That's good—"

"There's a thing we do, Alyssa. There's a thing shifters do sometimes." He grimaced. He'd never understood it before, but now he felt it. To the depths of his bones, he knew exactly what was going on. And it terrified him.

"You mean besides going furry?"

He looked her in the eyes and said the words. "We lock on to a mate. It's one-sided, Alyssa, but it's all consuming. We lock on to a mate and we don't let go."

Her lips curved into a soft smile. "That sounds nice."

"Really? You ready to commit to me for life, Alyssa? Because I'm already half locked on. If we do this now, if I put myself inside you again..." He thrust up against her groin for emphasis. "If I do that, I'll lock in completely. I won't let you go no matter what you want. You won't have a say in the matter, and when it's bad..." He swallowed, but forced himself to go on. "When it's really bad, you won't get a say in anything."

It took a moment for his words to sink in. He wanted to leave it alone. To let those words be enough. But she had to see where he could go.

"Think of the worst stalker tales you've ever heard of. Those were shifters."

She jerked back from him, and his hands tightened instinctively, keeping her exactly where she was.

"That's bullshit," she rasped. "They can't all have been crazy shifters."

"True. But enough were. Enough that you need to think very carefully. Do you want to commit to me now? For life? If not, then you better leave right now."

She blinked at him. "What are you saying?"

He huffed out a breath. "I'm half mated with you right now. It's the grizzly half, but the human part isn't far behind. It's going to see you as mine no matter what you want, how you want it, or anything. You'll be mine and I won't give you up. Ever."

Her eyes narrowed and her cheeks flushed. She was thinking romantically, and yeah, that was definitely there. But there was a darker side. A stalker side.

"You have to be ready to take me forever right now. Or you need to give me distance and I'll slow this down." He took a breath and forced his hands to release her. "Decide."

CHAPTER 19

Alyssa blinked, her mind reeling. She was straddling his lap, her core already wet as he ground against her. But this time when he tightened his thighs, she lifted up to gain some distance.

"You're saying I have to choose now? You for life or not at all? That's crazy. We've been together for what? Twenty hours?"

He swallowed and she could feel him struggling to control himself. His muscles were tight with tension and his eyes seemed to burn into hers. But when he spoke, he kept his voice level.

"That's the way it is with my kind. We just lock in. And when we do, it's for life."

"So I have to pick, right now." It wasn't a question, she was just repeating his words until they made sense to her. "Or you'll what? Stalk me? Lock me in a basement somewhere?"

He closed his eyes and breathed through his nose. "I'm trying to give you a choice, Alyssa. I'm afraid it may already be too late."

God, he was serious. How many nights had she gone to sleep imagining this? Not this conversation, but him telling her he loved her. He needed her. And could they be together forever? Except that wasn't what he was saying. He was telling her he'd stalk her if she refused him. Unless she bolted now.

Which is when she figured out the truth. And once she understood, she didn't hold back.

"You are so full of shit."

He reared back, startled enough that he bared his teeth. But she didn't give him the chance to talk. Instead she started ticking off his excuses on her fingers.

"You're an animal. Your mother left you because you're a bear. The Griz are coming to kill you. You're a crazy stalker. Have I missed anything? Hell, Simon, you've pulled out every excuse you can think of to push me away. What's next? You don't put down the toilet seat down? What a load of crap!"

She pushed back from her position. It took some time, especially since his hands were gripping her thighs like vises. But she forced the issue and he released her. Even as the air between them cooled, her heart was hammering in her throat.

"I want you," she said even though she was still backing away. "The whole thing. Church wedding and kids. I want to raise a family the way I'm raising up this building and maybe even the neighborhood. One upgrade at a time. One family at a time."

He swallowed, his gaze wary. "I might be able to do that," he said softly. "Many of my kind do."

"But I have to decide now? Doesn't that feel a little crazy to you?" She leaned into his space. "I thought you didn't feel for me. You denied our relationship, said I was your assistant—"

"I was trying to give you space. Time to decide—"

"Bullshit. You're running scared. Because this is happening so fast and neither of us can keep up. So you're trying to scare me away."

His cheeks flushed and she knew she had scored a hit. But his jaw was locked hard and a moment later, he pinned her with an angry glare.

"The danger is real," he said.

"I know!" And she did. But that wasn't going to send her running from the most amazing man she'd ever met. "And yeah, I might have to think a while about it. You know, after things settle down. But I've handled everything so far and haven't turned tail. So why are you?"

His expression tightened and his gaze slid away. "My father locked in on my mother young. She was only seventeen. That's rare, but he's a strong shifter and it happened. She didn't know anything about shifters, but he pursued her like she was nirvana. He was devoted to her. Desperate as only my kind can get. And in the end, he bowled her over."

His voice was hoarse as he spoke, and she knew he was talking from a place of fear because he wouldn't meet her eyes. So she settled on the coffee table and tried to listen with both her heart and her eyes. "That sounds nice. Like he…um…loved her."

He softened his tone. "It was love, I think. He loved her obsessively, at least. But she was young and timid." He shook his head. "She had no idea how to stare down a bear and win." His expression turned bleak. "He terrified her."

She touched the back of his hand and it felt like ice. "She couldn't have been that scared. She had two kids with him. You were a teenager when she finally left."

He nodded. "There were good times, but then Dad lost his job.

Started drinking." He glanced at her. "Alcohol is a bad idea for shifters. Always."

"Because they lose control. But you don't need to be half bear to be an asshole drunk."

He looked at his hands. "She left and nobody blamed her. Not even my dad. But it destroyed him. He couldn't find her and that made him insane. She must have been planning it for a while." He leaned back against the couch, his body tense even though he seemed to flop there. It was in the way his hands clenched on his thighs and his neck tightened as if he were forcing out the words.

"You're afraid I'm going to bail like she did. I'm not. Because you're not your drunken father. And I'm nothing like your mother."

She wanted to touch him, to hold him. Except the moment she started to lift off the coffee table, he stopped her.

"Don't," he said and there was enough pain in his voice that she froze.

"But—"

"You can't. Not until you decide." He looked at her, pain in his eyes. "I need to know you're not going to change your mind."

She stared at him, anger mixing with all the other emotions churning inside her. The man was giving her an ultimatum. Stay forever or don't touch me at all. They'd been together for less than two days. Fortunately, she could focus on her anger and not face the fact that she hadn't exactly bared her soul either.

"I don't know how you can be so incredibly strong and so whiny at the same time!" she huffed.

His head snapped up at her tone and his brows drew together. Good. Let him get pissed. Let them have a good rip-roaring fight because that was better than this quiet agony. But he wasn't a man to break easily. He didn't speak, so she poked at him again.

"You've got everything Simon. You're smart, powerful, and you just got control of a clan of bear-shifters. And yet you sit there miserable because you can't decide what you want. Boo-hoo, it's a dangerous life. Boo-hoo, I'm a dangerous man."

"I'm trying to protect you," he growled.

She was getting to him. Good. She pushed harder.

"I don't need your protection! I make my own choices. And here it is: I'm not committing to a man who's too afraid to say he loves me."

His eyes widened and his jaw worked. It took him two tries before words came out. And when they did, they were so hot, they burned her with hunger, with fear, and with flat out lust.

"I want you, Alyssa. Because you fight me and you don't run. Because you're sexy and smart. But you're so fucking stubborn, too! You run your own business, you run your own brother, and you're not going to surrender to me easily. You're going to tease me and drive me fucking crazy while I pant after you. But I'm dangerous, Alyssa. And I'm alpha to a dangerous clan. And if you push me any harder, I'm going to take you and never let you go. Is that what you want? Is it?"

Yes. A thousand times, yes. But damn it, he hadn't said he loved her. She knew it was stupid of her, but she wanted love. She'd had men after her before. Rich ones, smart ones, slick ones. She'd refused them all because they'd loved themselves way more than they loved her. She needed Simon to love her because she already knew she was head over heels for him. She had been for years.

But there wasn't any softness in him now. No tenderness that gave her hope that he had such an emotion in him. He was all logic and brutal animal necessity. It wasn't like she was asking for candy and roses. The words would be enough, but only if he said them.

So she took a deep breath. She smelled his scent, felt his heat, and let the strength of her desire make her bold.

"Do you love me, Simon?"

His eyes widened in surprise and maybe yearning. He stared at her while her heart thrummed in her throat. "Alyssa—" he began, but her name was drowned out.

A boom reverberated through the building. An explosion that made her furniture jump and her body reel. It tore through her body and his, but he was the one who reacted. His head jerked up even as his hands kept her steady. And then he abandoned her to rush to the door.

"Simon?"

"Get your gun."

CHAPTER 20

Shifting gears had never been easy for Simon. If he was in the middle of an intense relationship discussion with Alyssa, it would take something significant to jolt him into a fighting place. Something like a bomb going off in the laundromat. Still, his mind lurched as it tried to realign into tactical thinking. What he really wanted to do was grab Alyssa and run to the nearest bolt hole where they could finish what they were doing.

But as the acrid scent of gunpowder and smoke hit his nostrils, he knew that wasn't possible. So he rushed to the door and ordered Alyssa to get her gun.

She switched mental gears faster than he did. He saw her blanch and then nod. And while he was quietly slipping open her front door to see what was out there, she returned to his side with her gun and a grim expression.

"What—" she began, but he cut her off with the answers she needed.

228 Kathy Lyons

"I think that was a bomb," he said softly. "How many other people in the building?"

"Um, a couple dozen, give or take." Then she held up her phone. "I'll call 911 and—"

He shook his head. "Call Detective Kennedy. Then get those people down here to go out your bedroom window." It was opposite the fire, but more important, it was nearest the dumpster and other cover. "Tell them there are snipers at the doors. They have to go out here."

"Snipers!" she gasped.

"Maybe."

He watched her put it together in the time it took her to blink twice. Sure, it was possible that something had gone wrong in the laundromat. Or that this was random bad luck. But it was way more likely that Joey was making his move. With the quarantine, the cops were stretched thin. Perfect time to stage an attack on a cash business and be pretend sad when Simon was killed in the crossfire. Damn it, the man had even tipped his intention when he left, saying that he hoped Simon wasn't inside when everything went boom. Why hadn't he guessed that the bastard would act quickly and without care for the innocents in the building?

He had to get Alyssa far away from him. That was the safest place for her. He eased the apartment door open again. The smoke was thick, but no more than before. And he could hear a couple people hitting something hard in the laundromat. Probably trying to break into the vending machines to gather whatever money they could find. That meant if there was a fire, it was contained. But he still couldn't take that risk.

He was about to dash forward when he saw a dark figure coming down the hallway. That was the last thing he needed to lock him into fighter mode. Someone was coming for Alyssa.

The grizzly in him stirred and pressed forward with murderous intent. It knew how to protect a mate. But Simon kept it locked down. He needed to think, not be a huge furry target. So he suppressed the claws that tried to burst through his fingers and though his mouth was pulled back to show his teeth, he didn't grow a snout. He'd wait. The figure was slipping closer.

Another foot and he'd be able to kill him.

Six inches…

One…

"Vic!" Alyssa whispered.

Vic?

Yes.

Simon reached out and hauled the man inside. He came with a gasp and a struggle, but Simon was quick to muzzle him with a hand over his mouth. Then he leaned in and whispered, "Quiet. It's me."

Vic stopped struggling immediately and Simon dropped his hold. They both had their adrenaline amped and their hearts racing, but a quick look told him Vic was human and under control.

"What did you see?" Simon asked Vic.

"Smoke through the laundromat, but there are people in there. Robbing the place."

"Fuckers," Alyssa cursed. Vic ignored her.

"If we leave them alone, think they'll just take the vending machine money and leave?"

He wanted to say yes. He wanted to reassure Alyssa, but he knew it wasn't true. "If they were just thieves, they would have broken the door and robbed in quiet. These guys made a big, bad boom to get everybody running outside where they can be picked off one by one."

Alyssa frowned. "But why kill my tenants?"

"Just a few. Cover for when they shoot me. That way it's not a shifter revolt; it's an accident because of a psycho. A shifter killing his alpha gets attention, but a random crazy person…"

"Is just crazy," she murmured.

Vic's eyes widened. "The Jacksons are already headed out. And Mrs. Cooper. They were in the hall—"

Alyssa shouldered forward. "I got them. I know what to do."

Simon's heart lurched at that. His brave woman pushing forward like the boldest army ranger. He had to stop himself from grabbing her back. But she was safer away from him, so he stepped aside.

"Vic, go with her. Guard her six."

"No. It's not me they want." That was Alyssa, her voice hard and quiet. Then she looked at her brother and the two communicated something silently. It was quick and intense, and though Simon didn't understand how it worked, he could see when Vic locked into her opinion.

"She's right," Vic said. "I'm your beta. My place is with you, guarding your six."

Simon didn't like it. Hell, everything in him rebelled at it. He wanted his mate safe, and he sure as hell didn't fight with a team. But the military had drummed that particular idiocy out of him. They needed to end the mastermind behind this attack. And that would require stealth and coordination. Much easier done with a partner.

So he bowed to the logic of the situation, though he still hated it.

Worse, they were out of time. He could hear people upstairs coming out of their apartments.

"I've got this," Alyssa said, and he nodded.

"Go fast and quiet. And be careful."

"Roger that," she said. Then she flashed a quick grin. "I've always wanted to say that." Before he could manage to process her humor, she was slipping out and down the hallway. Which meant he had to focus on what he needed to do.

"Got any rope, Vic? Mountain-climbing equipment? Something?"

"Yeah, in my apartment." Then Vic nodded his understanding. "You want up on the roof."

"I need to see what's going on."

"This way."

Vic led as they eased out of Alyssa's place and up the stairs to the second floor. All of Simon's senses had been attuned to where Alyssa went ahead, whispering to people on the stairs, and sending them toward her apartment. He wanted to protect her, but he needed to trust in her strength. She was calm and smart. She'd be fine so long as he kept Joey away from her.

But he had to find the bastard first, assuming this wasn't just a random robbery. So he crept after Vic and tried to listen to the sounds coming out from the laundromat. Even in the stairwell, he could hear coins tumbling on the ground. Guess they'd broken at least one machine. Then a voice, muffled and faint from the distance.

"Hurry your asses up. I told you five minutes, no more."

He knew that voice. It wasn't Joey's, as he expected, but someone else he'd talked to recently. One of the shifters.

Hell. He paused, wondering if he should burst in there and take the bastard out now, and then look for Joey. But there were too many unknowns. And a ton of people still in the building.

Best to stick to the plan.

He followed Vic up the stairs, stopping another three from running toward the front door. Whispered communication sent them scrambling for Alyssa's bedroom window. And then they were upstairs in Vic's quarters.

His place was surprisingly organized. Messy, for sure, but in controlled areas. That corner for papers and books. That corner for entertainment of all kinds.

"All the climbing gear is in the hall closet," Vic said as he gestured. Simon was already there pulling out rope and equipment when he realized Vic was running water in the kitchen. Even though he knew the answer, Simon spun around and demanded an explanation.

"What are you doing?"

Vic put a full glass of tap to his lips, pausing long enough to say, "Gearing up."

"Negative!" Simon snapped. "I don't need you drugged up and smelling to high heaven. I need you thinking."

Vic paused, but he didn't put the glass down. "I'm a better fighter as a hybrid. Stronger. We don't have a gun. We'll have to fight hand to hand."

Simon snorted. "Bullshit. You always have a gun. Where is it?"

Vic sighed. "Locked up behind the desk in the laundromat. You know, where the bad guys are right now."

Great. So now they had well-armed bad guys. "I still don't want you amped up."

Vic grimaced but set down his glass. "You're the boss."

Just then another boom rocked the building and that one hit the foundations. He could feel it in the way it concussed around them. Vic knew it too because his expression tightened. He stopped arguing and grabbed the gear. They both knew that whomever was doing this was making sure the building came down around everyone's ears.

Then it was back into the hallway. One sniff told him that Alyssa was up here, too. Then he heard her bang on someone's door.

"Mr. Pinero, it's Alyssa. You need to come out. I know it's scary, but there's a fire in the building. Mr. Pinero."

She banged again and Simon pivoted, intending to help her. But one step in her direction, and she abruptly waved him back.

"I've got this!" she hissed. And apparently she did because right then the door swung open and she jerked back. "Mr. Pinero!" she said with a shaking voice. "You've got your…um…blunderbuss. Okay. Just point it to the ground as we get out."

Even in this chaos, his heart warmed with pride. These were Alyssa's people and she knew how to lead them. He had to let her do her job while he attended to his. So he turned and followed Vic up to the roof. They were stopped two more times by others who needed to be told not to go through the front doors. It was a measure of how scary life had become that no one argued at the possibility of snipers. They just nodded grimly and headed downstairs.

By the time they made it up to the roof, Simon could smell the acrid scent of smoke. The building was on fire, all right. The laundromat was likely a gaping hole right now, and it pained him that Alyssa's building was going to be destroyed because of him. Worse, they both heard the pops of gunfire. They had no idea who was shooting where and didn't have time to figure that out as Vic eased open the roof door. As soon as it was cracked far enough, Simon slipped through.

And just as he expected, someone was waiting right there for whomever came up. It was a young man who smelled of sweat and aggression. The BO was thick, indicating he was a hybrid, but he wasn't in control. Which made it easy enough for Simon to end him. If there'd been more time, he might have tried to simply knock the kid out, but the hybrid was ferocious.

Once the hybrid was down, they made a quick circuit of the roof. No one else was up here, but looking down gave them a wealth of information.

The building was on fire, and there were people down at the front and back of the building. People who obviously hadn't met up with one of them or simply hadn't listened. They didn't look dead, thank God. Just wounded as they crawled to lie beside cars in the parking lot.

A quick look to the side where Alyssa's window stood showed a couple people slipping out and running hard for the safety of the dumpster. It didn't appear that anyone had seen them yet, and that was good news. Simon picked out the likely places where the snipers were hiding. Thanks to the city light and the moon, they were pretty easy to spot. None of them was trained, and most of them were too hopped up to remain still. They danced on their feet, adjusted around cars, and one even hit the roof of a car in glee when he shattered a second story window. Apparently, he was bored with waiting for targets and was now just shooting out windows.

That was good for the people still running to the dumpster, but bad for Simon who intended to rappel down a wall. The last thing he needed was for that bastard to look up.

He needed to pick his best point of attack. He wouldn't do anyone any good if he was shot while descending from the roof. But at
that moment, he ran out of time.

There was a shout as someone bellowed, "Over there!"

They'd seen the fleeing people. He heard Alyssa scream, "Run!"
and then Vic cursed as another boom rocked the building.

Shit. Things were going south fast. Which meant he'd have to
do his best with what little intel he had. So he pointed to a spot
on the wall. It was to the side of most of the action, then gestured
to Vic. Without another word, he secured his tether and leapt. He
didn't wait for Vic, and he sure as hell didn't slow his descent until
the last possible second. This was about speed.

He landed on the top of a carport with a thud that would be
heard by anyone who was listening. Then he stripped off the rope
and dashed over the side, dropping down to sprint across the parking lot. Someone did see him. The ping of a bullet hit nearby, but by
the time he registered it, he was already across the lot and starting
his own hunt.

More shots. Same shooter. He zeroed in on it and began an
oblique approach. He glanced behind him once, hoping to see
Vic coming in safely behind him. He would have heard the drop
if the man had fallen, but sirens sounded in the distance and
so he might have missed it. Fortunately, he saw his friend slipping in beside him with a nod. *Damn.* Vic wasn't even winded.
Which meant he'd either been working out more than he ever
had in the military or he was a lot stronger now that he was a
hybrid.

Either way, it was a good thing and Simon gestured to coordinate.

A moment later, he came up behind a thick man with ugly tats who stank of the taint in the water. He was jittery and uncontrolled. Simon took him out. Vic handled his partner.

Meanwhile more people had spotted them. Shouts came from either side. All variations on, "The bastard's over there!"

Confirmation that the bad guys were looking for him. Simon zipped around another car and crouched to see who was coming. He hated this urban warfare crap. A thousand ways to patrol and evade in trees surrounded by natural scents. But this was cars, brick buildings, and the stench of exhaust. He made it work though and he and Vic steadily advanced to where he guessed the shooter was.

Next came the guys who had raided the laundromat. He knew that from the clink of coins in their pockets and the smell of explosives. They went down too easily.

Too late he realized that they'd been the bait. He'd barely turned away from the thieves when a shifter attacked. It was the one who had spoken in the laundromat, and now he remembered the bastard's name. Richard Howell. Plumber who smelled like beer and sewage. And amped-up testosterone.

He clocked Simon with the butt of a sawed-off shotgun and Simon careened against a car hood. Vic was too far away fighting another shifter, and the air was suddenly filled with stench. Vic had gone monster, but Simon didn't have the time to pray that the man kept it under control. He was busy recruiting all his strength to roll off the car hood and defend himself. He had enough time to see that Dick was aiming the weapon straight at him and there wasn't room to duck away.

He kicked up some gravel. It was his only hope as he dove to the side. And then the weapon went off with a deafening roar. Simon tensed, waiting for the impact, but none came. It took him a moment to realize that someone else had come up from behind and knocked Dick over. The shotgun had discharged too high and that saved Simon's life.

Squinting, Simon saw an elderly black man with a very wide grin on his frail body. He'd used an old-style weapon as a club and was now raising it again just as Dick was coming around with fists the size of hams.

Simon leapt to attack this time. And if he'd been holding back before—trying to knock unconscious rather than kill—he let it all loose now. This bastard was a shifter who had sworn loyalty just yesterday. By shifter law, Simon had the right to do whatever he wanted to the asshole. And so he did.

He took out Dick's throat. Just swiped hard and fast while letting the tiniest part of his grizzly through. The part that had really sharp claws. Then he spun in a crouch. Vic had finished with his attacker, and they both looked about them. Where was everybody?

Then the old man spoke. "I think that was the last of 'em." There was clear glee in his tone.

"There were more," Simon said.

"Yup. We got 'em. Damned punks."

The man pointed and Simon saw some older men and women, at least three he recognized from the hallway, standing their ground and looking fierce. The youngest had to be sixty, but they were determined. And they all brandished weapons of some sort. Though Mr. Pinero's was the oldest.

"Is that a real blunderbuss?" he asked. He'd thought Alyssa had been making a joke.

"Yup. Been passed down from my four-great-grandfather."

He grinned. He couldn't help it. He'd never thought a blunderbuss would save his life. But even so, his mind was clicking through the possibilities. He hadn't found Joey yet, and he needed to find Alyssa. Though if he had to guess—

"Simon!"

A chill went down his spine. That was Joey's voice calling loud enough to be heard over the sirens. He spun to look and saw the bastard at the corner of the neighboring building. It was a single family home with an unkempt yard and a chain link fence around the back and far side. Joey stood in the light of a single yellow porch light and he had Alyssa in a choke hold, a gun to her head. And worse, on the opposite side of Alyssa stood another of his shifters, this one the brown bear.

With extraordinary luck, he could take out one before they killed her. No way could he handle both. Which meant Alyssa was dead.

CHAPTER 21

Stupid, stupid, stupid!

Alyssa damned herself for being an idiot. She'd brought her youngest tenants to safety—a pair of four-year-old twins—was coordinating with Detective Kennedy, and watching her home and her life savings literally go up in smoke. But she couldn't see Simon, and that ate at her. Also, her older tenants might be fierce in mind, but frail in body. She let them cover her retreat while she was hauling the twins, but now it was time to make sure they made it to safety, too.

So as soon as she could, she handed off her phone to one of the mothers and headed back toward the building. Then the shots had started and she freaked. Nothing stopped the images of Simon bleeding on the ground from parading through her brain. His flesh torn open, his eyes glazing as he struggled for his last breath. She couldn't block the thoughts and so she'd rushed when she should have been careful.

The asshole caught her just rounding the corner of the neighboring building. Her gaze had been on the parking lot as she searched for Simon. The gun had been lax in her hand, her attention too far away. Joey disarmed her before she even knew he was there. And then she was pressed against the building with his arm across her throat as he buried his nose against her temple.

His inhale was loud and disgusting. Worse was the way he pulled back with a sneer.

"He mated you," he spat. "A pot dealer in a better-off-dead suburb."

"We can't all be born in alligator shirts and ugly chinos." No sense in telling him she didn't deal pot. He wasn't listening.

But he was damn fast.

He backhanded her. Quick and harsh. Her head slammed back against the wall and her cheek burned. But that was all she needed to move her fear into an icy cold rage. It cleared her mind and brought with it every self-defense tactic she'd ever learned. And a few that were all about maiming her assailant permanently.

But she never got the chance.

He was a great deal bigger than she was and he had her pinned against a brick wall. Right when she was about to slam on his instep, he spun her around and shoved her face-first into the brick. And he held her there with his weight and his minty Altoid breath while someone came up beside them to report.

"We've got a problem."

"No shit, Sherlock. Who thought a bunch of old geezers could fight?"

Good for them. She hoped her friends had killed every single one of his henchmen. Just like she was going to do to him the second he gave her a chance.

That came a moment later when he turned to look over his shoulder at the building. She didn't have much leverage, but damn she could head butt like nobody's business. Or in this case rear her head back and try to break his nose.

It didn't work. Or at least not as well as she'd wanted. She nailed him but not hard enough.

"Ow! You fucking bitch."

She tried to squirm away, but his hold on her didn't ease. And then he was pissed enough to slam her head forward again hard enough to make her see stars. Strangely enough it was the other guy who spoke reason.

"You can't kill her," the guy said. "They're mated. He'll kill us for sure."

"He's going to try. And that's just what we want."

Alyssa wanted to argue that she and Simon weren't mated, but her face was pressed too hard against the brick. And she also guessed that she was the only one who cared about the distinction.

"But—" began the other guy.

"Shut up and do what I tell you. Find out who's left."

Bad guy bickering. God, could it get any worse?

She shouldn't have even thought the question because a moment later, her biggest fear came true. First, they had to wait while the henchman tried to phone their buddies. No response, which made Alyssa all kinds of happy inside. But before she could make any snide comments, Joey zip-tied her wrists behind her back then spun her around. His choke hold was tight enough, but then she felt the hard press of metal against her temple.

She would have fought. Hell, she tried. But he was bigger and stronger. Worse, his forearm was so tight against her throat, it was all she could do to draw breath.

"Stand on that side," he ordered his man. "The minute you can, shoot him." Then he marched her into the narrow circle of yellow porch light and started bellowing for Simon.

It didn't take long for him to appear. He stood in the shadows beside an old minivan, and she scanned every inch of him looking for bullet holes. Thankfully there weren't any, but there sure as hell was blood on his clothes and a murderous look on his face.

But he didn't move and he sure as hell didn't speak. Thank God because where he stood was too protected for the asshole to get off a shot. And though she strained to get enough breath to warn Simon, she never got the chance. It was all she could do to get enough air to keep from passing out.

"Come out, you illiterate hick," Joey bellowed. "You've got a decision to make."

Don't move, she thought as loud as she could. *Don't fall for it.*

She shouldn't have worried. When Simon got pissed, he got super rational, super cold. And at that moment, she was extremely grateful that he could shut off his emotions like a faucet. Meanwhile, she saw Vic step into the shadows on the opposite side of the minivan. His face was monstered up, but he seemed to be in complete control of himself. Good. Though it was bad that they were way too far away to save her.

And then Joey kept talking, his voice chilling in that he sounded bored and impatient. Like a kid in a Starbucks line rather than a guy threatening murder. "You know I just want you. You're not fit to lead the Griz. So step out from that car and I'll take care of it. Otherwise, she dies. And you still die a moment later."

Where the hell were the police? And fire department? She'd heard the sirens. But in Detroit, they might just as easily be responding to a freeway pileup. And this wasn't exactly an area of town anyone rushed to. But still…

"Last chance."

It was those words that made up her mind. There was no rescue coming for her. Joey had his weapon pressed to her temple. And the other bastard had his gun out, pointed at Simon. She was dead for sure. At least she could try to save the man she loved.

Especially since Simon was moving. He was coming out into the light, but damn it, no way was she going to let him do that.

She took a moment to mouth the truth. She didn't even have breath to put sound to it. Her lips shaped the words, "I love you," and she prayed Simon saw it. Either way, there was no more time.

She went completely limp.

She'd once babysat a child who did that to her. Whenever she went to pick up the kid to force him do to what she wanted, the boy went completely boneless. Dead weight. Spaghettilike limbs. He would slide right out of her grasp.

She did that now and though she didn't think it would save her from the bullet, it would at least distract the maniacal asshole for the moment it would take for Simon to do whatever Simon was going to do. Especially if the bastard thought she'd passed out from lack of oxygen.

It worked.

Joey cursed and tightened his grip, but she was spaghetti. She kept repeating that in her brain. A limp noodle. See how good he was at holding up dead pasta with one arm.

He wasn't. But he also wasn't bothering with her. Suddenly, he dropped her on the ground and started shooting. The other guy, too, and she had a split second of complete shock that she was free. But then she began fighting. She kicked. She punched. If it was near her, it was a bad guy and she was going to give it pain.

She fouled their footing and got kicked in the chest for her trouble. She landed a solid blow on the henchman's knee and he went down with a curse. And still the deafening explosions above her until there was a wet splat. And silence.

Hell, the booming was still echoing in her head, so the silence seemed to pound on her. And she was still hitting Joey the bastard even as he crumpled before her. Didn't matter. He wasn't going to hurt Simon. He...He...

He didn't have a face. Or at least not a recognizable one. And there was blood everywhere.

Oh shit.

She didn't have enough time to process anything but that sight when suddenly she was scooped up again, this time from behind. Strong arms wrapped around her and she began to struggle, but a voice she recognized was murmuring her name.

"Alyssa Alyssa Alyssa Alyssa."

Over and over as if it were one word.

Simon. Whole and strong as he carried her away.

She held on to him. She gripped his shoulders and buried her face in his neck. She shuddered against him even as she felt the steady tempo of his feet as he carried her far away. He was here. He was holding her. And they were both miraculously alive.

They were nearly two blocks away before she lifted her head. His breath was heaving like a freight train but his pace hadn't slackened. And she knew it was time for him to stop.

"Simon," she said against his ear. "Simon, you have to stop."

He didn't. But he did tighten his hold on her. She squeezed back, but she kept talking to him.

"I'm fine. I'm fine, but you have to set me down. You're going to kill us both running like this. Simon, I'm fine." And she had to see if he was fine, too. "Let me touch you. Let me know that you're okay."

"Alyssa. Alyssa. Alyssa." Except instead of coming out as one word, her name came out as heaving exhales. Gasped as he tried to run.

"Simon," she said. Then she pressed her mouth to his.

He couldn't breathe like that. Neither could she. But she kept licking his lips until he came back to himself. Until the steady pound of his feet slowed. Until he pressed her against the siding of someone's home and held her there while he breathed.

And still she whispered to him. "I'm fine. Are you okay? Are you hurt?"

"Alyssa."

One last time. Spoken with a finality that told her he was calm now. Or at least more rational.

"Are you hurt?" she asked again.

"No. You?"

He was patting her down as he spoke, checking for wounds. His touch was frantic, but thorough, and she let him do it mostly because she could see how he moved, too. She watched for where he was tentative or jerky. She looked for scrapes or bruises and found a few, but none that was deep. Same for him as he touched her face. He probed gently at the swelling on her jaw and temple, but she covered his hand with hers.

"I've gotten worse playing basketball with Vic."

"You're safe now. He's dead."

She jerked. "Vic? Vic's dead?"

"What? No. Vic's fine. Joey's dead."

She winced at the memory that flashed through her mind. But with it came a huge wave of relief.

"I'm sorry," he said as he stroked her cheek. "I'm sorry you had to see that. That he—"

"Don't care about the visual," she said. "Glad that he's gone." Then she stretched up to place a kiss on his mouth. "Thank you."

"Wasn't me. Vic grabbed the gun off the thieves. They would have noticed if I had one."

She chuckled. Trust Simon to correct the details. "Doesn't matter. You saved me, and I—"

He kissed her. Hard. Fast. Thoroughly. She returned it a thousand-fold and soon they were panting for another reason. But then he pulled back and she held onto his shoulders to keep herself steady.

"You're mine now," he said. "You know that right? You said you loved me. I saw it, and now you're mine. Mated. *Mine.*"

So he had seen. She was glad. So glad that she said it again. "I love you. I always have. And I'm glad we're mated or whatever—"

Her words were lost in another desperate kiss. It was like he was trying to imprint himself on her. Or her on him. It didn't matter. They were together.

But then he slowed. Eventually he stopped as they separated to breathe. And in the quiet, she spoke the question that had been hovering in the back of her mind. The one she'd tried before but they'd been interrupted. But now, after what they'd just been through, she couldn't imagine not knowing the answer.

"Do you think, Simon, that maybe…you know…" Lord, it

wasn't like her to get tongue tied, and he clearly knew it. He drew back with a frown.

"What?"

She took a deep breath and forced the words out. "Do you think you could love me, too? In time?"

He stared at her, his face expressionless. Then his eyes widened in shock as he dropped his forehead to hers. And then the most amazing sound came out. A chuckle. A low chuckle that turned into a laugh.

"Simon?"

He sobered at that, but he was still smiling as he answered. "I thought you understood. Mating is love. Think of the most amazing feeling you've ever had. Like, I don't know, the first time you tasted ice cream or had a really good orgasm. That full body tingle that comes with intense pleasure."

She frowned. Okay, so she understood that. But that wasn't love in the way she was thinking. But before she could express that, he continued.

"Mating is like that only with need underneath. And it's hunger, desire, and lust, too. But it's also the kind of love that lasts for decades while kids and grandkids and great grandkids come around. That's what finding your mate is like."

She stared at him, shock echoing through her soul. He loved her like that? She didn't think that was possible, not in the short time they'd been together. But she saw it in his eyes. He really felt like that. About her.

"What if it doesn't work out between us?"

"I'll still love you, but from a distance. If that's what you really want." His voice broke on that, but she didn't doubt his words.

"What if I get Alzheimer's or go crazy?"

"I'll care for you every day. And I'll love you every moment."

She shook her head. "That's crazy. You can't have formed a bond like that already."

He grinned. "I can. I have. And don't think you can run away and it will fade. It won't. This is locked in now. It's done. And…" He took a deep breath. "I really hope you meant it when you said you loved me."

She smiled. "Of course, I did. I do. I love you." She was prepared this time for his kiss, but she lifted her hand up to stop him. She didn't want to get distracted again. Not just yet.

"Simon, wait!"

He froze, his entire body expectant.

"Could you maybe say the words back to me? Just once?"

He blinked then grinned. "I love you, Alyssa. I love everything about you. And I'm going to love you with everything I am until the day I die. You're my mate, my everything. And I really need to take you back to someplace safe so that I can show you how much pleasure a man can give to his mate."

"I think you already covered that last night."

He chuckled, and again it was the most beautiful sound. "Honey, you have no idea how much better it can get."

"Then okay. Let's do that," she whispered. She might have said more, but he was kissing her. And she was kissing back. And they kept kissing until flashing red and blue lights illuminated them. Plus the bright spotlight of a high-powered flashlight.

And when Alyssa was going to ignore that, Simon abruptly broke their kiss to glare hard at the interruption. Then the spotlight pulled off their faces and she could finally see Detective Kennedy with his hands raised in an I-surrender gesture.

"I was just trying to see if you're okay."

Alyssa giggled, embarrassment making her spout words that she would normally keep inside. "We're mated."

"Yeah," the cop said with a smirk. "I figured that out. Yesterday."

She grinned, but rational questions were pushing to the fore of her brain. "How are you here? Is everyone else okay? How bad is the damage to my building?"

"Looking for you. The wounded are already on the way to the hospital. The rest are all fine. Including that high-as-a-kite hybrid. And as for the apartment building." He exhaled with a sigh. "Fire's there now, but the damage is pretty bad. You have insurance, right?"

She nodded, feeling a little sick inside. "I do. But my whole life was in there."

"No," Simon said as he touched her face and brought her around to look at him. "Your life is here." He touched her chest, right above her beating heart.

She mimicked the gesture on him. "And here."

He nodded. "We'll figure out the rest." Then he smiled. "Besides, I've been trying to think of what to do with the rest of Nanook's money. Why not use it to build again? And maybe in a better neighborhood."

"No!" she said, her voice sharp. "This neighborhood is my home. And those people are my family." Then she smiled. "But I like the idea of rebuilding."

"Good. Because I like the idea of making you happy. No matter what."

She smiled and together with Detective Kennedy, they started walking back toward what used to be her home. She knew there would be lots to do. She had a whole building of people who needed to relocate. They had statements to make and details to iron out. Plus Detroit was still under quarantine, so that was going to make everything more complicated.

Even so, she smiled like a giddy school girl. He loved her. And she loved him.

"I think I can get used to being mated," she said with a smile.

Simon drew her close and whispered into her ear. "As soon as I get you alone, I'm going to…" His words were graphic and very detailed. They made her blush hot and giggle while Detective Kennedy tried to look anywhere but at them. And all the while, Simon kept talking. Damn, the man was very logical and very thorough.

And she loved him all the more for it.

Then his words slowed, though his hold on her body remained intimate. And when his words stopped, she looked at him, a question on her lips. It died the moment she saw his face. It was wrinkled up in disgust.

"The water," he said flatly. "It's still bad."

Kennedy straightened, his nostrils flaring as he inhaled the air. The fire truck was dumping gallons of water in a thick stream onto her laundromat. And though Alyssa couldn't smell anything wrong, she believed that their grizzly noses could.

Meanwhile, Detective Kennedy was turning toward them, tilting his head close as he spoke in a low tone.

"About that," he began. "I have an idea…"

When an alpha meets his match…

Don't miss *THE BEAR WHO LOVED ME*, the first book in the Grizzlies Gone Wild series, by *USA Today* bestselling author Kathy Lyons, available now.

See the next page for an excerpt.

CHAPTER ONE

*M*ore. *Power.*

Thoughts came slowly to Carl Carman, but each word reverberated with power. That was the best part of being a grizzly bear. Simple words meant simple, strong deeds. Human complexities were nonexistent in this state, though they echoed in the back of his mind. He was on a mission, had come to this Christmas tree field on a clan purpose. That he took joy in what he did was a trivial detail.

Now.

He braced his legs, shoved his claws deep, and then he thought it. One word, and the power crashed through every cell in his body.

Destroy.

He did.

What he held, he uprooted.

What he gripped, he crushed.

Whatever he touched, he tore apart.

Joy.

He grinned though he grunted with effort. He tasted blood—his own—and the coppery tang was sweet. Human language tried to intrude in this moment, but the grizzly had no interest in it. His language was action, power delivered with thrilling ease. And it liked to rip things apart. So he continued and was content.

Until something else disturbed him. Red and blue flashes across his retinas. At first he flinched away from the lights, but they roused the rational part of him. Red. Blue.

Police.

With a roar of fury, he began to tuck the animal away. His bear fought the shift, holding onto his shape with every ounce of his determination. But in this, the man was stronger, the mind crueler. With steadfast will, he folded the grizzly into an envelope in his mind. It had taken him years to master it. Things that large don't origami into a tiny flat rectangle easily.

His bones shifted, most of the fur thinned and disappeared, though some fell to the ground. His face tightened, and the strength in his arms and claws pulled inside, shrinking as it was tucked away. He straightened, the grizzly hump now gone as the energy coiled tight inside. His eyes burned. Damn, how they burned. But in time that last vestige of dark power would fade and his normal cool green color would return. Quiet control and long, complex sentences would be his norm. Though his first words as human were always the last snarl of his bear.

"Shit."

"And Merry Christmas to you, too," said a familiar female voice, though that particular holiday had passed months ago. His vision settled, and he saw Tonya dressed in her patrol uniform as she leaned against her squad car. The lights were still flashing, and in the early morning dawn, those colors would be seen far and wide.

"Flip off those lights," he growled as he started searching for his pants. He was out here swinging in the breeze for all to see, and though that rarely bothered him, naked and vulnerable was not a good idea around her.

She opened the squad car and used one hand to flip off the lights while the other aimed her phone at him. Jesus, she was taking pictures.

"I'll tear that thing out of your hand," he snarled, "and I won't be gentle."

"Promises, promises," she said with a sigh. But she did drop the phone. "Doesn't matter. I already got my holiday screensaver." She pushed off the car and sauntered over, her hips swinging in a tantalizing rhythm. Tonya Kappes had short honey-blond hair, modest curves on her tall, muscular frame, and a dangerous look in her eye that had once tantalized his grizzly like honey. Now it just made him tired. "See?"

She was hard to miss. He might not want to marry her, but that didn't stop him from appreciating her feminine charms. But then a moment later, he realized she was talking about the image on her phone, flipped around for him to see.

Hell. "Give me that."

She tried to pull away, but he was faster and stronger. He caught her wrist and squeezed until the cell dropped into his other hand. She might have fought him more, but a glare from him had her quieting, her head tilted to the side in submission. Then he looked down. There, full screen on the phone, was a video of him as a grizzly bear methodically destroying a field of Christmas trees. The telltale silver streak down his back flashed clear in the dawn light.

"Why would you record this?" he asked.

She flashed him a coy look that only pissed him off. "I like watching you work."

Bullshit. She liked collecting blackmail material on people. She'd never used it as far as he knew, but that didn't stop her from gathering intel on everyone. It was just part of her character and probably helped her be a good cop. But that didn't mean he had to like it. With a quick flick of his thumb, he initiated a factory reset of her phone.

"Hey!" she cried when she saw what he'd done. "That's evidence!"

"You here to arrest me?"

"You did just destroy Nick Merkel's best tree field."

"It had to be done, and you know it."

Her lips compressed into a flat line. "The Merkels' farm brings a boatload to the local economy. Hurting this field damages everyone." "He refused a direct order to fix his pesticide platform." Pesticides were a fact of modern agriculture, and most farmers were extra careful about the area where the chemicals were mixed and stored. Not Nick Merkel. Spills were common and his platform leaked like a sieve. But he didn't seem to care because the runoff went away from his property. Too bad for him that Carl cared. A lot. "He's leaking poison into the groundwater."

She nodded, grim anger on her features. "So kill him and be done with it."

"You'd rather I murder him than destroy his prize field." It wasn't a question. He knew that shifter law gave him the right to kill anyone in his clan who openly disobeyed him. But the man in him kept looking for a more civilized punishment. Not so for Tonya.

"He's got a wife and two sons to carry on the farm. They'll fix the platform and still bring in money to the area."

Carl didn't answer. Tonya was a cop through and through. That meant black-and-white law and swift justice. If kids vandalized a building, they went to jail. If a man poisoned the land, he got killed. For the most part, shifter law bowed to human law, but there were two unbreakables. Don't hurt the land. Don't disobey the alpha. Nick Merkel had done both.

Something in the Merkel bloodline was just ornery. The man had been a thorn in Carl's side since Carl had stepped into his position as the alpha of the Gladwin grizzly-shifters, eight years ago. But Carl had seen firsthand what happened when a leader took the law into his own hands. He had sworn his tenure as Maximus of their mid-Michigan clan would not be one of terror and vigilante justice. So he'd done one step short of murder. He'd destroyed a field of Merkel's Christmas trees, cutting the bastard's pocketbook instead of his jugular.

"It won't work," Tonya said. "You'll have to kill him eventually."

"And then they'll crucify me for killing one of our own." He knew because that's what had happened when he'd taken control of the clan. Another idiot had challenged him, and he'd let his grizzly out. One bloody death later, and Carl was the acknowledged alpha. But then the widow had started grumbling. And before long, others had agreed that an alpha should never kill one of his own.

"It's an endless cycle," Tonya agreed. "You can't stop it. So get on with the next step and kill him. Deal with the next step when it happens."

"Just help me find my damn pants," he grumbled, unwilling to admit that there wasn't a way out.

Her lips curled into a slow smile. "They're locked in my trunk."

Carl's head whipped back to her. "Why?"

She shrugged, a roll of her shoulders that set her breasts to bouncing. "Evidence."

"Blackmail, you mean."

She chuckled, a low throaty sound. "Or just a way to keep you naked for a little bit longer."

She took a step back, her gaze rolling slowly down his torso. Jesus, she was bold. She had a way of making even the most exhibitionist of his set feel dirty in a completely teenage horny, fuck-'em-fast-and-furious kind of way. But he'd left those hormones behind years ago.

Then he caught her scent. "You're in heat."

Damn it, if he hadn't been so absorbed in dealing with Nick Merkel, he would have noticed it right off the bat. No wonder he was keyed up around her.

She arched a brow. "Ticktock goes the biological clock."

"Give me my clothes. I am not fucking you. And especially not in the middle of a destroyed Christmas tree field."

She chuckled. "I don't care where we do it, Carl, but we gotta do it."

"No, we really don't."

He watched hurt flicker in her eyes. It didn't even touch her face, but her eyes flinched, and it was more telling on her than a scream on anyone else.

He didn't want to insult her. He had some warm feelings for her. They'd known each other all their lives, but cuddling up to her was like snuggling with a live hand grenade. He could control her. She always submitted to him eventually, but who wanted to spend their off-hours in a constant game of dominance and submission? He wanted someone he could relax and have a beer with. Around Tonya, he'd be on duty as the Gladwin Max 24/7. "All right," she said as she folded her arms across her chest. Her breasts plumped nicely, and his bear took notice. The rest of him was seeing that despite her words, Tonya had not given in. "Let's look at this logically." She almost sneered the last word. Grizzly clans were not known to be deep thinkers. Something he daily tried to change.

"Not until I'm dressed."

She didn't move. "Our bears are compatible. We established that as teenagers."

"Everyone's compatible at sixteen." And back then, they had "compatted" as much as possible for a hot, horny month. But even at sixteen, he had grown tired of the constant power play.

"You're Maximus now, but you need a strong wife at your side to hold the position. Merkel openly defied you. Unless you do a massive show of strength, more will follow. The last thing we need is a civil war inside the clan."

He knew this. It had been burning through his brain ever since Merkel had refused to fix his platform. Carl had tried to sic the EPA on the man, hoping that human justice would help him out, but the organization was overloaded and undermanned. The earliest they could get someone out to check on violations was three weeks away. Hence his morning rampage.

"We're short on numbers as it is," he growled. "I'm not going to murder my own people."

"You don't have to," she said. "I will."

"Tonya!"

"I'm a cop and the strongest she-bear in a hundred miles. Get me pregnant and my brothers will line up to support you."

"They could line up without me getting you knocked up."

She shook her head. "That's not how it works and you know it."

True. Family loyalty trumped clan groupings all the time. It was the reason Merkel's wife and sons hadn't taken care of their father themselves. That kind of betrayal was nonexistent within shifter communities. Tonya's family was large and powerful, and there were rumblings of them splitting off to establish their own clan. Or of them taking over his. That would all end the moment he impregnated Tonya. If she became his Maxima, then that would fold her family into his, locking up the leadership for generations to come.

But he just couldn't do it. They'd drive each other insane inside a year. Besides, he had a better idea, but first he had to end any romantic ideas between the two of them.

"I think of you like a sister," he began, and it was the God's honest truth.

She didn't argue. Instead, her gaze drifted down. The shift was slow and deliberate, and he forced himself to let his hands go lax, opening up his entire body for her perusal.

Flat. Flaccid. And absolutely uninterested despite the fuck-me pheromones she gave off.

She didn't speak. There was no need to. She simply lifted up the car key fob and pressed a button. The trunk popped open, and he finally got his hands on his clothes.

They didn't speak as he dressed. He didn't even want to look at her. He'd hurt her, and the guilt weighed heavy on him. Maybe the others were right. Maybe there just wasn't enough bear in him to effectively lead the clan. His uncle had been so much bear he was almost feral. When he'd been Max, he'd killed with impunity, destroyed at random, and taken the most powerful she-bear by force. It had been human cops who had killed him—with his own father's help—opening up their clan to another way to rule. Logic and law—human concepts that the Gladwin shifters desperately needed.

Ten years later, Carl had stepped into power, but everyone seemed to think he was more man than bear. He couldn't kill without exhausting all other possibilities. And he couldn't fuck the most powerful she-bear around just because she was in heat. Which left him with a fracturing clan and his best ally hurting as she answered a call on her radio. Some drunk teens were cow tipping a few miles to the east.

"I have to go," she said as she climbed into her cruiser and shut the door. But the window was still open, so he leaned in.

"Tonya, you're still a valuable member of the clan. Maybe my most—"

"Save it. I've heard it all." They'd had this argument in one form or another since they were old enough to marry. The only sop to his guilt was that she wanted the power of Maxima way more than she wanted him.

"I have a better idea," he said. "Be my beta."

She froze, her eyes widening in shock. "Alan's your beta."

His brother, Alan, had served as his second from the very beginning. It kept the power in the family, but Alan had never shifted. The grizzly DNA had missed him, and the man couldn't hold the position for much longer. Privately, Carl believed that's what had sparked Merkel's latest round of disobedience. The idiot hoped to force Carl's hand into making a compromise and giving him the beta honor.

Never going to happen. He needed someone he could trust as his second.

"I know it's unorthodox," he continued, "but I can't think of anyone better."

"Unorthodox? A female beta is unheard of! You think you have problems with Merkel now? Every shifter in the state will be calling you a pansy-assed *human*."

A big insult in the shifter community. Everyone seemed to believe that the animal side was the power center. The *male* animal. But if any female could change their minds, it was Tonya.

"A female beta makes the clan look weak. Those Detroit bastards will be on us in a split second."

"The Detroit clan has their own problems. They're not looking to start a war with us." He hoped.

"You should ask one of my brothers."

He'd thought of that, but he didn't trust them like he trusted Tonya. He'd known her since they were children. Everyone expected them to marry, so they'd been shoved together from their earliest moments. He knew the way she thought and which way she would jump. In most things their opinions aligned, though she tended to more to a black-white rule of the jungle, while he tried to think a problem through. All of that added up to her being an excellent beta.

"I chose you. Swear unwavering loyalty to me, and we can hold the clan together without marriage. That's what you really want, anyway."

She arched a brow. "You underestimate your attraction as a mate."

"Bullshit. You want the power."

"And the hot sex."

Carl rolled his eyes. "So get a gigolo and be my beta."

She shook her head slowly, not in denial but in stunned amazement. "You're trying to drag the shifter community into a modern mind-set. It's going to backfire on you. We're just not as logical as you." To her credit, she didn't sneer the word "logical" like most shifters would.

"Will you do it? I can announce it at the next clan meeting." He needed time to tell Alan, and that was not going to be a comfortable discussion.

"Yes," Tonya said, being typically decisive. Then she pushed the car into drive, but she didn't move. "One more thing: You had a message. That's why I came out here to find you."

He frowned. Damn it, she should have told him that first thing instead of trying to trap him into mating. "What?"

"There's trouble in Kalamazoo."

"What?" The word exploded out of him, but Tonya didn't hear it. She'd already hit the gas and was roaring away.

Just as well, he thought as he sprinted for his truck. Even clothed, there was no way to hide his reaction at the mention of that place where *she* lived. He hit the freeway with his erection lying hard and heavy against his thigh.

About the Author

Kathy Lyons is the wild, adventurous half of *USA Today* bestselling author Jade Lee. A lover of all things fantastical, Kathy spent much of her childhood in Narnia, Middle Earth, Amber, and Earthsea, just to name a few. There is nothing she adores more than turning an ordinary day into something magical, which is what happens all the time in her books. Winner of several industry awards, including the Prism Best of the Best Award, a *Romantic Times* Reviewers' Choice Award, and Fresh Fiction's Steamiest Read, Kathy has published more than fifty romance novels, and she's just getting started.

Check out her latest news at:

KathyLyons.com

Facebook.com/KathyLyonsBooks

Twitter: @KathyLyonsAuth

9 781538 762103